she has

my child

BOOKS BY EMMA ROBINSON

The Undercover Mother

Happily Never After

One Way Ticket to Paris

My Silent Daughter

The Forgotten Wife

My Husband's Daughter

His First Wife's Secret

To Save My Child

Only for My Daughter

To Be a Mother

My Stepmother's Secret

Please Take My Baby

she has my child

emma robinson

bookouture

Published by Bookouture in 2024

An imprint of Storyfire Ltd.
Carmelite House
50 Victoria Embankment
London EC4Y 0DZ

www.bookouture.com

ISBN: 978-1-83790-877-6
eBook ISBN: 978-1-83790-876-9

For my St Clere's Girls
Anita, Ashlie, Felicity, Hayley, Kerry, Louise, Theresa and Tracy
Thank you for your unwavering support (and for the book merch)

'There are only two lasting bequests we can hope
to give our children.
One of these is roots. The other, wings.'

—JOHANN WOLFGANG VON GOETHE

PROLOGUE

Mark was incredulous when she'd first told him about Sophia's offer. 'You're not seriously considering this?'

At that point, Megan hadn't known what to think about it. 'I don't know. I mean, if we're going to use a surrogate, wouldn't it be better that it's someone we know?'

He'd held out his hands in amazement. 'But we *don't* know her. That's the point. You haven't heard from her in over twenty years, Megan. You don't know what kind of person she is, or if we can even trust her. She ran out on you and never came back. With everything you've been through, how can you forgive that so quickly?'

She hadn't been able to explain it to herself, much less to him. She hadn't forgiven Sophia. How could she when she still hadn't really explained what had happened on that night all those years ago? But the more Sophia had offered to carry her child, the more she'd felt the flicker of hope being kindled into something possible.

Then they'd opened that box of her mother's and found what she'd kept all those years. Like a talisman from the past, it had felt like fate. As if her mother was giving her permission to do this thing. Because wasn't this proof that Sophia wasn't as selfish as Megan had thought she was? *It's okay now. You can trust her.*

When she'd tried to explain it to Mark, he might've stopped short of calling her deluded, but his tone had made it clear that he didn't see things the same way. 'Nothing has changed for me, Megan. We still don't know what kind of person she is. Whether we can trust her. Tell me this: if you'd met a woman on a bus three months ago and *she* offered to be your surrogate, would you accept *her?*'

This wasn't the same. It wasn't.

Sophia was her sister.

And this was her only chance to be a mother.

ONE

MEGAN

Seeing her face made it real.

Megan couldn't tear her eyes from the monitor. That square electronic screen that framed the first glimpse of how her baby might look. They'd been warned that the 4D scan didn't always work. That the baby – that real, live baby – might be facing the wrong way or have its arm – its tiny, chubby arm – across its face. But there she was in black and white. Her child.

Before beginning the scan, the technician had asked them if they knew the baby's sex. 'At twenty-eight weeks, it can be quite difficult to hide it, if you know what I mean.'

It was obvious from Sophia's face that she wanted to know – she'd tried to persuade them into it at the twenty-week scan. But Megan and Mark hadn't thought it was important. All they wanted was a baby. 'I'm not sure.'

Sophia groaned. 'You don't have to, but I really want to know. And I'm really good at keeping secrets.'

That decided her. If Sophia knew, she'd want to know. 'Okay. I do want to know.'

'Right, then.' The doppler moved across the gel on Sophia's stomach. 'I can see quite clearly that you have a little girl.'

Megan gasped. Until that moment, she would've said she had no preference. But now that she knew the baby was a girl – a daughter – she couldn't wipe the smile from her face.

As Sophia squeezed her hand, Megan pulled her eyes away from the screen to see her own grin reflected back at her. 'She's looks pretty great, doesn't she?'

Megan had to swallow hard before she could reply. 'She does. She really does.'

The technician smiled at them both. 'Is this your first baby?'

Sophia laughed, the deep throaty laugh that usually attracted half the room in her direction. 'We're not a couple. We're sisters. I'd be way out of her league, anyway.'

The technician blushed, then frowned. 'I'm sorry. You were just so excited, that I thought... well, it's lovely that you're so pleased for your sister.'

Ironically, the last was directed at Megan. Wasn't this on their notes? 'The baby is mine. Mine and my husband's. He couldn't be here today because he had a big thing at work.'

Sophia patted the side of her stomach. 'I'm just the oven.'

The confusion cleared from the technician's face. 'Ah, I see. How wonderful. What a wonderful gift.'

This time Megan was the one to squeeze Sophia's hand, then kiss it. 'It is. The best, most generous gift in the world.'

After they'd collected the photos, they had an hour until they had to leave for Gatwick. Megan suggested the canteen in the building, but – as always – Sophia had seen a quirky coffee shop from the car window on the way to the clinic and took them on a fifteen-minute detour to find it.

After the fresh March air, the tiny cafe was stuffy but welcoming. Inside, there were only five tables, and four of those were taken. It took much shuffling around to make their way to the back and find a seat each. 'Happy now?'

'Come on, you have to admit this is nicer than the cup of dishwater we'd have got from that instant coffee machine at the clinic.'

Rather than admit she was right, Megan picked up the menu and ran a finger down the multitude of choices of coffee roast and milk. 'Should you be drinking coffee anyway?'

Sophia rolled her eyes. 'I'll get decaf. Don't panic.'

On the table next to them, a young mother was breaking apart a cheese sandwich for a chubby toddler who was squeezing it between his tiny fingers before squashing it in the general direction of his mouth. Megan had always known she wanted children, but since their fertility struggles, she'd been drawn to any child in her orbit, as if she were punishing herself for her inability to make one of her own.

Sophia nudged her. 'That'll be you before you know it.'

Another wave of love for her sister almost consumed her. Within weeks, this ache she carried around with her like a heavy coat would be set down. She'd be a mother and would have her sister to thank. As soon as she opened her mouth, though, Sophia held up her hand to silence her. 'If you thank me again, I'm going to change my mind.'

Anyone watching them would assume that they were as tight as thieves and maybe they were. Or would be. These last two years, with Sophia back in her life, had been good. And what could bring them closer than Sophia carrying her longed-for child?

Spread out on the table, the photographs looked even clearer than they had in the clinic. 'It's so strange that we can see what she looks like already.'

Sophia leaned closer to look at them. 'Wouldn't it be weird if she looked a little bit like Mum?'

Megan felt the familiar squeeze in her chest. Two years on and she still found it difficult to talk about their mum. Sophia was able to do it seamlessly, as if the pain of her loss could be navigated with ease. It was different for her, of course. For so many reasons. 'If she's dark like Mum, she'll look like you, too, Soph.'

Sophia had lucked out in the gene lottery by inheriting their mother's thick coffee-brown hair, but their father's build. At twelve, Megan had stood in front of her bedroom mirror sucking in her pale cheeks and stomach, resenting her sister for inheriting their father's long limbs and slim torso, where she was short and solid like their mother.

When the waitress brought their drinks to the table – black decaf for her, something complicated and foamy for Sophia – Megan scooped up the precious photos. The waitress smiled at Sophia. 'Congratulations.'

It was a fight not to feel jealous. All the attention and warmth directed towards Sophia from complete strangers should rightfully have been hers. She should be the one plumped up with happiness, smiling benignly on a world that was about to change. This was her baby. Even if the pregnancy wasn't. At home, she'd pushed a pillow underneath her shirt, squinted her eyes, tried to imagine what it would feel like.

Still, she'd learned pretty quickly that there was little to be gained by explaining the surrogacy to every stranger that they met. Sophia, too, merely nodded her thanks at the waitress but, as soon as she'd gone, leaned in towards her. 'Did you see the look on her face. Shocked that someone as old as me was pregnant?'

Megan smiled at her attempt to make light of these awkward moments. 'Forty-one isn't *that* old. And, anyway, you look younger than that.'

Sophia laughed. 'Maybe the extra fat in my face is pushing out the wrinkles.'

She could joke, but she did look younger than her age. Especially right now, she practically glowed with prenatal health. No one would guess that there were seven years between the two of them. Even she'd been surprised at how little Sophia seemed to have changed since that awful day over twenty years ago.

Oh, but it was so lovely to have her big sister here with her now; she lifted everything and everyone around her and made this whole crazy thing more real. Megan's stomach pricked with the fear of letting her out of her sight. 'Do you really have to go back to Italy tonight? Come back and stay at the house. Please. I really want you to, and Mark would love to see you.'

Mark should have been with them today. He'd booked the day off and she'd made sure that it was in his work diary, his phone diary and circled three times on the calendar at home. *6th March. 4D Scan. Do not miss.* But then his father had announced a *vital* meeting in Milton Keynes that required Mark's presence and, yet again, he had acquiesced. A little too easily. Sophia was shaking her head. 'I need to get back to the cafe. They've got someone new starting to take over from me when I go on maternity leave, and I want to be there to help train him up.'

How much training could it take to make coffee and slice cake? Megan wasn't about to open that conversation again. 'How long will you keep going?'

Sophia shrugged. 'I'll last out as long as I can. Although my ankles are starting to puff like an overcooked soufflé if I stand for too long.' She looked down at her feet with a grimace.

Megan didn't take for granted the physical sacrifices that Sophia was making, though she herself had never got further than the first few weeks of a pregnancy; hadn't even experienced morning sickness. Listening to Sophia's recounting of nausea and cravings and backache, she devoured each detail as if hoping she could induce the experience in her own body. Trying not to let envy sour her sympathy, she reached over the table for her sister's hand. 'We are grateful, you know. It can't be easy. We can never repay you for this.'

'Hey, it's okay. Of course I wanted to do this for you; it was my idea, remember?'

It had been Sophia's idea. Just two days before their mother's funeral. When everything in Megan's world had become truly dark, Sophia had been the light, the hope, the lifeline she needed. Whatever Mark's reservations, and her own uncertainty that Sophia would stay true to her word, she'd come through for them. And here, just over a year later, they were. Twenty-eight weeks into a pregnancy which, apart from its unorthodox beginnings, had been textbook. Even though she said she looked like a sausage bursting from its skin, her sister had never looked more beautiful than she did right now. Her eyes were bright, her skin glowing from the Italian sunshine or the pregnancy hormones or the top-quality vitamins that Megan had been sending her and begging her to remember to take. Even her bump was a perfectly smooth and neat little orb.

An older waitress brought over a glass of tap water for them both. She smiled at Sophia. 'Enjoy your quiet time. Once the little one is here, you won't have a moment to yourself. Isn't that right, Shannon?'

The last remark was directed at the waitress clearing the table next to theirs. Megan shook her head at Sophia to stop her from explaining. It wasn't necessary. She knew that the waitress meant it as a friendly warning, but – to her – it sounded like the dream. She was so ready to immerse herself in motherhood, to focus on every little demand this tiny human would ever have.

Shannon was wiping so effusively that she was out of breath. 'Yep, but it goes by in a flash and then they're gone and all you've got is an empty bedroom and a broken heart.' She paused mid-wipe and looked at Sophia. 'Enjoy every moment when they're small, love. It goes so fast. You only get them for a little while.'

Her smile showed that her words were meant kindly, but they were like cold water flicked in Megan's face. The baby wasn't even here; she couldn't think about losing her already. She forced a smile until both women were off serving someone else, then leaned in towards Sophia. 'You're going to come back in two weeks, right? There are risks if you fly too late in pregnancy.'

Sophia scooped the foam from the top of her coffee and licked the spoon. 'I'll be back in two weeks. There's plenty of time. Stop worrying, Meg.'

That was easy for her to say. Worry had been Megan's unwanted companion for so long, she'd be lonely without it. 'I just want to spend time with you. Your room is ready and I've researched loads of Italian recipes that you'll like.'

Sophia bit into the hard caramel biscuit from her saucer. 'The room is lovely. But I need to spend a little time pacifying Richard before I settle into my confinement.'

She said the last in her best Victorian lady voice to make Megan laugh, but she was so desperate to have her sister stay with her, where she could keep an eye on her, make sure that she was looking after herself and, by extension, the baby. 'Okay, but please take care of yourself. I'll miss you so much.'

Though she'd promised herself she wouldn't, it was impossible to keep the tremble from her voice. A thick layer of emotion threatened to break through to the surface at all times. Sophia tilted her head, her dark-brown eyes that looked so much like their mother's were full of a love that Megan wanted desperately to trust. 'I'll miss you, too. I'm so happy that we're doing this.'

Megan nodded. 'Me, too.' Every inch of her wanted to grab hold of her sister and not let her go, but a glance at her watch confirmed that they needed to move. 'We'd better finish our drinks and get you to the airport. You're in no condition to be running through departures this time.'

Goodbyes were always difficult. If Sophia was going home,

Megan wanted to get it over with as quickly as possible. The sooner she went, the sooner she'd be back.

Sophia wrapped her long purple scarf twice around her neck. 'Good idea. I'll be back before you know it, Meg. I promise.'

Megan believed her; she had to. If only Sophia hadn't said those exact same words over twenty years ago before disappearing without a trace.

TWO

SOPHIA

The heat of the late afternoon welcomed Sophia back to Italy like a warm embrace. Everything about this place was perfection. The people, the architecture, the food, the apartment: all of it. Of the many places she'd lived, this was possibly her favourite.

Richard used to collect her from the airport – sometimes with flowers or a funny handwritten sign – but the last few times he'd been too busy, their lives more disparate. It was understandable, her flights to and from the UK were more frequent now with hospital appointments and scans, but it was hard not to feel uncared for. Last time she'd taken the train then bus to their town, but the effort involved in that was beyond her right now so she'd booked a taxi. Though she hadn't hated pregnancy as much as she'd anticipated, it was starting to get more cumbersome and she could only imagine that it was going to get more difficult.

Matteo, the kind taxi driver, had been more than attentive to her needs, jumping out to grab her bag and holding the rear door open, pushing the passenger seat forward to allow as much leg room as possible in the back. The acidic scent from the lemon-shaped air freshener swinging from the rear-view mirror hit the back of her throat. Once she'd had the baby, she wouldn't miss the way random smells assailed her like this.

Somehow, gentle Matteo managed to squeeze his car into a tiny space directly outside her apartment building. If she'd let him, he would've followed her in with her small suitcase, but she insisted – in semi-fluent Italian accompanied by hand gestures and repeated shakes of the head – that she'd be fine, lying that her apartment was on the ground floor and she wouldn't have to climb any steps.

Once he'd given in, with many shakes of his head at her independence, she slotted her key into the large wooden front door. After almost a year of being here, the novelty of living in this beautiful building hadn't worn off. The heavy wooden door opened onto a cool marble floor in front of a staircase that curled around to the left, the wrought-iron balustrades topped with polished wood. There were two apartments on each of the four floors; theirs was on the third. For a moment, she contemplated calling Richard to see if he was at home and could help with her bag, but then remembered he was on-site today. The dig he was working on had got to a crucial stage apparently. When she'd met him a year ago, she'd thought an archaeological director would be an exciting job. Turned out, it's pretty slow going.

She'd just bent to pick up her case when the front door opened behind her and a man she'd never seen before bustled through with a bag of groceries: tall, slim, blond and, at first glance, probably around her age. Welcoming a new arrival to the building was a good excuse to wait a little longer and catch her breath. '*Ciao.*'

Behind a pair of wire-framed glasses, he looked startled to see her. 'Oh, hello, I mean... *Ciao.*'

He had the clipped short vowels of a lot of Richard's colleagues.

'You're English?'

Shifting the grocery bag into his left hand, he held out his right. 'Yes. Sorry.'

She laughed and took his hand. 'No need to apologise. I'm English, too. Sophia.'

'Hi, Sophia. I'm Alex.'

His handshake was firm and efficient and accompanied by a nod of the head. She decided to like him. 'Are you at the university?'

The only English people she'd met here were connected with the university in some way, either as a lecturer or student. Dressed in jeans and an open-necked shirt, this man had that academic charisma that she always found attractive – the Henry Higgins effect – so she'd guess the former. But he shook his head. 'No, I'm just staying here for a while.' He blushed, which only made him more handsome. 'I'm trying to write a book.'

How wonderful to have a creative job. At nineteen, she'd been a month away from starting a fine art degree before she'd had to leave home. Sometimes she wondered where she'd be right now if she hadn't made the decision to go and follow Jed Northover's backpack and pretty blue eyes to South America.

'A book? That's exciting. You must meet my partner. He's published a few things on archaeology. He's working with the university on a dig near here.'

He looked impressed. 'That's pretty cool.'

She didn't like to tell him that she'd thought that too until she had to hear about it on a daily basis. 'So, what are you writing?'

He scratched the back of his head and pulled a face. 'It's a novel. Well, it will be. Historical. About a doctor who worked around here. I'm hoping to get a feel for the place. I'll be here for three months.'

'Great. I'm going on maternity leave soon, so I'll be able to show you around if you'd like a guide?' She stopped herself.

'Actually, no, I won't. I have to go back to England to have the baby. Well, I'll be around for the next week or so if you want any info.'

'Thanks. I'd like that.' He nodded at her suitcase. 'Do you want a hand up the stairs with that?'

She wanted to decline, but the case was pretty heavy with the expensive organic soaps and a book about pregnancy health that Megan had insisted she take home. 'That's kind, but I'm on the third floor.'

He picked it up with the hand that wasn't full of groceries. 'I'm on the fourth, so I'll have to pass your place anyway.' He nodded towards the staircase. 'After you.'

It was a little embarrassing having him follow behind her as she made her way cautiously up the stairs like an old woman; the shiny steps felt more precarious now that she was front-heavy. Once they'd made it to the third floor, he dropped her suitcase on her doorstep.

'Thanks so much. You must come for dinner soon and meet Richard, my partner.'

His long legs were already on the way up the next flight of stairs to his own apartment. 'No problem. And yes, that'd be great. Thanks.'

Sophia was expecting an empty apartment, but as soon as she pushed open the stiff wooden door, she could hear Richard in the kitchen. Leaving her suitcase just inside, she resisted the urge to collapse onto the sofa and poked her head into the kitchen. 'You're home.'

Richard turned away from the coffee machine. 'Yes, I had to get some paperwork done, so it was easier to do it here. How was your trip?'

No hug. No kiss. Not even much of a smile. 'It was good. Meg wanted me to stay, but I said I couldn't bear to be away from my boyfriend for any longer than I needed to.'

One of them had to make the first move. He'd returned his

attention to the coffee machine, so she slipped her arms around his waist and laid her face against his back. Well, as best she could with a bowling ball between them. Possibly protesting at being squashed, the baby chose that moment to kick her. The first movements had started after the twenty-week scan. Flutters to begin with. But over the last two weeks, those gentle prods were turning into fully fledged kicks.

Richard stiffened in her arms. 'Was that what I thought it was?'

'Yep. You just got kicked.' It was the strangest thing to have another living creature move inside her. She was enjoying it in a strange, almost scientific, way, trying to work out what position the baby would be in to be able to get a toe – or was that a finger? – right between her lower ribs. It was actually quite exciting to think about her growing bigger each day, becoming her own little person. And seeing the scan picture had been more thrilling than she'd expected.

But Richard pulled away from her arms. 'Well, that's a turn-off.'

Again, it was understandable. Just like she understood why he no longer wanted to sleep with her. The doctor had confirmed that it was perfectly safe, that many couples enjoyed a physical relationship until late into a pregnancy. It must feel different when it wasn't your baby in there, though. Or even your girlfriend's. But she didn't want to start another argument as soon as she'd arrived.

'How's the project going?'

He sighed as he turned to face her and leaned against the counter. 'Terribly. Two steps forward, three steps back. There's so much red tape and no one is listening to me.'

Leaving half her brain on autopilot listening to his – seriously dull – work talk, she tried to remember what they'd been like before she was pregnant, when they wouldn't be able to keep their hands off each other, tearing off their clothes before they'd even closed the front door. She'd tried to understand how difficult this was for him, made allowances for his behaviour in the last few weeks, but it was getting to the point when she was going to have to face facts. This wasn't just about her being pregnant, it was about seeing their relationship for what it was when sex was off the table. Not, it turned out, what she'd hoped.

Now he was looking at her expectantly and she needed to say something soothing. 'I'm sorry you've had a tough time. They'll come round to your way of thinking eventually; they always do.'

His face softened a little. 'I hope so, or it's going to take three times as long and we'll run out of funding.'

She'd need a recharge before the necessary stroking of his ego. 'I'm going to have a quick nap and then let's go out for dinner and we'll plot their demise.'

She could still make him smile at least. When she'd told Megan that she needed to come home and spend time with Richard, she hadn't added that she wondered each time whether there'd be a relationship to come back to.

Dinner was gnocchi at Roberto's Trattoria on the corner of their street, with its bare wooden tables and choice of two dishes every day. Mismatched chairs wobbled on the cobbled floor and the last few inches of a candle burned between them in the neck of a dark-green bottle. All around, the chatter and laughter of family groups wove in and out of the strains of a slightly stuttering violin played by one of Roberto's many grandchildren. It was everything she loved about Italy in one place and, closing her eyes, Sophia absorbed the moment. 'It's good to be back.'

Richard tore a slice of olive ciabatta and sank the larger part into a pool of oil and rich, sweet balsamic vinegar. 'Even if it's only for a short visit.'

Sophia had allowed herself a half glass of Chianti, although she could almost taste Megan's disapproval with every sip. Richard's less-than-subtle digs were starting to irritate. 'We've got two weeks before I have to go back. It makes sense for me to stay with Megan. For a start, I can't fly if I leave it too late in the pregnancy and, anyway, I want her to be as involved as she can now that the baby is moving around. I don't want her to miss anything.'

He didn't look up as he took the second part of the bread. 'As long as *Megan* doesn't miss anything.'

That was unfair. And childish. He knew as well as she did how much Megan was missing out on. 'You knew what I was getting into, Richard. This was always the plan.'

He looked up at her then, with that hooded gaze which had always burned to the depths of her. And beyond. 'But what about me?'

Choosing to translate that as him needing her, she reached across the lake of oil to take his hand. 'I miss you, too. But it won't be for much longer. And, after the baby's born, I'll be home again and we can get back to normal.'

Even as she said it, she wasn't sure if she believed her own words. Things had been so precarious between the two of them for the last few months that she didn't even remember what normal was. Seven months in, she wanted this pregnancy over as much as he did. The difference was, she didn't regret it for a second. She owed it to her sister.

Because it didn't matter what the truth was, Megan had been led to believe that Sophia had abandoned her. That she'd left that night and hadn't given her a single thought. However guilty she felt about what Megan had been through, she couldn't go back and change those years. But maybe, by giving her this chance to be a mother, she could make sure the next twenty would bring her the happiness she deserved?

THREE

MEGAN

Glad she'd booked the whole day off work, Megan headed straight home from the airport. It got more difficult to say goodbye to Sophia whenever she left. Old anxieties fluttered up each time they said goodbye, memories of Sophia rocking her awake in her childhood bedroom.

When she'd opened her eyes, Sophia's face had been close to hers, her voice only a whisper. 'Megan, I'm leaving for a while. You won't see me in the morning.'

She'd rubbed at her face to wake herself up. 'What do you mean? Leaving where?'

Even at twelve and barely awake, she could tell that Sophia's smile was fake. 'I'm leaving with a boy called Jed. We're going on an exciting adventure.'

Megan could still remember the way her bottom lip had wobbled. She hadn't looked excited. 'Where are you going? When will you be back?'

Across the hall, the sound of their mother's cough had made Sophia freeze. Then she'd leaned forward and pulled Megan close, her thin arms cold against the short sleeves of Megan's pyjamas. 'I have to go. But I'll be back for you. And I'll send you a postcard.'

She'd tried to be brave, but when Sophia had reached her bedroom door, she'd begged her to stay. 'Please don't go. I'm scared. Please stay.'

Sophia had come back for one last squeeze, and it'd been obvious that she'd been trying not to cry. 'I can't stay. You'll be okay. I'll come back for you.'

As she'd done so many times, Megan forced these memories from her mind. She knew more now, understood that things had not been as she thought. *She's coming back this time.* She repeated it to herself like a mantra. *She's coming back.*

It was only a short drive back from the airport, so she was home long before Mark. Their cleaner had been and the air was still fresh with disinfectant – Megan's favourite smell. Mark still teased her for tidying up before their cleaner came, terrified that she would think her slovenly. It was easier for him; he'd grown up with money. He'd never lived with the shame of poverty just below the surface of his skin.

As she often did these days, she made her way up to the bedroom they'd set aside as a nursery. Other than a fresh coat of paint, nothing had been changed in here since it was just an anonymous spare bedroom. She hadn't dared to start the nursery before now. Even after the twenty-week scan, when Sophia was definitely showing a bump, she hadn't been able to believe that there was an actual baby in there. A baby who belonged to her. But today, seeing her little girl in that eerily beautiful scan, it was safe to push aside the curtain of worry for just long enough to let in a little sunny excitement. Even if the baby was born right now, she would almost definitely survive. Not that she wanted her born right now, when she was in a completely different country.

In the middle of the room, a large box held the cot they'd ordered last week. Mark had dragged it up the stairs two nights ago, but she'd asked him to hold off putting it together until today's scan. Of course, at that point, she'd assumed he'd be there with her at the clinic, holding her hand as she held Sophia's. Now he wasn't here, she'd just put it up herself. Surprise him when he came home. Maybe seeing the cot up would make it more real for him, too.

On the windowsill, she found the radio he'd brought in for her when she'd painted the walls. When she switched it on, the blare of one of those dire discussion programmes filled the room and two strident voices argued about the government's reaction to this new virus that was on everyone's mind. She quickly snapped the dial to a music channel; there was enough to think about without that scaremongering added to the mix.

She found a station playing the Backstreet Boys, which brought with it a memory of Sophia singing along to them as a teenager. Sometimes she'd even ask Megan to do the backing vocals. Despite their seven-year age difference, they'd been close back then. When they got in from school, Sophia would look after her until their exhausted mother came home from her second cleaning job. Sometimes she'd bring a friend back from school and they'd make brown sugar sandwiches and talk about boys. For an eight-year-old Megan – arms wrapped around her shins, chin on her knees, staying quiet so they'd forget she was listening – it'd been thrilling.

The heavy rectangular box containing the crib was made of thick cardboard held together with vicious industrial staples, so it took some getting into. Once she was in, she pulled out the four sides of the cot, the base and the various sized screws and checked them off of the inventory list on the instructions. There were two spare nuts, but everything else was as listed. She could do this. First thing was the dowels into the holes on *Side A*. Easy.

Mark – not the most practical of people – had suggested they pay someone to paint the walls and put up the furniture.

But she'd flatly refused. If she couldn't be the woman who grew the baby, she was definitely going to be the one to decorate the nursery. She'd also rejected the expensive brochure his parents had sent. Partly because she didn't want them to dictate any more of her life and partly because the prices were obscene. Even though they'd offered to pay for it, she couldn't justify that amount on a cot when she'd seen a perfectly nice one for a quarter of the price.

She slotted another dowel into a hole, but this one didn't want to go in. She pressed it harder. Still nothing. Then she banged it with the end of the screwdriver; that did it.

It was all very well her in-laws wanting to throw money at them for the baby, but what she'd really needed was to have Mark there today. It was cruel for his father to demand his attendance on his trip to Milton Keynes. She was angry with Mark, too. When he'd told her early this morning that he wasn't coming, she'd had to keep her voice to a hiss so as not to wake Sophia who was still sleeping in the next room. 'Just tell him you can't. Doesn't he know that we have the scan today?'

He'd fiddled with his tie, pulled it out from his collar in irritation then started again. 'You know what he's like, Meg. There's no point. At the end of the day, he's my boss.'

As usual, they had their priorities wrong. 'He's also your father. The grandfather of this baby. You can't miss it, Mark.'

It'd been difficult to convey how cross she was in a whisper, and he'd clearly thought a smile would be enough to placate her. 'You'll get a video, won't you? You can show me tonight. I'll only get in the way, anyway. Three's a crowd.'

She'd known he was trying to lighten the mood, but she hadn't been playing. When he'd leaned towards her, she'd turned over in bed and hadn't replied as he'd kissed the back of her head and whispered goodbye.

Both ends of the cot were assembled now, but two attempts at propping one against the wall, balancing the base on her knee

while she tried to connect the other end, proved that this was
going to be a two-man job, so she would have to wait for Mark to
come home after all. That was annoying. She checked her
phone but there were no messages from Sophia or anyone else
to reply to. What was she going to do now? Maybe she could fit
in a session at the gym? Or a run? Before she made up her mind,
she heard Mark's key in the lock and she jumped up to try and
meet him at the door.

At the bottom of the stairs, he was barely visible behind the
huge bunch of white roses in his arms; they were her favourite.
He peeked around the side of them. 'I'm sorry about this morning. I should've been there.'

Today's scan had been too wonderful for her to keep up her
anger with him. She skipped down the stairs, took the flowers
from his arms and motioned towards the kitchen door. 'I've got
something to show you.'

Spread out on the kitchen worktop, the photos of the scan
looked like an uneventful comic strip. Mark's eyes scanned from
the first to the last and back again. 'Wow.'

It was disappointing that they weren't nearly as clear as the
video had been. 'They're sending through a link to the video,
too.'

Mark ran his hands through his hair as he stared at the
pictures. 'Still. Wow. That's a baby alright.'

She stroked the side of the first picture, still entranced by
that tiny nose, those precious fingers and toes. 'Not just a baby.
Our baby. Our little girl.'

He smiled at her; were those tears in his eyes? 'A girl? You
found out?'

'Yes. I'm sorry. I know I should have checked with you, but I
just kind of got carried away.'

He shook his head. 'It's fine. Are you happy?'

What a strange thing to say. 'Of course! Aren't you?'

'Yes. Of course, I am.'

He might want to tell his face that. 'You don't seem happy. I thought I was the one who was the worry wort in this relationship.'

It was like role reversal; Mark was usually the *glass half full* side of the partnership. 'I'm sorry. It's been a full-on day with my dad. And then, you know... Sophia and everything. It still feels really strange. It's not that I don't trust her, obviously.'

Heckles rose on the back of Megan's neck. 'Obviously. Because she's my sister, Mark. And this is a huge thing she's doing for us.'

He held up his hands. 'I know. I know. But these last two years have been a bit of a rollercoaster. I mean, your mum, and then Sophia back in your life and now the baby coming.' He reached for her hand. 'I am pleased, sweetheart. I am. Just ignore me.'

It was difficult to ignore that he wasn't reacting as she wanted him to. Wasn't jumping around the room with excitement as prospective fathers were supposed to. The circumstances were difficult, she knew that. All the baby books she'd read had suggested that fathers be encouraged to feel the baby kick as much as possible, sing or read to the mother's stomach, feel as close as they could. But Mark felt awkward doing any of that to Sophia and she was here so infrequently that he hadn't had the chance to get over that.

He looked so contrite that she softened. 'I think it'll be easier once the baby arrives. When she's here with us.' She stepped closer towards him, her arms cradling an imaginary child. 'This'll be us soon. The three of us.'

He swallowed and circled her in his strong safe arms. His voice was thick and heavy. 'The three of us.'

She forced herself to believe that he just needed to meet their daughter to be as happy as she was. He'd wanted this as much as she had. They'd both been surprised by Sophia's offer and, yes, he'd taken longer than she had to get on board with it.

But everything would be okay again once the baby was born, wouldn't it? This was a night to celebrate. 'Have you eaten? Or shall I make some dinner?'

'Dinner would be great, thanks. I'm just going to get changed out of my suit.' He reached towards her and placed a dry chaste kiss on her cheek. 'I am pleased, Meg. It'll be great.'

She reached out to pull him close, but he'd already gone.

It'll be okay when the baby comes had become a new mantra to add to her others. Just a few more weeks and she'd have everything she'd ever wanted. This was all going to work out, wasn't it?

FOUR

SOPHIA

On Monday morning, the March sun was bright and warm for Sophia's walk to work. Every morning, an aroma of pastries and coffee accompanied her along the Via del Rosa and now pregnancy hormones were making scents stronger, they were joined by the freshness of the produce on the market stalls. Nodding and smiling at the men and women who worked there, she enjoyed the familiarity of the faces and their wares. The deeply wrinkled old lady on the end stall pressed an orange into her hand and nodded at her stomach *'per il bambino'*.

These last eleven months in Italy were the longest she'd spent in one place for decades. It was a big world, why stay in one corner of it? Megan might have a huge house and a great job but, to Sophia's mind at least, she was stuck in it. Sophia preferred the thrill of somewhere new, the honeymoon stage of a new city, a new home. Where you could fall in love with an unfamiliar accent or food or architectural style. Still, there was something about the way of life here that soothed her soul. Maybe, even if things didn't work out with Richard, she'd find a way to stay a little longer in this town of limoncello and gnocchi, old buildings and cypress trees, gruff but kind restaurant owners and old ladies with oranges.

She'd planned to be the first one at the cafe this morning. Her temporary replacement was due at 8.30 a.m., and she wanted to be there to greet him. The cafe was cool after the warmth of the morning sun and the exertion of the walk. She locked the door behind her then poured herself a glass of water, running the tap until it was ice cold.

She'd lain awake last night thinking about Megan. Leaving her to come back here, she'd seen again how fearful she was. With everything that'd happened in the last twenty years, was it surprising that she had issues around people leaving? Since Sophia had returned home, they'd talked about their lives while they'd been apart, but – thanks to a conversation with their mother – she knew that Megan had skirted around reality. Not that she could judge her for that. Guilt still punished Sophia for the half-truth she'd told about her own departure. If Megan knew what had happened, would she trust in Sophia more or less? If only she could make her believe that she would've come back sooner if she'd known. But, without revealing the real reason for her departure, it was impossible to expect Megan to understand. All she could do was try her very best to make it up to her now.

She flicked on the switches for the coffee machines and toaster, then pulled the vat of butter from the under-counter fridge to let it soften. Heralded by the scrape of a key in the front door, Natalia bustled in carrying two large cake tins. '*Ciao*. Good morning.'

Though Sophia's Italian was improving, Natalia always insisted they speak English to one another. Her dream was to travel to America one day to visit her aunt in New York: 'So I must learn.'

Natalia slid her cake tins onto the counter. A lifelong insomniac, she claimed to do her best baking around midnight.

Perhaps that's what made her lemon cannoli so good; there could easily have been witchcraft in their creation.

She waved a hand at Sophia's midriff. 'How is everything with the baby?'

Unconsciously, Sophia put a hand on her stomach, then pulled it away as if she'd scalded herself. Damn. Why did she keep doing that?

'It was good. Everything is fine with it. I mean, her. Everything is fine with her.'

Now that she knew she was carrying a girl, something had shifted. This was no longer an anonymous baby: it was a real-life person. A girl.

Natalia clapped her hands together. 'A baby girl! How wonderful. Your sister will have a best friend for life.'

Sophia was familiar with the idea that mothers and daughters stayed close. It hadn't been like that for her, but it had for Megan: she'd looked after their mother her whole life. Sophia wouldn't have even known that their mother was dying if Megan hadn't tracked her down online. 'I think my sister was pretty pleased.'

She'd got in the habit of doing this. Referring to Megan each time someone asked about the baby, keeping her distance. Making it clear that this was not her baby. Not with strangers, obviously. It would have been too weird to respond to every kind remark on the bus by saying 'My sister can't carry a child so I am being a surrogate.' It just wasn't necessary.

'And you? How do you feel?'

'I'm fine.'

Natalia raised an eyebrow at Sophia's hands, which were again – traitors – circling her stomach. 'Maybe you'll enjoy having a baby more than you think.'

Natalia was nothing if not blunt. Sophia knew she was expecting her to break down and admit that she was going to find it difficult to hand over the baby. Though she'd tried to explain that she wasn't maternal, had never wanted a child of her own, she could tell from Natalia's eyes that she didn't believe her. How could she? Coming from a sprawling Italian family – and with three grown-up children of her own – she had no idea why Sophia was so sure.

She was saved from answering by the appearance of a slim young man with the kind of smile that would be melting their younger customers' hearts by that afternoon, and she beckoned him in with a smile. '*Benvenuto.*'

The rest of the morning was a blur of showing Carl what to do and chatting to some of their regulars about the pregnancy and how she was feeling. In the last couple of weeks, a few of their older customers had been anxious about a virus that was affecting some of the larger towns. Several had even started to wear the kind of face masks beloved by Japanese tourists. On the news, they were talking about curfews and closing shops. It would be a lot of fuss about nothing, she reassured them. Just talk.

It wasn't until later in the afternoon that Natalia nudged at her foot with the broom. 'So, you have a photo? Of the baby?'

Though Megan had offered her one, Sophia hadn't kept a paper copy of the scan photo, but she had taken a snapshot of one of them on her phone. She pulled it out to show Natalia. 'It looks a bit strange.'

Natalia leaned in with a frown. 'Looks like an alien.'

Sophia had to laugh. She could only imagine Megan's horror at this honest description. She'd thought something similar herself. 'I've found it looks better if you kind of squint at it from an angle.' She tipped the phone slightly. 'Like this.'

Natalia tilted her head one way and then the other; she didn't look convinced. Sophia had had more time to get used to it; she'd found herself drawn to the photo on the plane home on

Friday, several times over the weekend and again this morning. There was something about the baby that looked familiar to her. Not like someone she knew exactly, just... like she'd met her before. Maybe her joke about the baby looking like her and Megan's mother wasn't totally unfounded. It would be strange to see that face again.

The last time she'd seen her mother had been the day she'd passed quietly away, Sophia and Megan by her bedside. But, if she closed her eyes, she could still remember her mother's face twenty years before, on the day before she left. She hadn't told her she was going; she hadn't deserved to know.

Natalia had given up trying to make sense of the scan picture. She waved away the phone. 'I will wait until the baby comes and I meet her.'

She wasn't going to meet her, though. Sophia was returning to England to have the baby so that Megan and Mark wouldn't miss a moment. They'd talked through the whole thing. Megan and Mark would both be present at the birth. The baby would be handed to them as soon as it – she – was born. Megan wanted Sophia to stay with them after the birth, for a couple of weeks at least, before she had to return home, but Sophia wasn't planning on doing that. She hadn't told Megan, but the last thing she wanted was to be trapped in England in her spare bedroom. She was banking on the fact that Megan would be too caught up in life with a newborn to really mind. After all, surely they would rather start their life as a family of three without her hanging around like stale bread?

The coffee machine hissed behind her and made her jump, Carl raised a hand in apology, and she laughed as she shook her head. Without realising it, her hand was resting on her stomach again. This time she didn't remove it. It felt natural. Despite the weirdness she'd felt during the insemination process and then the early stages of pregnancy, she'd actually settled into this pregnancy more than she'd anticipated. She'd never wanted a child, but there was definitely something going on with these hormones raging through her body. It was as if they were working on her brain to make her consider what it might be like to have a baby of her own. Another good reason to come straight back here after the birth. The last thing she needed was for some sorcery of a post-birth hormone surge to make her feel maternal. Motherhood was not part of her future and that was the best thing for everyone.

Carl was handing an espresso to one of their regulars when a hush came over the cafe. Natalia reached up to the shelf above the sink and turned up the radio. Sophia's Italian was good enough for conversation, but there were too many words she didn't recognise for her to understand what was going on at first. As the cafe cleared of customers, she turned to see Natalia's face frozen white as a marble grave.

FIVE

MEGAN

All weekend after the scan, Megan couldn't settle her mind to much else. Mark was busy with work, the nursery was finished and she was trying to limit the number of times she sent a text to Sophia checking that everything was okay. Her mind was everywhere except her job, so she'd completely forgotten that Bethany's sister Petra was starting on the Monday.

Megan and Bethany had started their company nearly ten years ago. They'd met in the PR department of a US computer software company and, when Mark's father had told her over dinner one night that she was 'just lining someone else's purse' and offered to invest a healthy amount in getting her started with her own business, she'd known that Bethany would be the perfect partner. Where Megan was good on the details, Beth was strong on the vision.

A couple of weeks ago, Bethany had floated the idea of bringing her sister on board. 'She's ready to go back to work part-time now her kids are at school. I thought, with you planning to take time off when the baby comes, it might be a perfect fit.'

In the past, this would have triggered negative thoughts in

Megan's mind about women who got to have it all – the family and the career – but soon that was going to be her, too. Her stomach twinged with excitement every time she thought about it. 'Good idea. Why don't you ask if she wants to start soon? That way she'll be up to speed when I leave.'

She wasn't sure yet how much time she was going to take off when the baby came. Due to Mark's job, she had the luxury of giving up altogether if she wanted to. But she and Bethany had worked hard to get the business to where it was, and she enjoyed what she did. Plus, she'd be able to dial in from home when she needed to, anyway. That was another luxury of being your own boss.

When she arrived at the office, she could hear laughter behind the door. Bethany and her sister must be there already. As she walked in, their faces turned towards her and Bethany grinned. 'Morning, Megs. This is my sister, Petra.'

There was no need to announce they were sisters: Petra had the same dark hair and pale skin as her sister. She held out a hand. 'Nice to meet you. Beth talks about you all the time.'

It felt rather formal to shake hands, but she was pleased that Petra was professional. 'She talks about you all the time, too. But don't worry, I didn't believe any of it.'

It was a lame joke, but Petra did her the courtesy of laughing. 'Big sisters, eh? You can't trust them.'

The ease between the two of them stirred old feelings in Megan. The morning after Sophia left, she'd woken to absolute silence. When she'd tried to ask her mother if she knew when she was coming back, her father had forbidden that they speak about her. Later that night, and many nights afterwards, she'd cried in her mother's arms as she'd rocked her to sleep and whispered soothing words. *She'll be back. Don't cry, Megs; she'll be back.*

But she hadn't come back. And Megan had looked

endlessly for the promised postcards that never came. Missing her sister like a lost limb.

The easiness between Bethany and Petra was something she envied. 'Beth tells me you've got lots of office experience, Petra, so I'm sure you'll find this pretty straightforward.'

Petra pulled a face. 'I have, but that was pre-children. I'm a little worried that baby brain might be a permanent issue.'

Meg's body prickled in response to this before her mind could catch up and tell it to relax. *You're having a baby, too.*

The morning flew by as she explained everything to Petra. 'Basically, your main job will be to ensure that your sister doesn't blow the clients' budgets by hiring a fighter jet to write their company logo in the sky or booking George Clooney to open their latest store.'

Beth stuck her tongue out and Petra laughed. 'Don't worry. I know exactly what she's like. I'll keep my beady eye on her.'

They were so close even as adults. What must that be like? As much as they'd tried, it'd been difficult for her and Sophia to make up for their lost years. It wasn't only the times she'd cried herself to sleep those first few months, it was the years afterwards. When their father had left, the tough time she'd gone through in her late teens, when she'd married Mark... how did you catch up on a lifetime of missed moments? How do you rebuild a relationship that had been torn apart? Especially when you were never told the truth about why.

Petra seemed to be getting the hang of things pretty quickly. 'You'd better watch out, Beth. Your sister's going to be taking over the company.'

Bethany laughed. 'Well, we'd better keep her in her place. Send her on the coffee run.'

Petra was straight on her feet. 'I can do that.'

'You really don't have to.' Megan shook her head. It wasn't fair to treat her like an office junior.

But Petra was already pulling on her coat. 'Honestly, I don't mind.'

Bethany held up her arms and stretched. 'I'll come with you. Show you where we go. We can pick up some sandwiches for lunch, too.' She turned to Megan. 'Usual black coffee for you?'

'Yes, please.'

'And a sandwich?'

Megan shook her head. 'No, I'm going to call Mark and see if he wants to meet for lunch.'

Beth's voice crept back to her from the door before it closed. 'Good idea. Make the most of it before the baby comes.'

Even Beth was starting on this now. Why did everyone make it sound as if your life was over when you had a baby? She was hoping it might begin.

It wasn't that she and Mark weren't happy, but the last few years had put quite a strain on them both. They'd been told to expect that, but nothing could prepare you for the rollercoaster of hope and disappointment of fertility treatment. She'd grown to resent Mark's resolute pragmatism; she was pretty sure he'd found her emotional outbursts a strain.

The place she and Bethany rented was only a ten-minute walk from where Mark worked, and he'd told her he was in the office today. But when she called his phone it went straight to voicemail. Rather than leave a message, she sent him a text to see if he was free for lunch.

Things had been particularly tense between them again this week. His reaction to the scan picture had underlined how nervous he was about the baby coming. There was no reason for that: he was going to make a really great dad. Ever since she'd known him, when they were barely twenty, he'd been taking care of her.

They'd met at a theatre group of all places. Her mother had sent her there to try and build up her confidence; it'd been her doctor's suggestion. Mark had been a human crane fly: all arms and legs. He'd probably been the only person there with less talent than her, which is why they'd always been left alone when the group had to pair off.

His screwed-up expression was all apology. 'I'm really sorry you got lumbered with me.'

As opening lines went, it was hardly *Romeo and Juliet*. But he'd made her laugh and she'd wanted to put him at ease, too. 'Don't worry. I'm only here because my mum made me. How about you?'

'Same.' His smile had changed his face entirely, lifting his delicate features. 'My dad read somewhere that acting skills can help you to become a better salesman.'

'Is that what you do?'

'It's what my dad does. And what I'll be doing when I finish university next summer.'

She hadn't known then how different their families were. When they'd first become friends, he'd had holes in his clothes and lived in a flat share with three other boys. It wasn't until the friendship had graduated to a relationship and he'd taken her home, warning her before they got there that their house was 'ridiculously big'. She'd been amazed. How had this gentle, reticent boy come from so much money?

She tried his number again. This time it rang and rang before clicking into his voicemail. That was weird: he was never more than a foot away from his phone. Part of his father's expectations were that every customer had their call answered within three rings.

Three rings. That phrase always made her think of her mother. Whenever she'd go out. 'Give me three rings when you're there.'

She used to roll her eyes. 'Do you mean send you a text?'

Every memory of her mum made Megan ache. Without Sophia there, her mum had been all she'd had. Especially after her father had left, just over a year later. That goodbye had been a relief. Without him in the house, they'd both been able to breathe easier. That was, until his absence brought other problems.

Since her mother's death, there'd been a huge hole in her life. So many times, she'd gone to pick up the phone to tell her something, only to realise that she couldn't. Mark had been kind and supportive, but there was nothing he could do. He'd watched her like a hawk for the first few months and that'd made her feel worse. Like a child who couldn't be trusted.

During those dark early days after the funeral, her need to have a baby had become so desperate that she'd spent many late nights trawling websites over the world for cutting edge fertility treatments. She'd researched adoption and surrogacy. But Mark hadn't been keen on the idea of effectively employing someone to carry their child. When Sophia had offered, though, she'd begged him and he'd relented. 'If you're happy, then I'm happy.'

And she *was* happy. She *was* excited. But it was normal to feel scared too, surely? If Sophia had come to live with them already as she'd asked her to, it would've been far less stressful for everyone. The room she'd planned for her to stay in had been totally redecorated with her in mind. The posters on the wall of European cities were not to Megan's taste, but she'd hoped they'd make Sophia feel at home. She'd chosen a dressing table with lots of little drawers for all her bracelets and pendants, a wardrobe with space at the bottom for her endless supply of shoes, an eye-wateringly expensive Anglepoise lamp so she could read easily at night. What more could she have done to tempt her to stay?

But no. Sophia had wanted to go home to Richard. Which, as Mark had been keen to point out, wasn't a huge surprise. Unable to see her and check on her, Megan couldn't help but worry. Was she looking after herself? She always ate well, but was she tempted to drink alcohol? Stay out late? Hang around in smoky bars? What did she really know about Sophia's life in Italy? Was the neighbourhood in which she lived even safe?

The door to the office opened and Petra brought pastries and news. 'Have you heard the latest about this coronavirus everyone's talking about? Apparently, there've been lots of deaths in Europe. Italy is bad.'

Megan froze. Did she hear that wrong? 'Are you sure they said Italy? Where in Italy?'

She tried to keep breathing. If it was Italy, surely it would be in the cities. Sophia was out in the countryside.

Bethany fired her sister a warning glance. 'It's probably just our news ramping it up, Megan. You know what they're like. It'll be a different story next week.'

Megan pushed away the paper bag that Petra had put on her desk. Just the sight of the butter stain on the paper made her nauseous. 'Where in Italy?'

Looking from Megan to Bethany and then back again, poor Petra was only now picking up on the atmosphere. 'I don't know. I'm sorry. It was just on the news in the bakery.'

The plastic wheels of Megan's chair squeaked as she slid towards her laptop to look up BBC News. She turned up the volume, trying to listen to the reporter, but she couldn't focus. All she could see were the words running at the bottom of the screen: *Italy in Lockdown.*

Megan's heart thudded in her ears, blocking out well-meant but uninformed comments from Bethany and Petra. What did this lockdown mean for Sophia and the baby? Would they let Sophia come home? Could she fly? Take the train? Her hands trembled as she fumbled in her bag for her mobile, a small tin of mints clattering to the floor. 'I need to call her. I need to call my sister.'

SIX

SOPHIA

Within seconds of the announcement, the cafe had cleared. Natalia sent Carl home and then gave Sophia her marching orders. 'You are pregnant. Go home.' The streets were full of people hurrying home, white-faced and confused. It was surreal. Like something from a disaster movie. By the time Sophia arrived home, she had six missed calls from Megan.

Megan would be worried, she'd need reassuring, calming down, but that would take more emotional energy than Sophia could muster at present. She needed the mental space to make sense of what was going on. Instead, she fired off a quick text: *I'm fine. I'll call you very soon.*

When she pushed open the door, she almost bumped into Richard who was pacing the floor of the apartment like a caged tiger. He growled like one, too. 'Have you heard?'

Of course she had; why else would she be home at this time of day? 'Yes, we had to close the cafe. It's so weird, isn't it?'

'Weird?' He looked at her as if she was mad. 'Weird? It's absolute craziness is what it is. The whole dig, shut down. As if it wasn't going slow enough as it was. Months of work and I've got nothing. Nothing.'

Right now, she was worried about the baby, whether she could get back to England, about Megan who she knew would be in a terrible state. She didn't have the capacity to soothe him, too. 'I know it's frustrating, Richard. But this might only be a couple of weeks and it'll still be there. You can pick it up again.'

He twisted around to face her. 'You don't know what you're talking about. This delay could cost thousands and we're already over budget. The university could shut it down altogether.'

It was difficult not to see a selfish tantrum in his behaviour. How had she not seen this side of him from the beginning? More and more she'd become aware of how one-sided their relationship had been. 'People have died, Richard. They are dying.'

He stopped pacing, took a breath. 'I get that. Of course, I do. But this is my work, Sophia. I've planned for this for months and months. I don't expect you to understand when you only work in a coffee shop.'

That stung. He was the reason she 'only' worked in a coffee shop. It was his work that'd brought them both here. 'I'm going to pretend you didn't say that. I know you're upset.'

He was across the room in two strides. 'I'm sorry. I didn't mean that. But you have to understand how serious this is for me. This could be the end of it all. And then what? You're only as good as your last published work. This affects both of us, Sophia. I was hoping for a professorship after this. You know how this works.'

She knew how it worked because she'd had to listen to it ad infinitum for the last twelve months. How universities had less money. There were more people going for the same positions. The need to be current and innovative and blah blah blah. 'The whole country is affected by this, the rest of the world is dealing with it, too. They can't hold that against you.'

'You're right. I need to see what I can do from here. Write up the notes I have. I'll make some calls. Thanks. I needed to hear all of that.' He kissed the side of her head and disappeared into the bedroom.

For a few moments, she remained standing in the middle of the sitting room. He hadn't once asked her how she felt. Whether she was worried about the virus. How this was going to affect her plans. Instead, she'd been merely a sponge to absorb and mop up his concern. The whole way home, she'd just focused on putting one foot in front of the other, getting home so that she could process all of this, speak to him about it, wanting to get it all clear in her own head before she called Megan back. And Richard hadn't even attempted to check how she was coping with the news. Not one word about how she was feeling, or what she planned to do next. She shouldn't be surprised; his absolute lack of care and support in the last few months had made her wonder if he'd ever loved her at all.

Megan would be going up the wall by now. It was cruel not to call her back, but Sophia couldn't yet cope with the emotional fallout. She needed to be calm for her, not feed her anxiety. But she couldn't do that until she got her own head around it.

Megan had always been sensitive. Even when she was small. Their mother used to joke that she was her shadow; everywhere she went, Megan would follow. After school, when their mum was still at work, Megan would want to sit wherever Sophia was and she couldn't bear being left out if Sophia had friends over. When she'd complain to her mother, she would just ask her to be kind. 'She looks up to you. She wants to be with you.'

She closed her eyes and tried to just breathe and think about what she could do. Gradually, her heartbeat returned to normal, until the shrill ring of her phone interrupted her serenity. She opened one eye to check the screen and – with great reluctance – answered it.

'Sophia! Thank goodness! I've been trying to call you. Why aren't you picking up?'

She needed to calm Megan down as quickly as possible. 'Well, I don't know if you've heard, but there's rather a lot going on over here.'

Her attempt at humour fell wide of the mark. 'What's happening? Can you leave? I've been looking at flights online and there's nothing, no seats. What about trains? I haven't checked trains.'

Megan's panic poured into her ear; this was not helping her own mood. *Breathe in. And out.* 'You need to calm down, Meg. Just take a breath. No one knows anything at the moment. There's no point panicking about something that might not be a problem. This could all be over soon and then we can go back to our plan. I'll come to you and have the baby and all will be fine.'

She was reassuring herself as well as trying to calm her sister. But Megan wasn't even listening, Instead she was winding herself tighter and tighter. 'But is it even a good idea for you to get on a plane or a train? Confined spaces would be worse, wouldn't they? You'd be more at risk of catching it. Where are you right now? Are you at home? Please tell me you are at home. Is Richard with you?'

Words spilled out of her so fast that Sophia's head swam with them. 'Megan. You have to calm down. This is not helping.'

It was as if she'd lit a fuse. 'Calm down? There's a pandemic, you're carrying my child and I can't get to you. How can I possibly calm down?'

It was natural that she was upset, but yelling wasn't helping matters. In her mind, she could see the small child who'd clung to their mother's leg, begging her not to go anywhere. But Sophia wasn't their mother, and she wasn't about to roll over and let Megan take control. 'Megan. I am fine. I am at home. I will keep safe. The baby will be fine.'

Megan was still firing questions like arrows. 'But what if you can't come home in time? What if the baby comes early?'

These were the same fears that'd been running through Sophia's head on her walk home. But what was the point in getting themselves so upset about something that might not happen? 'It's too early to think about that. We have time to—'

'We don't have time!' Megan cut her off. 'This is why I wanted you to stay. This is why I begged you not to go back to Italy. I wanted you here, safe. Why didn't you listen to me?'

She was hysterical now and, just like Richard, there was no point in trying to reason with her. 'Megan, you must calm down.'

Megan had stopped listening. 'When you were here, you said you weren't even sure it was going to work out between you and Richard. So why were you so desperate to get back to him? I should've known this was going to happen. Why do you have to be so selfish? You always do what's best for you. And you always leave. You always leave.'

As Megan's anger subsided into sobs, a cocktail of emotions fought for precedence in Sophia: anger at being called selfish when she was carrying her sister's child; sympathy for her despair; but overriding them both was a dull, heavy guilt. Guilt that she had left. Not a week ago, but two decades before. Because, according to what her mother had told her before she died, wasn't that why they were in this position at all?

When you've felt pain yourself, seeing someone else suffering is almost unbearable. In the days after their mother's funeral, Megan had been inconsolable, as if a darkness had fallen on her from which she couldn't emerge. It was only after Sophia had overheard a conversation between her and Mark on her way to bed one night that she'd realised why she was struggling to cope.

The following morning, Megan had told her herself. Three days after the funeral, she'd had the final confirmation from their fertility specialist that her chances of carrying a baby to term were practically zero. She'd almost choked on the sobs as she'd tried to get her words out. 'It just feels so cruel. To lose my mum in the same week as finding out that I'll never be one myself. I mean, what did I do that was so terrible that I deserve this to happen to me?'

Sophia had tried to put an arm around her. 'It's not your fault, Megan. None of this is.'

Megan's face had contorted with pain. 'Maybe it is. Maybe it is all my fault.'

It'd been agony watching her beat herself up about it and Mark had been almost useless. He took a stiff upper lip to an extreme: she hadn't seen him shed a single tear and he'd seemed almost relieved that she was there to listen to Megan cry. 'I just wanted a baby, Sophia. That's not a lot, is it? Just a little baby of my own to love.'

Sophia hadn't been ready to give up. 'There has to be something they can do. Another treatment. Mark has enough money to fly you to America or anywhere they have a special programme.'

Megan had pulled at the tissue in her hand, shredding it into pieces. 'I've asked all of those questions. The answer is the same. Our only choice is surrogacy or adoption.'

To begin with, it'd been an impulse, an instinct to make things better for her sister. 'I'll do it. I'll be your surrogate.'

Megan had stared at her. 'You can't. That's too much.'

The more she'd thought about it, the more she'd wanted to do it. 'Why not? I don't want a child, but there's no reason I can't carry one for you.'

Despite Megan shaking her head, Sophia had seen she was interested. 'You've only been back a few months. We hardly know each other.'

That was true. But wouldn't this be a wonderful way to get them back on track? 'I'm still your sister. If you can't carry your baby, then your sister has to be the next best person to do it, doesn't she? It's biology.'

As the days had worn on, it had become a longing to do this for her sister. Since the conversation with her mother weeks before, she'd carried a guilt that she hadn't known what to do with. This was her penance, her sacrifice and her offering all at once. 'Please let me do this for you, Megan. Please.'

Would Megan have ever accepted her offer if they hadn't found that box that their mother had brought from home? Was that the turning point? It certainly seemed to be, because the next day she'd sat next to Sophia on the sofa, taken her hand and looked her in the eye. 'Yes. Please. Yes, we would like you to be our surrogate.'

That's why she didn't respond with anger to her sister's harsh words now. She understood why Megan was upset and, whatever the cost had been to Sophia and Richard's relationship, she didn't regret offering for one moment. Because wasn't this the one big chance to put everything right?

SEVEN

MEGAN

Within moments of her conversation with Sophia, Megan was pulling on her trainers to go for a run.

She couldn't blame Sophia for ending their call with an abrupt, 'I'll call you later.' She hadn't meant to lose it with her like that. Hadn't meant to blame her for going back to Italy. How could Sophia have known what was about to happen? She winced at the memory of calling her selfish. Was she the one being selfish, expecting Sophia to do any of this? Had she done the wrong thing going down the surrogate route?

It'd been such a surprise when Sophia had offered. Only three months into her return, they were still getting to know one another. Not for a moment had she expected her to suggest such a huge and generous thing.

After twenty years of no contact, it'd been a big shock how quickly Sophia had responded when she'd messaged her online. It had taken Megan about fifteen attempts to get the wording right, explaining about their mother's diagnosis and asking if she'd like to see her while she still could. Allowing for the time difference to California, where she'd happened to be, Sophia's response had been instant. *I'm on my way.*

Outside, the cool March air was welcome on Megan's hot face. She flicked her right foot up onto the low garden wall to stretch it out. Then the left. Pulling her muscles as far as she could to release the tension in her body.

When she'd opened the door on the day Sophia arrived, she'd almost gasped. Despite telling herself that they were effectively strangers, the little girl in her had reached out immediately to her older sister and she'd had to hold on to the edge of the front door to prevent launching herself at Sophia. With perhaps a few more lines around the eyes and a slightly softer silhouette, she'd looked just the same as the teenage sister who'd cuddled her asleep and read to her from romantic books that were probably inappropriate for someone her age.

Almost immediately, she'd taken her into their mother's bedroom. Seeing the joy on her mother's face when Sophia had walked into her room had made Megan's chest ache. She'd slipped away to give them time alone. In those first few days, Sophia was in that room for hours on end; not knowing how much longer their mother had left, it was more important that they had that time together. Megan and Sophia had longer to get to know each other again.

Stretches done, she turned out of their garden and started to jog her muscles into readiness, the firm tattoo of her feet on the paving settling her thoughts, shuffling them into an order she could understand.

In the evenings, when their mother had slept, she and Sophia had got to know one another as adults. To begin with, they'd avoided the difficult questions – their mother's last days were hard enough without that – and it'd been so nice just being together, laughing about the time Megan had coated herself in Sophia's make-up, or when Sophia had snuck in the window of Megan's bedroom and fallen on top of her. Megan hadn't wanted to bring up the years they'd lost, the difficulties she'd faced. A few times Sophia had asked vaguely how things had been and the way she'd searched her eyes had made Megan think that she knew the answer already. But she didn't know all of it. Didn't know how bad it had gotten.

Then the night had come, three days after their mother's funeral, when she'd opened up about the fertility problems. Sophia's offer had been instant. 'I'll do it. I'll be your surrogate.'

Muscles warmed, Megan began to pick up the pace, the thud of the pavement travelled up her legs and started to shake the anxiety loose. Deeper breaths pushed the tightness from her lungs.

Mark had been amazed that she'd even contemplate Sophia's offer. 'You haven't heard from her in over twenty years, Megan. You don't know what kind of person she is, or if we can even trust her.'

But then they'd opened that box of her mother's and it'd felt like fate. As if her mother was giving her permission to go ahead. *It's okay now. You can trust her.* Megan had needed to make him understand. 'I can tell you something, Mark. I can tell you that I stay awake sobbing into my pillow some nights grieving for a child that I've never even had. That every day I hate myself for having a body that won't give me a baby. That I felt overwhelmingly lonely every time my body rejected that whisper of possibility inside. And now I have no mother and no child and maybe, just maybe, my sister has come back into my life to give me the one thing I want – no, the one thing I *need* – more than anything else in the world.'

As the sobs had come, he'd taken her into his arms. Held her close in a way he hadn't in months. 'Okay, Megan. Okay. If you want to do this, we'll do it.'

Instead of continuing to the park, Megan turned left at the end of the next road and circled back towards home. The run was doing its work; already she felt calmer and more able to deal with the situation. The most important thing was that Sophia and the baby were fine. This was just a geographical problem –

a pretty huge problem, admittedly – that she needed to solve. She'd find a way to get her and Mark to Italy or to bring Sophia here. It wasn't as if she was going to be held captive there, was it? She'd be as eager as they were for her to have the baby in England.

By the time she opened the front door, her body was loose and she could breathe again. Her laptop was open on the kitchen counter, and she checked again online for a flight or train ticket out of Italy. There was still nothing. Trying to stay calm, she took a shower, before checking again. Still nothing.

Irritation itched at her. Where was Mark? She needed him here. He would be able to think of something, she was sure. His phone was still going to voicemail. Had he not heard the news?

The flight schedules on her laptop started to blur before her eyes: she needed to look at something else rather than a screen. There was nothing to do here except wipe over surfaces that had already been scrubbed by their efficient cleaner that morning. And she didn't want to go to the gym when she'd just had a run. Maybe Elsie needed something. She'd give her a knock and see if she wanted anything from the supermarket.

Elsie was the first neighbour Megan had met when they'd moved into the house four years ago. She'd lived there since her son was small and, although her husband had passed away six years before, she had no intention of leaving the house 'where all my life has happened'. When she knocked on her bright-red door, it took a while for Elsie to open it and, when she did, she was out of breath.

Megan's first thought was her heart. 'Are you okay?'

But Elsie waved away her concern with a laugh. 'Fine, fine. I was in a downward dog when the bell went so I had to untangle myself. Come in.'

Of course, she was. Elsie was over a decade older than Megan's mother would've been, yet her vim and vigour made her seem younger. In her plum velour tracksuit and professionally highlighted hair, she could have passed for a woman twenty years younger. Megan felt like a fraud offering help. 'I was just going to Waitrose and I wondered if you wanted anything?'

Hands on hips, Elsie shook her head. Even when she was home alone, her face was always fully made up in case of company. 'No, I'm fine. I had a delivery this morning so the cupboards are fit to bursting. I've got a nice coffee and walnut cake if you've time for a coffee? You look like you need one.'

She didn't fancy the cake, but an hour in Elsie's company was exactly what the doctor ordered. 'A black coffee would be great, thanks.'

There was a beautiful orangery on the back of the house, which Elsie's husband had put in – 'that man would give me anything I wanted' – and Elsie brought the coffee and cake through. Though the March air was crisp, the light and warmth in here was welcoming; Megan let her shoulders drop from where they'd lifted to her ears.

'I heard the news. About Italy. Your sister is over there, isn't she?'

Though Elsie knew everything about the surrogacy arrangement, Megan had never told her the reason why she couldn't carry a baby and Elsie had never asked. She belonged to a generation who believed in people's privacy. Now her mother was gone, the only other person who knew the full story was Mark: even Sophia had just accepted the little she'd told her. 'Yes. I'm terrified. She was supposed to come home next week. I've got her bedroom ready for her and now...'

She couldn't stop the tears from coming. Elsie leaned forward and patted her hand. 'There, there, love. I can understand you being worried.'

Worried didn't even come close. Megan didn't have enough synonyms for terrified in her vocabulary. 'I don't know which I'm most anxious about: whether she catches this virus, or whether she's trapped over there, or she can't get to a hospital or...'

So many disaster scenarios were running through her head.

Elsie nodded. 'It's the unknown, isn't it? We can deal with anything if we know what's coming.'

That was exactly it. Well, part of it. 'I wanted to be there. When the baby was born.'

'Of course, you did. She's your baby, isn't she?'

The kindness of Elsie's tone brought tears to her eyes. *Her baby*. Even thinking about it hit every nerve in her body. They were so close to the birth that she'd dared to imagine the day that her baby would be placed in her arms – at last! – and now it felt as if it were all slipping away again. 'I know it's selfish, because so many people are really at risk from this awful virus, but I'm angry at how unfair this is. I thought that we were finally going to get our baby and now...'

Again, she couldn't finish. She knew that she sounded like a petulant child.

But Elsie didn't seem to be judging her. Instead, she smiled kindly. 'Did I tell you how I was born? Or where I was born, I should say.'

'No. I don't think you did.'

'Well, I was born during the Second World War. My dad was away fighting, and my mum was living above a shop in the East End. When she went into labour, her neighbour was helping her but then the sirens went off. She had to stumble towards a public underground shelter leaning on her next-door neighbour. She ended up having to give birth in there.'

'Oh my goodness. That must have been horrendous.'

'That's what I said when she told me, but she was made of stern stuff, my mother. They all were.' She sipped at her coffee. 'I know this is not what you wanted, Megan, but it's better that she stays where she is right now, don't you think? You don't want her catching this wretched thing.'

She was right. If this virus was still rife in the coming weeks, Sophia would be safer staying where she was. They had to put the safety of the baby first, however much it hurt that she wouldn't have the birth they'd planned. 'You're right. I know you are.'

'You're allowed to be upset, though, I'm not saying you shouldn't. But you've waited a long time for this little one. It's just a bit longer.'

Megan swallowed down the lump in her throat with the scalding black coffee. It wasn't the waiting that upset her, it was the fear of missing out on those first moments of her daughter's life. She'd rehearsed it so many times in her head that it felt as if those precious minutes were being stolen from her. 'I'm not sure that Sophia would cope giving birth in an air raid shelter.'

Then something else occurred to her. What if Sophia wasn't able to even get to a hospital? What if the hospitals were full?

Elsie picked up the cake slice and held it over the coffee cake. 'How big a slice would you like?'

Megan was aware that she needed to eat soon, but even the thought of that sugary cake made her nauseous. 'Not for me, thanks. I'm fine with the coffee.'

She glanced out of the front window, but Mark's car was still not there. As soon as he got home, she'd go back and explain the situation. Then she'd call Sophia in the morning, tell her to stay where she was. That was the right thing to do, wasn't it? And, if Sophia couldn't come to her, they would have to find a way to go to Sophia. Mark had done so little towards preparing for their baby so far, but now was the time she needed him to step up and help. He'd do it, wouldn't he? He'd find a way to get them over there in time?

EIGHT

SOPHIA

The third-floor apartment in a quiet side-street had been offered as part of the package when Richard and Sophia had moved to Italy. Though there was only one bedroom, it was high-ceilinged and spacious: a balcony looked across to the buildings opposite and the bathroom was marble-tiled and elegant. In the lounge, a gold velvet sofa, patchy but decadent, was half-covered in the clothes that Sophia had been sorting through in order to find something that would cover her burgeoning stomach without making her look like a battleship.

The first week of lockdown had proved to be surprisingly pleasant. After months of getting up early to work at the cafe, these lazy mornings in bed with no alarm to jolt her awake were an absolute – if rather guilty – treat. She'd finished a novel for the first time since coming here and had even found a couple of art history podcasts to enjoy. Once this was all over, she'd finally make that trip to the Uffizi Gallery in Florence. With, or without, Richard.

For most of the last few days, he'd been shut up in their bedroom with his laptop, firing emails to anyone who might have any power to get the dig reopened or, at the very least, allow him and a couple of the more senior members of the team on-site. He wasn't having much luck. Unsurprisingly, to everyone except Richard, ancient pieces of pottery weren't at the top of anyone's priorities right now. Aside from their first passionate weeks together, this was the longest they'd spent in close proximity. She was glad that the bedroom door was thick enough to keep his negative energy enclosed and away from her.

Ignoring his barbed comment about tidying up the mountain of shoes in the bedroom – swollen feet was making that choice a minefield, too – she'd found an episode on Italian Renaissance painting and had spent a very pleasant hour clearing out and cleaning the spice cupboard. The glass spice jars chinked together as she rearranged them into alphabetical order.

Despite the calm she was manifesting in the apartment, she'd been unable to avoid a couple of intense conversations with Megan over the last few days. Repeatedly, she'd promised not to leave the house in case of infection and assured her that she'd keep using antibacterial gel after touching anything that Richard had brought home with the shopping and would call Megan immediately if she felt unwell. She even resisted the urge to ask her sister what she could possibly do from hundreds of miles away if she did actually call. She remembered her mother's words before she died. 'Megan is fragile, Sophia. She's not like you. You need to look out for her.'

The reconciliation with her mother had been pretty intense. Though she'd jumped on a plane as soon as she could, it wasn't until the taxi ride to Megan's house that she'd wondered how their first meeting would go. In all the years she'd been away, Sophia had pictured her mother in many different ways: the kind fun mum of her early childhood; the loving mum who'd tried to help her through boyfriend breakups and friendship fallouts; and the last mum – the one who'd failed her. She'd wondered many times what she'd do if she saw her again.

But, when Megan had suggested she go straight in without taking a breath, all of her preconceived ideas had gone out the window. Seeing her mother laying there, frail but still the same, she'd realised – in a rush of heat and tears – how much she'd missed her. 'Hi, Mum.'

She'd frowned before she'd opened her eyes, as if trying to place the voice. 'Sophia?'

She'd swallowed, trying to keep her voice steady. 'Yes, it's me.'

Fighting to push herself up on her elbows, her face had been an indecipherable mixture of joy and pain. 'Oh, baby girl. You're here. You're really here.'

In two steps, Sophia had reached the bed. 'I'm here.'

For the first couple of days, Megan had thoughtfully left them alone, knowing that they had a lot to process. It was good that she had because, after their tearful embrace, the things they'd talked about – the apologies they'd made – were not destined for Megan's ears.

On the second day, still sore from the conversation of the day before, Sophia had assumed that all the secrets had been discussed. But she'd been wrong.

As well as the chair by their mother's bed, Megan had set up a small table with water, a box of tissues and a bowl of mints. It'd made Sophia smile. 'She's good, isn't she?'

Her mother had nodded. 'She's always been a good girl.'

Sophia had tried not to feel that there was an unspoken comparison. 'And this house is quite something. She fell on her feet when she met Mark, didn't she?'

It hadn't been meant as a jibe, she'd only been making conversation, but her mother's face had been serious. 'Life hasn't always been easy for your sister. She feels things very deeply.'

The last time Sophia and Megan were together, she'd been a shy and gentle twelve-year-old. It was hardly a surprise that she was still sensitive. 'I know, Mum.'

Her mother had reached for her hand and held it. The day before, when she'd explained – as best she could – her own part in their rift, she'd done the same thing. As if, now she had Sophia back, she'd wanted to make sure she wouldn't lose her again. 'No. I mean she's really struggled. I need to tell you because I need someone to look out for her.'

It'd been difficult not to feel envious about her mother's concern. Where had that been for her twenty years ago? And since? But they'd been through all of that yesterday; this hadn't been the time to bring it up again. 'What kind of struggles?'

Her mother had tried to swallow but it'd made her cough, so Sophia had poured a glass of water and held it to her lips. It had been hard to watch her attempt to lift her head high enough to drink. Megan had told her the night before that there were good days and bad days.

After the tiniest of sips, she'd continued, her rasping voice so quiet that Sophia had to lean forward to catch it. 'After you left, we had a difficult time of things. And your sister... well, she missed you a lot. We both did.'

Now it had been Sophia's turn to swallow. She couldn't bear to imagine Megan alone in that house, thinking that Sophia had forgotten her. 'I missed you both, too.'

Her mother had squeezed her hand with the little strength she had. 'And then your father left and we really struggled. Life was difficult. And then Megan got ill.'

Sophia had been staring at the pale-pink bedcovers, but her head had snapped up at that. 'Ill? What kind of ill? Is she okay?'

Her mother's eyes had filled with tears, one of which spilled down the side of her face to the pillow. 'She had anorexia. She got very poorly.'

Anorexia? She'd stopped eating? But that made no sense. The twelve-year-old Megan had been the first one to plead for ice cream or cake every time they were out together. 'How did that happen?'

The guilt on her mother's face had been an exact copy of her expression the day before when she'd begged Sophia to forgive her. 'I don't know. I didn't notice for so long. She wore baggy clothes. She told me she'd eaten when I got in from work. I just didn't see it until she was really poorly.'

It had been almost unbearable. The Megan of Sophia's memory was such a sweet round-faced girl with an infectious giggle and a love of anything sugary. How terrible had she felt to get to that point? 'How bad was it? Did she have to go into hospital?'

'No. We avoided that, but it was close for a while.'

Sophia had tried to picture Megan that morning. Had she looked ill then? She'd wanted to run downstairs and check her over. 'I should have been there.'

Her mother's smile had been weak, but kind. 'Oh, Sophia. You couldn't have done anything. She had doctors. She got better.'

I would have noticed. Wasn't that the truth? She would've known if her sister was sick. She would've made sure she got help quickly. Or – and this made her feel even worse – maybe, if she'd been there, her sister wouldn't have been ill at all. She'd put her hand to her throat and tried to massage away the tightness there. 'Is she still okay now?'

Her mother's nod had been almost imperceptible. 'Yes. But I don't think it ever really goes for good. When things are difficult, it rears its head.'

'Like now?' Sophia couldn't imagine things getting any worse than watching your mother slowly slip away.

Her mother had closed her eyes, but she'd frowned. 'Strangely, I think she's coping right now. She's busy. Making my meals and measuring out my medication. I think it'll be harder for her... after.'

Sophia's eyes had filled, her chest tightening. Even with all the anger she still felt, she couldn't bear the thought of her mother's death. How much worse was it going to be for Megan? Looking at this empty bedroom every day. It was that image that had decided her. 'I'll stay. I won't go back to California. I'll stay here as long as you both need me.'

Her mother had shaken her head. 'That's not what I'm asking.'

'I know. But it's what I want to do.'

And she had stayed. Megan had been shocked but, she believed, pleased to have her around. It hadn't been easy – her sister liked everything done a certain way, would wipe crumbs from the counter before Sophia had finished making a sandwich and seemed to think a five-kilometre run was the quintessential good time – but she'd stuck it out. Then, when the question of surrogacy had come up, she'd grabbed the opportunity with open arms.

And wouldn't Megan be surprised – and impressed – to see her right now, enjoying this rearrangement of the spice cupboard? She'd got as far as the T herbs and counted four opened jars of tarragon. The sweet grassy liquorice smell made her crave tarragon chicken as she tipped the contents of three of the jars into the fourth, gave it a wipe and slotted it into place. She should put chicken on the shopping list for Richard. Even in the midst of his frustrations, he couldn't complain about being the one to go out for food rather than her. He may not agree with what she was doing, but he wouldn't put an unborn baby at risk.

Almost full jars of thyme and turmeric rattled back into place and she was done. She leaned back on her heels and stretched her arms into the air. She'd kept her promise to Megan to stay at home, but she really needed fresh air. If it was empty, the small shared garden behind their building would have to do.

Richard was mid-shout on the phone when she pushed open the door to the bedroom and he waved her away irritably when she tried to convey in hand gestures where she was going. If it wasn't for the fact she couldn't go anywhere, and was over seven months' pregnant, she wouldn't put up with it. For now, they'd have to just navigate this as best they could.

Thankfully, the garden was empty; the cool air must be deterring any but the most desperate. It was a square of lawn surrounded by shrubs, bushes and terracotta pots. When they'd first moved there, Sophia had intended to get involved with the older couple who tended the plants, but since before Christmas, the garden had been a little neglected. Propped against the wall, she found a wooden fold-up chair and dragged it to the back corner into a patch of sunlight. With her head tilted backward to warm her face, the first she knew of Alex's arrival was hearing the back door bang.

She sat up and squinted at him. 'Hello.'

He almost jumped. 'Sorry, I didn't realise you were out here. Do you want me to go?'

She was actually pretty desperate to speak to someone who wasn't at the end of a telephone or the other side of a closed door. 'No, stay. We can keep our distance.'

According to the English press she was reading online, the safe distance was two metres apart and Alex was a lot further than that away. He crouched down until he was sitting on the back step, an open paperback in his hand. 'Thanks. I just needed to get out in the fresh air. I'm still not sure what the rules are about being outside in public. I'm scuttling to the shops and back like a nervous cockroach.'

Sophia smiled. 'I'm not even doing that. Richard is getting

our shopping. I've got practically a year's supply of pomodoro sauce if you want any of that.'

With time on her hands, Sophia had enjoyed cooking batches of sauce, slow roasting vegetables and had even been experimenting with making pasta by hand. Life at a slower pace was agreeing with her much more than she'd have anticipated.

'That sounds great. I'm not a particularly proficient cook. To be honest, one of the other attractions about coming here to write was the promise of eating out. Timed that wrong, didn't I?'

He smiled, but there was something about his tone that made him sound lost. 'Are you okay?'

Behind his wire-rimmed spectacles he raised his eyebrows. 'Me? I'm fine.'

She didn't believe him. 'Really? Because you don't sound it.'

He sighed. 'I'm not good at being cooped up like this. Plus —' he looked as if he was wrestling with himself '—I've got some stuff on my mind.'

Sophia knew that she shouldn't pry, but someone else's problems would actually be a relief. 'Anything I can help with? I have a friendly ear, which is all yours. From a social distance, obviously.'

He was kind enough to laugh at her feeble joke. 'The thing is, I trained to be a doctor. Well, I didn't complete the training, but I know my way around a hospital.'

That was surprising. 'I see.'

He looked down at the ground, smoothing over the gravel path with his foot. 'Yeah. It got too much for me, if I'm perfectly honest. I trained in the UK and the hours, the pressure. I couldn't hack it, so I just left.'

Head still down, he looked up at her from beneath his eyelashes as if waiting for judgement. She had none. 'I can understand that. It must be an incredibly challenging job. There's no shame in saying it's not for you.'

He coughed a dry humourless laugh. 'Well, that's what I've been telling myself, too. But it's pretty difficult when the whole of your family is in the medical profession. Especially now that they're all working round the clock in hospitals helping people who are contracting this virus.'

She was starting to understand his turmoil. 'I see.'

Now that he'd started, it was clear he wanted to talk about it. 'And the hospitals here are crying out for staff, but I no longer have any kind of licence to practise, so I can't offer to help. I feel utterly useless.'

His forehead creased as if a sharp pain had run through him. She wanted to make him feel better, but how could she? 'There's nothing you can do about that. You can't offer to help if they won't have you, can you? I mean, I understand. I really do. It's difficult to sit back when you might be able to help.'

Megan came to her mind. This was why she'd had to offer to be her surrogate. She could help, so she did.

His voice cracked as he spoke. 'But people are dying. And I'm just... just sitting here doing nothing.'

It must've been the hormones that made tears rush to her eyes so fast. As a rule, she wasn't a crier. Social distancing – and the fact that this was only the second time she'd met him – prevented her from hugging him, so she tried to convey that sentiment with her voice. 'Please don't beat yourself up. We're all useless in the face of this thing. I've done nothing except make pasta sauce and tidy up.'

She'd never been a homebody. That had always been Megan's personality, not hers. She remembered Megan playing with dolls when she wasn't much more than a baby herself. Putting them to bed, rocking them, pretending to feed them from one of those bottles that made the milk slowly disappear when you tipped it downwards. She would always have one of her 'babies' with her. At thirteen, Sophia was far more inter-ested in clothes and make-up than toys, but she would indulge her sister sometimes and hold her baby for her when she asked. How ironic that was now.

Even then, their mother had pigeon-holed them both. 'I know which of you is more likely to look after me in my old age,' she used to say. Megan would climb on their mother's lap and hug her close. 'I'll look after you, Mummy.' Sophia would just roll her eyes.

Now Alex was wiping at his eyes with the back of his hand. 'I know. You're right. It's the old saviour complex, I suppose.' He nodded at her stomach which, again, she had her hands on like a parody of a pregnant woman. 'How are you feeling?'

Now it was her turn to look down at the ground. She wasn't ashamed of what she was doing; on the contrary, she knew that it was a gift that she was giving her sister. But she'd had mixed reactions from people and Alex was a doctor; he probably had strong opinions about this one way or another. There was no point hiding it, though. 'Physically, I'm fine. But this baby doesn't belong to me. She's my sister's. I'm carrying her embryo.'

He raised his eyebrows. 'You're her surrogate?'

She still couldn't gauge his reaction. It was odd that she wanted him to approve. 'Yep. She had some... health issues. She couldn't carry a child so, here I am.' Again, the memory of six-year-old Megan passing over a doll for Sophia to hold came to her mind.

'Wow. That's quite something. Would you believe that I've never actually met a surrogate in real life? I mean, I had to do a rotation on maternity – I've even been present at a few births – but I've never spoken to anyone carrying a baby for someone else. That's pretty amazing.'

She was pleased he approved, but his praise was making her blush. 'Yeah, well. She's my sister. It's not completely altruistic. I'm not donating a kidney to a stranger or anything like that.'

'Don't underplay it. I've been around enough pregnant women to know that it's not a walk in the park.'

Something prickled in the depths of her; it was definitely time to steer this conversation to a lighter tone. 'I'm glad you've got experience in the delivery room. If this situation doesn't improve, I might need you.'

She'd meant it as a joke, but he paled. 'You'll be much better off in the hospital.'

'I know. I'm only teasing.'

For a few moments, awkwardness floated in the air between them. Then he coughed like he was beginning a new paragraph. 'It's a great thing you're doing. You and your sister must be close?'

It was easier talking about this to a stranger. 'Not especially. I mean, we're getting there, but we haven't been close for a long time. There's an age gap and I left home at nineteen so, you know, we didn't exactly spend a lot of time together.'

'That makes it even more of a great thing you're doing.'

He wouldn't be saying that if he knew the real reason she was doing it. She shivered in the breeze. 'I'd better get in. Those tomatoes won't roast themselves.'

Alex stood further away from the door so that she could get inside without coming too close to him. 'I'll see you around. If I can help at all with any concerns you have, just shout. But I hope the hospitals are back to normal soon so that you get in to see your midwife.'

Despite his distance, she could smell the citrus of his after-shave on the breeze. Meeting his eye made her stomach fizz a little. 'Thanks. And if you need someone to chat at you from across the garden, just knock on the door.'

This wasn't flirting. She was about to pop out a baby and – even though she and Richard were on borrowed time – they were together right now. She might have racked up a few boyfriends in her time, but she wasn't the cheating kind. It would be nice to have a friend here, though. And, with his medical experience, it was comforting to know that there was someone in the building she could call on if she needed to. Alex hadn't seemed too keen to help out at a home birth, but maybe – in the present circumstances – it wasn't the worst thing that could happen. Women had been doing it since the beginning of time, it was a natural process, she'd had a healthy pregnancy. How hard could it be?

NINE

MEGAN

When the announcement was made, on the 23rd March, Megan was home alone.

At six that morning, she'd been to a spin class, followed by a HIIT session. Her appetite was non-existent, but she'd forced half of a green smoothie down on her way to the office. Now, more than ever, she needed to keep to regular mealtimes, routine and the repetition of the rules that kept her well.

Sitting beside Petra, she'd talked her through how to place ads on social media to boost their clients' posts. For someone who professed to still be battling baby brain, she picked everything up very easily. It was Megan who'd been distracted and lost her place a few times. They – like most of the country probably – had had the radio news in the background all day, waiting for updates. When they left the office around five, she and Bethany had taken home the files they'd need to work remotely, just in case. She was home by six and calling Mark. He'd been in Cardiff for a meeting, but he and his father were on the way home. At 8.30 p.m., she was in front of the TV watching Boris Johnson announce that everyone had to stay at home. Like Italy, the whole country was now on lockdown.

When Mark arrived home thirty minutes later, Megan was sitting on the bottom step in the hallway, waiting for him to make sense of all this. As soon as he was in the door he dropped his briefcase and came to sit with her on the stairs. 'How are you feeling? It's a shock, isn't it?'

She reached out her hand so that he could hold it. 'To be honest, I didn't think they'd actually do it. I mean, shutting schools and shops... It's really serious.'

Even though she'd been worried about Sophia, there was a part of her that'd thought that this would all be temporary. She'd held onto the idea that, maybe, she'd be able to bring her home before the baby came. Mark kissed the top of her head before he let her go. 'Yeah, it's serious. I called Brendan Ryan – my uni friend who works for the Health Department – and he thinks this is going to be in effect for a while.' He looked her in the eye. 'Weeks. If not months.'

Her stomach tightened; they didn't have that long. 'We have to go to her, then. They haven't stopped the flights yet. I checked.'

He sighed and rubbed at his eyes as if he needed to sleep. 'I just don't think it's a good idea. Planes, trains – they're going to be incubators for this damn thing. It's not worth the risk, Megs. For any of you.'

She knew he was right but missing the birth of their child was unthinkable. 'We have to be there when she's born, Mark. We have to go.'

He shook his head, watching her closely. 'I don't think we can.'

Throughout their marriage, he'd been the strong one, the one who made everything better, who helped her to make sense of the world when problems seemed insurmountable. Whatever he could do to make her life easier, he did. Which is why it'd been so difficult the last few months when he'd almost retreated from any discussion of Sophia's pregnancy. Still perched on the bottom stair, she leaned forward onto her thighs, wrapping her hands under her knees. She wanted to squeeze hard on the pain that soured her stomach. 'It's so unfair.'

Mark pulled her close again. 'I know, love. I know how much you wanted this. I'm so sorry.'

Want didn't even come close. Her desire, her *need*, to have a child had become so strong that it had taken over every part of her life. She couldn't walk in the street or speak to another woman without being reminded that she was outside this club of motherhood. Resentment would seethe in her if she saw a mother ignoring her child; jealousy would be worse if she was enjoying them. Just watching a mother spoon feed their baby in a cafe high chair could be enough to send her to the bathroom to close herself in a cubicle and cry.

'I wanted so much to be there when she was born. To have those first moments together.'

'I know. I get it. I do. But you'll still have a baby. Being there at the birth isn't as important as the rest of her life.'

How could he understand? He hadn't fantasised about giving birth the way she had. Hadn't struggled to make peace with the fact that their child would not come from her body. He was trying to make her feel better, but he was actually making it worse. 'You don't seem that bothered that we're going to miss out. I thought you'd be upset, too.'

Mark closed his eyes, longer than a blink, as if mustering the energy to answer her. 'I am. Of course it's a disappointment but...'

She frowned. 'But what?'

He sighed. 'I've been kind of expecting that something would go wrong. It's why I didn't want to do it. Your sister is... she doesn't strike me as someone you can depend on.'

Megan stiffened. 'That's hardly fair. She can't be held responsible for a global pandemic.'

'No, of course not. But she is responsible for being in an

entirely different country. We asked her to stay with us while she's pregnant and she didn't want to. Now this has happened, and we have no control whatsoever about where she's going or what she's doing and, yes, we won't see our child born.'

Megan had the same feelings of frustration, but loyalty to her sister prevented her from joining in. 'She couldn't give up her whole life for nine months, Mark.'

His laugh was unkind. 'What life? She works in a coffee shop and lives with a guy she's only known for a year. A guy she doesn't even seem that keen on any longer. Even you said her romantic history needs a revolving door.'

She had said that. But it was before she'd got to know Sophia properly again. Before she'd offered to do this amazingly generous thing for her, for both of them. 'She's giving up a lot, Mark. We're basically renting her body for nine months. And that's without the emotional side of it all.'

That was the part that worried her the most. It was all very well Sophia joking that she didn't have a maternal bone in her body, but what if that changed? Hormones did funny things to you. She should know, she'd been pumped with enough of them in the last few years.

Mark shook his head. 'Your sister doesn't strike me as the kind of person who is suddenly going to have a breakdown. She seems pretty strong to me.'

It was hard not to hear the subtext of *unlike you* in his voice. They rarely spoke about her eating disorder these days – she'd been so well for so long – but sometimes he treated her like a crystal vase that needed to be wrapped in tissue. Maybe she was being unfair. Either way, she didn't want to talk about Sophia's emotional state any longer. 'What are you going to do about work? You won't be able to visit any clients, will you?'

'I'll have to work from here. I assume you'll set up in the kitchen like you used to at our old place?'

Before the company was making enough to rent the office,

she and Beth had worked from their own homes. Meeting up a couple of times a week in a coffee bar halfway. She'd used the kitchen table as a workspace. 'I guess so. What about you?'

'I was thinking I'd set up the small room as an office space. That way I won't be in your hair.'

Her throat tightened. 'That room is the nursery now.'

Something that she couldn't name flashed across his face. 'Well, I know it will be. But I thought it was the easiest place to set up a desk. I'll just dismantle the cot for now. It's only temporary.'

Maybe she was overreacting, but there was no way she would let him take that cot apart. Right now, it was the only proof that they were expecting a child. 'I want that room to stay as it is. I don't want anything to spoil it.'

He took a deep breath and spoke slowly. 'I understand that, Megs, but I need to work somewhere.'

Lately, there'd been that tone in his voice, like she was an irritation. It pulled her right back to the way her own father used to speak to her mum. She'd grown up used to his dismissive, authoritarian tone. The day after Sophia left was etched on her brain. Peeping in at the kitchen door, she'd seen her mother crying at the table with her head in her hands, while her father had stridden up and down behind her, waving a piece of paper and doing that whisper-shout which had made Megan's stomach hurt. 'Don't ever mention her name again. She might as well be dead.'

But she wasn't her mother. And she wasn't giving in on this. 'You can work in the kitchen. Or the dining room.'

Again, that irritated sigh. 'That won't work. I need privacy. Some of the clients are sharing sensitive information.'

Privacy from whom? 'You don't need to worry about me. I wouldn't be interested even if I understood it.'

She'd meant this as a joke, but it didn't come off that way. More and more lately, they seemed to be running into a brick wall when they tried to communicate. His face was closed. 'You know what I mean. They're already going to be twitchy about not meeting in person. Dad thinks we're going to have a challenge on our hands with the more traditional clients who like to do business over a nice claret.'

The mention of his father made her even more cross; she still hadn't forgiven him for preventing Mark from being at the 4D scan. 'Can't you use the guest room?'

Aside from keeping the nursery sacred, she hoped that turning the guest room into an office might stop him from using it to sleep in. In the last year, he'd spent more and more nights away from their bed, saying that her fitful sleep was making it difficult for him to relax. Their sex life had been almost non-existent. Despite his assurances that he was just tired, it was hard not to feel that it was *her* he was tired of. Mark had grown more attractive as he got older and filled out the gangly limbs of his early twenties. While her mirror reflected how the anorexia, fertility treatment and years of anxiety had ravaged her face and body.

He frowned at her suggestion of the guest room. 'I thought that you were keeping that pristine for Sophia?'

At her sides, she squeezed her hands into fists. 'Well, that's not urgent now, is it? I'd rather you set up in there than the nursery.'

Mark shrugged. 'Okay. Suits me. There's more space and I won't have to disturb you if I work late. I can just crash in there.'

Her heart sank at his words. More than anything, she needed him to be strong right now, to sweep away the fears that were creeping over her like a cold draught. 'This is going to be okay, isn't it? I mean, the baby? Sophia? It's all going to work out?'

He brought her hand up to his mouth and kissed the back of it. 'It's going to be fine. You're going to have a baby, Megs.'

Was she reading too much into it, being oversensitive, in

noticing that he said that *she* was going to have a baby? More and more in the last few weeks, this had felt like something she was doing with her sister and that he was not involved. Still, she swallowed the question that she really wanted to ask. *Do you want this baby as much as I do?*

Mark wasted no time in bringing his laptop and files in from the car and setting himself up for work tomorrow in the bedroom. The sound of him dragging furniture around up there grated on Megan's nerves as far away as the kitchen, so – despite the darkness – she took herself outside with a glass of water.

The security lights they'd had installed in the garden must have alerted Elsie, unless she, too, had needed some fresh air. Her voice called out, 'Megan, is that you?' before her face appeared over the garden fence. 'Well, this is a rum old business, isn't it?'

That was an understatement of epic proportions. 'Yes. It's a bit scary.'

Elsie sighed. 'I'm none too keen on these staying home rules. I should have been at art club today, but they cancelled it. And if they don't have it sorted by Friday, I'll miss tai chi and there'll be hell to pay.'

Her tone was light but there was an unmistakable wobble to Elsie's lip that Megan had never seen before. Elsie was always upbeat and positive and glass half full. But, of course, the isolation of lockdown would be worse for people who lived on their own. Especially for someone like Elsie who spent most of her life shooting off to any event in a five-mile radius. 'We'll have to do some tai chi in the garden. You can show me from over there.'

She was pleased to see Elsie smile. 'Good idea, love. Although I must warn you that I tend to make up my own moves. I only really go for the tea and natter afterwards. I'm more about the chai tea than the tai chi.'

It felt good to laugh. And to talk to Elsie. This was when she missed her mother most: when there was a problem chewing at her brain that she needed to talk about. 'Oh, Elsie. I'm really worried about my sister and the baby.'

Her understanding was immediate. 'Of course, you are, love. You and Mark must be desperate to get her back here.'

Megan wasn't sure how to answer that question either. 'Well, I am.'

Elsie tilted her wise head. 'Not Mark?'

Though they were familiar enough for a brief hello, Elsie didn't know Mark that well. He was away with work a lot and wasn't one for chatting over the garden fence when he was home. 'He's just being so pragmatic about it all. Saying that we have to accept that we can't do anything about it. I can't understand why he's not more bothered about it.'

It felt disloyal, speaking about Mark this way. In all their years of marriage, she'd never talked him down to someone else, couldn't understand how some of her friends were comfortable with discussing their partner's failings as a form of small talk. But she needed to talk to someone about this or she knew it was going to eat away at her.

Elsie brushed a hair from in front of her eyes, her full face of make-up still carefully applied despite it being almost ten o'clock. 'It's not just Mark, love. Lots of men are like that before the baby's here. It's like they have to see it before they realise there's an actual child. It's different for us because... well, because it is.'

Megan knew why she'd faltered. Knew that she was about to say, 'because we carry the baby'. Because Megan wasn't, was she? But it didn't make any difference at all to how much she wanted to get to her child. 'Why, though? He's seen the scan just the same as I have.'

Although he hadn't seen the 4D scan. Hadn't made the effort to be there when she'd needed him to be. Elsie held on to the top of the fence as she leaned a little closer. 'It doesn't necessarily improve a lot when they're first born. My husband was useless when Peter was tiny. Not interested at all. He barely held him and he definitely didn't change a nappy. But when Peter got older, he loved the bones of him. Some men just aren't into babies. Maybe Mark's like that.'

She wanted to believe that Elsie was right. And it was more complicated for them, anyway. It wasn't as if Mark was lying next to her every night feeling the baby kick. Even when Sophia was there, Mark hadn't felt comfortable putting his hands on her stomach. When she'd asked him about it, he'd said he'd cuddle the baby 'once it's ours'. It'd made her feel annoyed back then because the baby was *always* theirs. Now, she felt even more worried. What if he *never* connected with their child? 'What happens if he doesn't see her born? Do you think that'll make it even harder?'

Elsie shook her head. 'Not at all. Lots of fathers don't see their child born. Goodness, years ago they were down the pub wetting the baby's head before it'd even arrived.'

It wasn't just Mark, though. 'He doesn't seem to realise how I'm feeling. I *need* to see her being born. I want those first moments with her so much.'

In one of her random trawls of the Internet, she'd stumbled across an article about baby ducks and how, after hatching, they'd be imprinted with an attachment to the first 'mother' they saw. It didn't even have to be another duck. It was such a ridiculous worry that she couldn't even repeat it to Elsie, but she also couldn't stop it nibbling away at her. What if that happened to her baby? When her daughter opened her eyes for the first time ever, she wanted it to be *her* face smiling down on her, whispering her welcome to the world. She'd dreamed about that moment for so long, persuaded herself that not carrying her daughter didn't matter as long as she was there when she arrived.

Elsie understood this far better than Mark. 'Oh, sweetheart, I'm so sorry. Of course you do. But don't give up yet. We don't know anything about how long this is going to last. And those idiots on the TV don't seem to have much of a clue, either. Keep hoping.'

Hope? It felt like that's all she'd ever had. An ephemeral, fragile, painful hope of being a mother. In the light of what was unfolding across the world, it was hard not to feel that the whole universe was against that happening. She was ricocheting between sobbing with grief and stamping her feet in anger about how damn unfair it was.

But she couldn't dump all this onto Elsie; she'd have her own worries to deal with. 'Thanks. You're right. I mustn't give up. I'll try and stay positive. And don't go stir crazy indoors on your own. I'm always here if you want a chat over the fence and I'll try not to be a misery next time.'

'Nonsense. You're totally justified in being upset. And likewise, I'm always here for you, love.'

Her kindness pulled at the part of Megan's heart that was still grieving her mother. She swallowed down the lump in her throat and tried to smile. 'And if you need anything from the shops, let me know.'

'I will love. But I've got enough food in the freezer to keep me going past Christmas.'

She left with a wave. *Past Christmas? Please let Elsie be right that it could be over much sooner than that.* And if it wasn't, then – whatever Mark said – there had to be a way for her to get to Sophia before the baby was born. She'd missed out on so much already. That was the moment she'd been pinning all her hopes on.

And it wasn't just the irrational duck thing. If Sophia had the baby and Megan wasn't there, how would she know what to do, how to look after her, to love her the way Megan would, did already, love her child?

No. She had to be there when she was born. Whatever it took.

TEN

SOPHIA

Through the large window that looked out onto the street, a shaft of early April sunshine made its way across the room, past the piles of magazines on the chair, to warm Sophia's toes. A year ago, the very idea of being cooped up in an apartment for most of the day would have made her run for the hills. But today, four weeks into lockdown, laying on the sofa with a long glass of lime and soda, she felt decidedly... content? It was not a word she used very often, equating it with dullness and repetition and at odds with her usual thirst for change and excitement. But it was the right word. She was content.

Richard, on the other hand, was not. He'd had a forty-five-minute telephone conversation in the other room which had got louder and louder until she could clearly hear him 'with respect' giving it both barrels to whoever was unlucky enough to be on the other end of the telephone. Now the door to the sitting room slammed open and he marched towards her with his hands outstretched. 'Unbelievable.'

'Thank you very much.' She winked at him as she bit into another glossy olive. She couldn't get enough of them at the moment.

He chose to ignore her joke. 'How can it be difficult to get permission for us to work on the site? It'll be outdoors. And we can work in different areas well away from each other.'

She was bored of having the same conversation with him about this. So she tried a different tack. 'If you were working with other people, we wouldn't be able to live together at the same time. The UK news is calling it a bubble.'

When her brain tired of translating the Italian news, she'd been watching what the UK press had to say about what was going on. It was troubling to see that the messages weren't always the same. Part of the reason why she wasn't venturing further than the back garden.

He screwed up his face. 'What the hell is a bubble?'

She was too tired to explain that either. 'Why don't you just accept it, Richard? Think of this as an enforced holiday.'

He dropped down into the armchair across from her. 'We can't all be earning money while laying on a couch eating olives.'

That was unfair. She hadn't wanted to accept money from Megan and Mark, but they'd insisted that she needed enough to live on while this was going on. She wasn't going to rise to his jibe; he was just looking for someone to spar with. 'I'm growing a human. That's very tiring, you know.'

'I would imagine it is.' For the first time, he seemed curious. 'Does it feel weird? When it moves, I mean?'

It was more strange that it *didn't* feel strange. In the first stages of the pregnancy, she'd wondered whether it would feel alien to have something moving inside her. Yet, now it was happening, it felt like the most natural thing in the world. 'I kind of like it. It feels... I don't know, wholesome? I'm not sure that's the right word. I'll think of a better one.'

Richard waved his hand. 'You don't need to. It's funny, seeing you like this. I never expected you to actually enjoy it. I thought it was an act of penance.'

She hadn't told him the whole truth about why she was doing this for Megan. He'd had the same story she'd given to her sister: that she was trying to make up for those lost years. 'I didn't say I was enjoying it exactly. It's just not as bad as I thought it would be.'

That was a lie. She *was* enjoying it. Once she was through those scary early months, she'd been really well and, judging by some of the complaints she'd heard from the pregnant women she'd served over the years, she was getting off very lightly in the pregnancy-symptoms department. Even the changes in her body were interesting. Now Richard was looking at her as if appraising a piece of pottery he'd just dusted the centuries from. 'It suits you, you know. You look – what is it they say about pregnant women? – radiant.'

He was mocking her, but he wasn't wrong: she did look good. At thirty-three weeks' pregnant, her skin was practically glowing and her hair was thick and shiny. Even her normally stubby fingernails were growing fast enough that she could enjoy filing and painting them as another way to while away half an hour. Speaking of which, her nails were dry enough for a second coat.

Richard watched her pick up the bottle of dark-green nail polish with almost a sneer on his face. 'How can you lay around doing that in all this mess?'

She followed the sweep of his hand, which took in the magazines, three empty glasses on the table, a pair of socks that she'd just taken off and a pile of laundry that needed putting away. It was hardly a cesspit. 'I'll tidy up this afternoon.'

He coughed out a sarcastic laugh. 'Don't you have plans to paint your toenails this afternoon?'

Sophia wasn't averse to a good row, it cleared the air sometimes, but Richard's passive aggressive jibes about her untidiness and general nit-picking about the teaspoon she'd left in the sink or that she'd forgotten to add his favourite shirt to the washing she'd done earlier – where was he going to wear it anyway? – had made her even more sure that it was starting again. The unravelling of another relationship. A loose thread of annoyance, a pinprick of irritation. It was the beginning of the end for her and Richard, she could feel it.

She stretched out her legs – they had that itchy restlessness that had begun to bother her at night – then pocketed the nail polish and pushed herself out of her seat and past his chair, calling back over her shoulder. 'I'm going to make a salad for lunch. Any requests?'

In the kitchen, chopping cucumber and tomatoes was cathartic. Did all relationships have this built-in obsolescence or was it just hers? Usually it was because – whatever they said about wanting to travel the world – most of her boyfriends had eventually wanted to settle down and make somewhere home and she never did. The few times that Megan had asked her that question – *but why did you not come back?* – she'd kept her answer vague. When this was over and Megan was finally happy, would she be able to tell her the whole truth?

Her mobile buzzed on the counter. She wiped tomato juice from her hands before swiping it. 'Hi, Megan. How are you doing?'

'I'm going a little crazy to be honest. It feels like we've been in lockdown for two months rather than two weeks. Any tips for dealing with cabin fever?'

She didn't want to admit that she was enjoying her time at home. 'I'm cooking up a storm. There's not a vegetable gone unchopped or a pastry unbaked in this house. We're going to struggle to get through the doorframe when this is all over.'

As soon as she said it, she could've kicked herself – what kind of insensitive idiot talks about weight to someone who's struggled with an eating disorder? – but Megan didn't miss a beat. 'Good for you. I'm trying to keep busy with work but it's driving me nuts not being able to get to the gym. I've been going for a run every day but it's not enough.'

She'd forgotten how obsessed Megan was with the gym. Should she be worried that she didn't have that release at the moment? When she'd last stayed there, Megan would have been to a spin class and back, making some kind of green slime smoothie before Sophia had even emerged from her bedroom. 'What about a YouTube workout video? You could do that at home.'

Megan pulled a face. 'It's being stuck at home that's the problem. There's only so much work you can get through before you need to do something else.'

'What about Mark? Isn't it nice being together?'

There was a pause on the other end before she replied. 'Yes. But he's having to put in extra hours. He's working in a different room. I can't just interrupt him every time I need a distraction.'

That was surprising. As much as Richard had been absorbed in his work, he hadn't complained about her wandering in and out of the room when she was bored. He himself emerged several times a day to regale her with his latest phone battle. Whether she wanted it or not. She glanced through to the sitting room where he was putting on his trainers. He pointed towards the door and mouthed, 'I'm going out.'

It really frustrated her when he did this in the middle of her making a meal, but she couldn't cut her conversation with Megan so she contented herself with a grandiose hand gesture of frustration, which he replied to with a wave before he disappeared.

Megan didn't really have much to say and the conversation was a little stilted. It wasn't as if either of them had done anything interesting since they last spoke this morning. Though she would've liked fewer calls, she knew it would break Megan's heart if she'd actually suggested that. Instead, she rummaged around in the fridge for mozzarella, while nodding along to

Megan's updates on the length of the socially distanced queue outside the local Waitrose that morning. Long, apparently. And as slow as this conversation.

A combination of her conversations with Richard and Megan left Sophia feeling a little claustrophobic, so once she'd chopped the tomatoes and torn the mozzarella, she took her salad bowl outside. The door to the courtyard was propped open with a man's large black boot. The owner of which was sitting at the other end of the garden on an upturned plant pot.

Alex held up a hand to say hello. 'I can go in now if you need some space?'

She leaned her back against the wall of the building and jabbed at the salad with her fork. 'No, stay. Actually, I'm glad that I've seen you. I need some medical advice.'

This time he held his hands up for a different reason. 'I'm not really qualified for that anymore.'

She rolled her eyes at him faux-dramatically. 'Calm down. I'm not going to ask you to sign a prescription. It's more of a biology thing. Could hormones make a woman want her baby more?'

If he was surprised at the question, he hid it well. 'Yes. I think so. I suppose it's a primordial thing designed to make the mother love her child and protect it from the moment it's born. Why do you ask?'

He'd probably already guessed the answer to that, but she approved of his tact. 'I've just been feeling a little strange. Like I'd expect a mother to feel.'

He nodded. 'Well, as far as your body knows, you are a mother.'

Though that was an obvious point, it hadn't hit her like that before. She'd spent so much time in her head about all of this – *it's not your baby, it's Megan and Mark's embryo, you're just a vessel* – that she hadn't considered that her body wouldn't have got the memo. 'Is there anything I can do about it? To stop it, I mean. It's kind of messing me up.'

He shook his head. 'I'm afraid not. I'm sure it will sort itself out once the baby's born.'

The baby must've known that she was talking about her, because she chose that moment to push a tiny little fist or foot directly out of the front of her stomach. Sophia ran her finger down the tiny bump it made before it disappeared again.

Alex grinned at her. 'Is the baby moving?'

She matched his smile. 'Yes. It's such a cool feeling.'

Keeping her hand there, she imagined the little person inside. What was she going to be like when she came out? Would she push and kick her way through life, or would she be passive and calm? She was actually pretty excited to find out.

ELEVEN

MEGAN

The shrill whirr of the hand-held vacuum threatened to give Megan a headache as she pushed it hard to the back of each step on her way up the stairs. They both left their shoes in the rack in the porch, so there was nothing to actually pick up, but the repetitive – slightly violent – movement was helping to push away the jealousy she felt at how happy Sophia sounded whenever she called.

She knew that she was luckier than a lot of people, of course she did. There was plenty of space in her house, they had a garden to sit in, rooms in which to work. But the space was part of the problem. Despite being in the same house, she and Mark had barely seen each other since lockdown began three weeks ago. He'd set himself up in the second bedroom as she'd suggested but, when she got to the top of the stairs and popped her head around the door, it twisted her stomach to see his laptop set up on the dressing table she'd laid out with tissues and candles and a bowl of peppermints. He'd relocated those to the windowsill, where they sat like relics of a more hopeful time. 'Do you want tea?'

He barely looked up from his laptop. 'I'm fine. I've got the old coffee machine set up over there so that I don't need to bother you in the kitchen.'

She *wanted* him to bother her. Lots of her clients were quiet at the moment, unsure how comfortable they were with promoting their businesses while the country was still in a state of shock. Plus, she'd hoped that she and Mark might get to spend a bit more time together; in the last six months, he'd been away with work so often that they'd barely had time to do what everyone had told them to do and make the most of nights out before the baby came. 'Shall we have lunch together? I can make something.'

'Maybe. Let me see how I get on. I'll give you a shout.'

Though he smiled, he turned straight back to his laptop, which was her signal to leave.

Downstairs, she sprayed the kitchen worktops with disinfectant and wiped hard. It was almost a relief that their cleaner, Gloria, couldn't come, because at least that gave her something to do. She'd been in tears over the phone yesterday when Megan had insisted that they still pay her. It wasn't her fault that she wasn't able to do her job and she had two young children at home. They had a two-bedroom flat without a garden; it must be so difficult keeping little ones amused. Megan felt guilty for her boredom.

On the corner of the kitchen island, she found something stuck hard and rubbed at it with the cloth. If her world was small, Mark's was even smaller. He'd worked into the early hours last night and slept in that room, telling her this morning that he hadn't wanted to risk waking her. How long had it been since they'd slept together? All the fertility treatment they'd been through had made sex a necessary hoop to jump through whether they'd felt like it or not. Even through the heartbreak of accepting that they would never conceive naturally, they'd both been relieved when they were no longer performing to a schedule. But it'd been over a year since then and, other than a handful of times when they'd had a few drinks, they hadn't really gotten back on track. Would they ever be easy around one another in the bedroom again?

Finally, the hard spot disintegrated under her cloth and she wiped it away. Maybe she'd call Sophia again. Though she knew she was probably calling too often, it was difficult to resist. If she could, she'd have had a camera in Sophia's apartment so that she could keep an eye on her. Ironic, really, with her being the younger sister.

A rhythmic thud of footsteps on the stairs heralded Mark's arrival. The door opened on his sheepish smile. 'Actually, I will have some lunch. Sorry, I wasn't thinking before. Too much going on. A sandwich together would be great.'

He slid onto one of the stools at the breakfast bar. Did he really want something or was he checking on her, making sure that she ate? 'What would you like? Cheese? Ham?'

He shrugged. 'How about both? I'll grab some of that chutney I brought back from Chester.'

The chutney was at the back of the larder cupboard. As Mark brought it down onto the counter, she was bobbing back up from the small fridge with the meat and cheese and they nearly collided. He held her arms before she toppled. 'Sorry.'

'It's okay.' Before, he would have held her closer for a few moments. Now he let her go immediately and returned to his stool. Every part of her yearned to be touched. Why was he being so distant? With her back to him, it was easier to talk. 'How's it going up there? Is this lockdown going to affect the business?'

Ever since she'd first started dating Mark, the family business had been front and centre of any decision or choice. His grandfather had started a small printing business over sixty years ago, then his father had grown it to include merchandising materials and now Mark was under pressure to put his own ideas into place to make it even bigger.

'There might be some problems with paper supplies, but we should be fine in the short term, at least. Dad's sounding off about it all, saying that we need to be able to have meetings, but it can all be done online. It might help to drag the old dinosaur into the twenty-first century.'

Mark's father was a force of nature. He might joke about him when he wasn't here, but standing up to him in the real world was another matter. In any case, Megan had only asked about Mark's work as an opener. She was far more interested in bringing the conversation around to the baby. 'I was going to call Sophia after lunch, see how she's doing.'

Mark had his head down, rifling through the cutlery drawer. 'Really? Didn't you call her this morning?'

The butter was hard and it tore the bread as she dragged it across. 'Yes. But I thought you might like to talk to her.'

The spoons clattered against one another beneath Mark's fingers. 'I'm okay. You can tell me how she is. Where's that spoon with the long handle that we use for the chutney?'

She reached into the drawer, plucked it up and held it out. 'When I spoke to her earlier, she wondered if we'd come up with a name for the baby yet. We need to do that.'

'Yes. Good idea. Maybe we can chat about it tonight.'

He did this every time she wanted to talk about the baby. *Tonight. Later. Tomorrow.* It was never *now*. 'Or we could go for a walk this afternoon and think of some ideas? We're allowed our daily exercise.'

He took the buttered bread from her and peeled a slice of ham from the paper for his sandwich. 'Oh, sorry. I already went for a run this morning.'

That explained why she'd woken up alone. 'I don't think they're checking us in and out. We might get away with it.'

'Sorry, Megs.' He was already smearing chutney across the ham as he glanced at his watch. 'I've only got about five minutes for lunch. I have a conference call in about fifteen minutes. I need to eat this and get my head in the game.'

She carried her own sandwich over to the kitchen island that she'd just cleaned. The sharp smell of disinfectant hit the back of her throat. 'We need to find some time to talk, Mark. The baby's coming soon. It's not just her name. There's lots of things to discuss.'

He chewed three more times and swallowed. 'Like what?'

Of course, she couldn't think of one single thing. 'I don't know. It'd just be nice to talk about it. How we're feeling. I mean, it's going to be a big change for both of us.'

Did she imagine his face getting paler as she spoke? And could he inhale that sandwich any faster? He barely met her eye. 'Okay, we can talk tonight.'

The small bite of her sandwich tasted like cardboard and the prickle of anxiety climbing her throat meant she had to concentrate to swallow. It didn't help that Mark was focused on her plate rather than her face. She had this under control. He didn't need to watch her eat like a potential criminal. 'Shall we watch a film together later, too?'

'Good idea. You can choose.' He picked up his plate. 'I'm going to take the rest of this upstairs. I need to read through a few emails before the call starts.'

His stool scraped on the granite floor tiles as he pushed it away before kissing the top of her head. A brief dry sweep of the lips that could only be described as brotherly. As soon as she heard his feet on the stairs, she tipped the rest of her sandwich in the bin and pushed open the back door to the garden.

Out here, the sun was warm at least. Closing her eyes, she offered her face up to the sky, breathing deeply as she'd been taught to. Feeling the feelings then pushing them away. When Elsie spoke, it made her jump. 'Is this what they call a staycation?'

She opened her eyes and smiled over the fence. 'I'm not sure you can call it that when you've been forced into it.'

Elsie looked as if she were expecting company; her hair and make-up were always polished, but she was also wearing a smart blue dress. 'I've just had a visit from my son. On the doorstep. He dropped off some shopping and we had a bit of a chat.'

A dull ache squeezed at Megan. What would she give to visit her mother's doorstep right now? 'That's nice of him.'

Elsie rolled her eyes. 'I tried to tell him that I've just had an online order, but he insisted. Goodness only knows what he's brought me.' She laughed. 'I'm not complaining. He's a good boy.'

That 'boy' was at least a decade older than Megan and had lost most of his hair. 'It's nice that he lives so close.'

Resting her arms on the top of the fence, Elsie nodded. 'It is. He's been asking me to move in with him, but I don't think that's a good idea. I think he feels it, being an only child. Since his dad went, he thinks he needs to look after me. Must've been nice for you having a sister to share it with when you lost your mum. I know she liked having the two of you here.'

In the last months of her mother's cancer, Megan had moved her from her small flat in Walthamstow into the guest room upstairs so that she could look after her. After she'd tracked down Sophia, she'd invited her to stay, too. She'd been amazed when she'd accepted. 'We aren't that close, to be honest.'

Elsie's eyes widened. 'Really?'

She could understand her surprise. Wasn't her sister carrying her child? 'I mean. We are now. But we weren't then. She left home when I was young. We didn't see that much of her.'

She didn't want to admit to Elsie that they hadn't seen her at all. Not when the explanation would put her mother in such a bad light.

Elsie raised an eyebrow. 'I didn't think there was that much between you in age.'

That assumption wasn't a total surprise. Sophia had a lightness to her that made her ever youthful; Megan's anxiety seemed to do the opposite. 'She's seven years older. When she left home, I was only twelve.'

At the time, she'd thought her world was coming to an end. Despite the age difference, Sophia had always been her heroine. Beautiful, adventurous, daring: everything that Megan wasn't.

'She was only nineteen? I bet your mum missed her.'

That's what Megan had assumed, too. When the days had turned into weeks and then months and then years, she'd seen her mother's grief every time the subject had turned to her sister. Which is why the discovery in her mum's belongings had shocked her so much.

It'd been about a week after the funeral. Sophia was still staying with them because there was a lot of paperwork to do and she was trying to persuade Megan that she could be her surrogate. Mark was back at work – obviously – and they'd decided to bite the emotional bullet and go through the last few boxes of their mum's possessions. It'd been Megan's idea. 'There might be something you'd like to keep. You know, a memento of Mum.'

Sophia had laughed at that. 'I'm not sure I want to remember those days, to be honest.'

Megan had tried to hide her hurt. Whatever reason Sophia had for still being resentful towards their mum, she knew from the stories they'd shared in the last few weeks that she did have some happy memories of their time together.

The third box they'd looked in was half empty. There was a cassette tape with Sophia's name on, some photographs of the two of them together and then a sealed brown envelope.

Sophia had picked up the tape. 'Oh, my goodness. I think I

know what this is. I remember listening to it once. It's a tape of me singing nursery rhymes when I was about three.'

Before Megan was born. That's probably why she'd never heard it. But she'd like to. 'I don't think we have anything that plays cassettes. We must be able to hunt down a tape recorder somewhere.'

Sophia had smiled at it, lost in thought, and Megan had really hoped she was remembering a happier time. Not wanting to interrupt, she'd popped open the flap of the brown envelope, expecting – from the feel of it – more photographs.

Instead, it'd been a whole collection of postcards from foreign countries, some more dog-eared than others. As they'd slipped out onto Megan's lap. Sophia had looked up and her hand had flown to her mouth. 'Oh, my goodness. They're here.'

The top postcard had a picture of the Colosseum. When she'd turned it over, Megan had been shocked to discover that it was addressed to her. And it was from Sophia.

She'd glanced up at her sister, but she was still frozen with her hand to her mouth, so she'd picked up a card with a mountain on it and turned it over. Also addressed to her. Also from Sophia. And the next one. And the next one. 'Sophia. What are these? When did you send them?'

Sophia had let her hand fall from her mouth. 'Every week when I first left. Then every month. Or few months. Until I gave up.'

It hadn't made sense. 'Why did I not get to see them? Why did Mum keep them?'

Sophia had clearly struggled to find the words. 'She had her reasons.'

None of it had made sense. Her mother had missed Sophia desperately. Megan knew she had. They'd needed her. Megan had needed her. The same question had come up in countless therapy sessions and in her brain during late-night insomnia. If Sophia had stayed, would her anorexia have ever reared its ugly head? No one knew the answer to that. And she was glad that at least Sophia didn't know about her illness.

She'd looked at one of the cards more closely. A few sentences of what Sophia had been up to and then: *I know you clearly don't want to speak to me. But in case you change your mind, here's my new address.*

Cold realisation had trickled through her. All these years she'd blamed Sophia for leaving them and never looking back. Yet, wherever she was in the world Sophia had reached out to her. It was her who'd been abandoned, her who'd been ignored. 'Oh, Sophia. Why didn't you tell me? You've been here for weeks. Why didn't you tell me?'

There had been tears in Sophia's eyes. 'Because I promised Mum that I wouldn't.'

TWELVE

SOPHIA

After making a half-hearted attempt to throw clothes into the cupboard and kick shoes under the bed, Sophia had spent the afternoon scrolling through the tsunami of information from Megan. Well, the parts that were nice, that is. She still hadn't mustered up the courage to watch the birth video. Did she really need to? It wasn't as if she could back out now if she didn't fancy it.

A hot and sweaty Richard pushed open the door and strode into the room. He'd left in a real funk a couple of hours ago, still muttering about the 'idiots making these ridiculous rules'.

Even if things weren't going to work out for them, they were stuck together here for the foreseeable future. Sophia needed to tie a knot in her feelings for now, patch their problems until lockdown was over. 'Are you feeling better? Did the walk help?'

He can't have seen her laying on the sofa because he jumped. Then blushed. 'Yes. I'm getting in the shower. Then I'm going to call the Dean again. There must be something he can do to get us back on-site.'

Maybe even the birth video would be less painful than listening to Richard's gripes again. But when she started it, the twanging background music made her tense. She hadn't actually planned to watch a birth at all. But when she'd seen Alex on the stairs yesterday, and mentioned that Megan had sent it, even he had agreed it was a good idea. 'It will help you to know what to expect.'

She hadn't been convinced. 'Really? Do I really need to watch? Can't you just give me a summary?

He'd shaken his head. 'I could describe it to you. But, having never given birth myself, I think that might be as useful as having my grandmother describe the Internet. Just watch it, you coward!'

She was a sucker for men who made her laugh; always had been. Obviously, this was just a friendship. But between the strained calls with Megan and the fraying mess of her and Richard's relationship, these conversations with him felt like a lifeline.

She was saved from putting on her big girl pants and watching the video, by yet another FaceTime call from Megan. She was still smiling about Alex when she picked it up. 'Hi.'

'Hi. You look happy.'

She stretched her legs and yawned. 'Relaxed, I think. I haven't moved from this sofa for about two hours.'

'Good for you. It's important to rest.'

How did Megan manage to make a pleasantry sound like a telling off? 'I probably need to move my backside at some point, though. How's things with you?'

Was she imagining it, or was Megan's face pinched? Unlike hers, Megan's eyes and lips were carefully made up and her hair its usual salon-like perfection. But there was no smile on her face when she nodded. 'Fine. I've just been thinking. I was talking to my neighbour last week. You remember Elsie next door? She didn't realise that you'd left home at such a young age.'

Oh dear. Megan wasn't going to start asking about that day again, was she? 'Oh yes?'

'I mean. I know you've kind of explained why Mum didn't want me to know about the postcards, but I still feel as if there's stuff I don't know. And I can't get it out of my mind.'

Sophia closed her eyes. When they'd discovered the postcards that her mother had kept, it'd been really difficult to explain to Megan why they'd been hidden from her. To be fair, she'd only had a few weeks to process it herself.

That first day she'd seen her mother had been a shock. Megan was right to have warned her. She looked as if a puff of a breeze might take her away.

After their initial hello, it'd been the first thing her mother had said to her. 'She doesn't know. Megan doesn't know why you left.'

Sophia had expected that. She hadn't ever revealed the reason to Megan in the postcards she'd sent and was pretty sure her parents wouldn't have told her. 'I know.'

Her mother had looked anxious. 'I don't think you should tell her. Not now. She's been through some things... It's not an easy time for her.'

More secrets. 'I don't suppose she'd want to know anyway. It's not as if she ever replied to any of my postcards.'

Pain had flashed across her mother's face. 'That's because she didn't get them.'

Sophia had frozen. 'What do you mean?'

'She never saw the postcards.'

An unanswered question that she'd lived with for twenty years had begun to unfurl itself in Sophia's mind. 'Why?'

Her mother had taken a few breaths before she'd continued. 'To begin with, your father tore them up and threw them out. But I rescued the pieces, kept them. I thought there might be a time when I could show them to her.'

It was as if someone had clawed at Sophia's throat. She'd barely been able to get the words out. 'You kept them?'

'You weren't there, Sophia. It was so hard after you left. Your father was...'

Hate had clenched Sophia's jaw. 'I know what he was.'

'I kept a look out for them after that. Hid them away. I couldn't show them to Megan. She would have given it away.'

That hadn't made sense either. 'But Megan told me that he left years ago. When she contacted me last week. She said he was long gone. Why didn't you tell her then?'

Her mother hadn't been able to meet her eye. 'Because she was ill by then. And I thought, if she knew where to reach you, if she spoke to you, I just... Well, I thought it would be more than she could cope with.'

This conversation had happened before her mother had told her about the anorexia, but she'd had bigger questions at that point. 'What about me? What about what I was coping with?'

Then her mother had looked at her. 'You sounded like you were having such a wonderful time. It was such a relief. I was happy that you were okay, that your life was good. Why would I want to bring you back here, when we were struggling? I'd already let you down once.'

Her eyes had held oceans of pain. It had felt cruel to make that worse, but she'd needed to tell her. 'I needed you, Mum. I needed you so much and you weren't there.'

Sobs had turned to coughs, which had wracked her mother's body. 'I know. I'll never forgive myself. I was weak, Sophia. I was so weak. I'm so sorry.'

Sophia had wrapped her arms around her body, holding herself as she'd done many times in the last twenty years. 'I needed my mum. When it... happened. I needed you. But you weren't there. And now... how could you have ignored me all those years? How could you just pretend that I didn't exist?'

Her mother had reached weak arms towards her, but she hadn't been ready for that. 'I never pretended you didn't exist. Every night I would think about you. I would imagine my brave beautiful girl out there in the world having the most wonderful life. You weren't weak like me. You were strong and independent, and I was so proud of you. Each postcard that came, I would look up the place you were in, imagine you there. In a cafe on a busy street, walking through ruins, laughing, joking, with friends, with lovers. You were the best of us, Sophia.'

'But I would've come home. If I'd known Dad was gone, I would've come home.'

Her mother's face had been red with crying, but still her voice was soft, weak. 'We never really knew whether he'd left. There was so much coming and going and he'd just turn up sometimes. Then, when he'd gone for good, there was nothing to bring you home to. Megan needed me to look after her. We were living in a two-bedroom flat. It was no place for you to be.'

These had felt like excuses. 'But later? When she married Mark. When everything was okay for her?'

Her mother had closed her eyes again. 'I was weak again. I worried that she'd never forgive me. I'd lost one daughter. I was terrified I'd lose the other. I missed you so much, Sophia. I don't expect you to believe me, but I never stopped thinking about you.'

Years and years and years of pushed-down pain had begun to flake away inside Sophia. The loneliness, the fear, the loss. 'I thought you didn't love me. When I didn't hear from either of you, I just thought you didn't want me back. I thought you were happy with Megan and glad that I was out of the way.'

'Oh, my Sophia, I've always loved you. You were my first child, my precious baby girl. You made me a mum and I was so so proud of you.'

Tears had fallen down Sophia's cheeks; she was still angry and hurt and jealous and all of the maelstrom of emotions that had governed her life, but here was her mother and she hadn't long left. This time, when she'd held out her pale, thin arms, Sophia had leaned into them.

For a long time, they'd held each other and wept, their tears mingling as her mother only pulled away to kiss her cheeks, her eyes, her forehead. Was there any kiss as gentle and full of unselfish love as a mother's? That is what Sophia had needed for so long. Who knew if she could every really forgive her mother? But if she wanted to have this love around her for the precious little time they had left together, she had to try.

Once the torrent of emotion had subsided, she'd sat next to her mother's bed with her head next to hers on the pillow. Her mother had stroked her hair as she had when Sophia was young. Sophia hadn't wanted to break the spell when she'd spoken. 'Megan and Mark will be back soon.'

There had been a few beats of silence. 'Sophia. I know this is a lot to ask, and I don't have a right to even say it, but please don't tell her any of this. She and Mark are having fertility treatment and I'm already worried how the stress of that might affect her. It's bad enough that I'm leaving her. If she finds out what I did, that I kept your messages from her, it might be too much.'

Again, Megan had been the one who needed looking after; Sophia could make her own way. But that hadn't been Megan's fault, had it? She'd been unaware that Sophia had tried to stay in contact with her. As far as she knew, Sophia had left that night and never looked back. Spell broken, the sadness had settled over her again. 'I won't, Mum.'

Even that hadn't been enough. 'And you won't tell her why you left? Because that could break her, too.'

Break Megan? What about what it'd done to her? Sophia had screwed her eyes shut. She wouldn't cry again. 'No. I'll never tell her why I left.'

When they'd found the postcards, she'd explained as much of this as she could to Megan without telling her the biggest secret: the reason why she'd left. Every so often, Megan would circle back to it. Like now. 'The thing is, I understand why you left to go travelling. But I still don't think you're telling me the truth about why you didn't come back.'

Sophia was saved by Richard in shorts, rubbing at his hair with a yellow towel that Megan had actually sent over for the baby. 'Sorry, Megan. I need to go. Richard needs me. I'll catch up with you later.'

Richard threw his towel on the back of the chair. Clearly it was okay for him to be messy. 'I'm enjoying being referenced as your Lord and Master but not sure what it is I need?'

She sighed and shook her head. 'I just had to get off that call. It was Megan. She's clearly got too much time on her hands and she's raking up the past.'

'The past? Now that is my department.'

He could be nice when he was in this mood. 'She suddenly wants to know why I didn't go to university. Why I left.'

He perched on the arm of the chair opposite. 'I see. And why didn't you go?'

After a year together, most people would have had these types of conversation, but they weren't most people. 'There were a few reasons. Mainly, I just wanted to get away. See the world.'

It was her usual lie, but he was happy to accept it. 'Totally understand. I'm assuming Megan doesn't?'

There were so many things Megan didn't understand. 'We're very different.'

They'd always had different personalities, even with the big age difference, that'd been obvious to everyone. Since those last days with her mother, she'd begun to wonder whether that wasn't so much who they were, or who they'd been expected to be.

Richard scooped up his towel and flicked it so it lay across his shoulder. 'Are you more like your father?'

The question was an innocent one, but not one she liked. Her mother had allowed that man to come and go as he pleased. Acquiesced to his every demand. Never thinking about her own happiness. Never would Sophia do that for a man. She would do what *she* wanted, *when* she wanted. 'No. I'm not like him. I'm not like him at all.'

She wasn't like her mother either. Because her mother was weak. Which is why there was the other thing. The real reason she'd left and never wanted to come back. That one mistake which had set the rest of it in motion. And she wasn't about to tell Richard that. Because she'd never told anyone.

THIRTEEN

MEGAN

It was lunchtime. But after her conversation with Sophia, Megan hadn't even the whisper of an appetite. Standing in front of the open fridge, she scanned the plastic containers for something that she could stomach. Celery – her old friend – a cube of cheddar, a wafer-thin slice of ham. She cut each of them into small manageable pieces and laid them out on a plate in three distinct pools.

Though she tried to focus her attention on chewing, and breathing, the heat of frustration still burned. Why was Sophia still keeping things from her? It was obvious that there was more to the story than she'd already been told. Finding those post-cards had turned everything she knew upside down. Her belief that Sophia had been skipping around the world without once thinking about them was a total lie.

If only she'd known about them when her mother was still alive and she could have asked her. As far as Sophia was concerned, her mother hadn't cared enough that she was gone, but it wasn't true. If only she could grab Sophia's hand and drag her back to see how their mother had felt. Once, she'd caught her holding the clumsy pottery bowl they'd used to store boxes of matches and toothpicks in the corner kitchen cupboard. She'd been crying.

'Mum, are you okay? What's happened?' At fourteen, it was scary to see her cry.

She'd sniffed and smiled a watery smile. 'I'm okay, love. Just worrying a bit about your sister. She made this when she was younger than you.'

Of course she had. There were so many things around this house that Sophia had made. Always the creative one. The clever one. They were among the many things she'd admired her sister for when she'd been there. Now she'd left them, those things had taken on the significance of holy relics. 'She's probably fine, Mum. And she's not thinking about us.'

Her mother's smile had turned down at the edges. 'You're right. She's probably having too much fun, eh? This place is too small for that one, isn't it?'

Too small for 'that one' but not too small for her. Her life – school, home, school, home – had to be enough. That's what Sophia hadn't understood. Her choice to leave had forced Megan to be the one who stayed. Did she not owe her an explanation at least?

The piles of food on her plate didn't seem to have reduced, but she couldn't eat any more. As the itch of irritation subsided, a cold anxiety trickled over her. Why had she been so short with Sophia on the phone? What purpose did it serve to remind her of why she'd left them in the first place? Would Sophia be angry? Upset? And that couldn't be good for the baby. What a fool she was. What a stupid, stupid fool.

In seconds, she'd tipped the rest of her food into the bin, slotted the plate into the dishwasher and made her way towards the front door. She needed to get out of here. She'd already been for one run that morning. Though the lockdown rules said only one trip out to exercise a day, who was going to know? She could have gone to the shops, but the thought of standing in a long queue outside the supermarket – each of them stood on a socially distanced sticker on the floor – made her feel even more twitchy.

As she stared at the front door, trying to make her mind up, a shadow appeared in the glass followed by the scrape of Mark's key in the lock. He'd been to deliver paperwork to his parents' doorstep. An unnecessary trip that his father had insisted on. When the door opened, he had his head down reading something on his phone and he jumped when he looked up to find her standing there like a marble shrine to indecision. 'Were you waiting for me?'

She wasn't, but she was glad that he was home. 'Just deciding whether to go out. How were your parents?'

He pulled a face. 'Fine. My dad doesn't get it. The lockdown. Keeps calling people snowflakes. But Mum is really anxious. She made me drop the paperwork on the step and then back away before she'd open the door. I felt like a spy delivering state secrets rather than a range of paper samples for leaflet production. What's up with you?'

She could practically feel the muscles in her face creak as she tried to smile. 'I've just had a bit of a crappy conversation with Sophia. She's so prickly sometimes.'

He nodded. Looked relieved. 'Well, that's just how she is. Plus she's pregnant. Doesn't that make you cranky?'

She knew he was trying to make her feel better, but he couldn't have chosen anything worse to say. 'I'm really worried about what's going on over there, Mark. I need to get there. Can't we go? They haven't stopped the flights.'

His sigh was deep as he shook his head. 'No. We definitely can't. I'm sorry, Megs. I know this is really hard, but it's all so uncertain at the moment. Try not to worry. We've got plenty of time before the baby comes. Hold on a bit longer.'

Hold on. Wait. Be patient. 'I don't think I can. I want us to be out there.'

He shrugged. 'I can't stop you. But I'm not going.'

Though he was easy-going, there was no moving him once he'd made up his mind. And he knew as well as she did that she wouldn't get on a flight without him. 'Then I guess I have to wait.'

He reached out and rubbed her arm. 'It'll be okay. Why don't you go for your run? I'm heading up to carry on working now anyway.'

He hadn't even realised that she'd been out today already. Did he pay attention to her at all? 'Actually, I need to get some work done, too. I need to call Bethany.' There was nothing to discuss, but she was irritated by the way he always seemed to view his work as more pressing than hers.

'Good idea. See you later.' He disappeared upstairs before she could say another word.

She no longer felt like leaving the house. But she needed to do something. She might as well call Bethany and see if there was anything that she could pick up.

It was good to hear her cheerful voice at least. 'Hello! Good to hear from you. I was just thinking about you actually.'

It was nice that someone was. 'Good things, I hope?'

'Always. I've been having a sort out while we're stuck in, and I've got a load of books you might want for the baby. A couple of baby and toddler recipe books, too. There's an Annabel Karmel one that was my Bible when Sam and Ella were small. Shall I keep them for you?'

'That would be great, thanks. I'll look her up online, too. Doesn't hurt to be prepared.' She was trying her best to sound upbeat. No one wanted a misery. Especially now that everyone was having a tough time. 'Is there anything you need me to do? I've been keeping an eye on the emails but it seems as if everything has gone a bit quiet.'

'Yeah, same here. I've asked Petra to do a bit of research online and see what other companies are doing. She's got it covered. Don't feel like you need to be doing much. Your maternity leave is due to start soon, anyway.'

Maternity leave. When she'd had so many plans to join baby groups and take her daughter swimming and then just enjoy their time alone. Now who knew what was going to happen. 'I need to do something to keep me occupied.'

Beth's voice was sympathetic. 'I can imagine. Well, I also have a ton of parenting books that I can drop off for you to read? When Sam wouldn't sleep, I basically bought the entire canon in the hope of a magic formula. Half of them I didn't even get round to reading. Do you want those?'

She'd already read a fair amount herself, but more information would probably not be a bad thing. And what else did she have to do? 'Yes, please. That would be great.'

Once their call ended, she was back to boredom. Maybe she should take a leaf out of Beth's book and take the opportunity to have a sort out. Maybe she could find an answer to her questions in those boxes of her mother's. Rereading the postcards might reveal something she'd missed. If Sophia wasn't going to tell her, she'd have to look for herself.

Upstairs, she remembered that the boxes were no longer in the third bedroom. They'd put them up in the loft when they cleared the room to paint it for the baby. Their loft was boarded out and well-organised, but she didn't like climbing the wooden ladder into the hatch and, from memory, the boxes had been pretty heavy. It would only take Mark a minute.

She always knocked when going into his office, but this time she was thinking about the boxes and just pushed it open. Mark had his back to her, wearing his large black noise-cancelling headphones and talking to a woman on the screen. He clearly hadn't heard her come in, because he continued his conversation. 'I can't tell her.'

The woman on the screen was talking, but the headphones meant that her words were only for Mark's ears. She was around fifty, Megan would guess, Blonde, attractive. She had kind eyes.

Mark's reply sounded pained. 'Because it will hurt her.'

This didn't seem like a conversation about printing or promotional materials. Megan remained completely still, watching as the woman on the screen talked, gesticulated, and Mark nodded in response. What were they talking about? And who was she?

The voiceless woman spoke for so long that Megan jumped when Mark's reply cut through the silence. 'She's fragile. And with the baby coming... I can't tell her yet. I need more time.'

They were talking about *her*. This was like being in a nightmare. Megan couldn't move. Couldn't stop listening.

'I know. But it's not just about us, is it?'

Megan's hand flew to her face. She might actually be sick. She turned and crept out of the room, down the stairs, out of the house.

Outside, the sun was so bright that it made her squint. Was Mark having an affair? Was he having a relationship with that woman on the screen? *I can't tell her yet. I need more time.*

It all made sense now. All the business trips he'd assured her were necessary. The lack of physical touch. His disinterest in the baby. How had she not seen this before? It was so obvious, wasn't it?

With no destination in mind, she walked down the street, moving out into the road to pass an old man with a stick, a mother with a slow toddler. She wanted to run but she was wearing the flip-flops she used in the house.

Shock made her numb, but it also made things clear. There were issues between them, that had been evident for months. Now, with both of them stuck in the house together, it had been impossible to avoid the truth. They had a problem. But never in a million years had she imagined that Mark would cheat on her. He'd never even looked at another woman, as far as she knew.

A sear of pain was so sharp that she had to stop and bend over, clutching onto the railing of the park. Her breath came in jagged, painful bursts. Was this her fault? Because she'd been so focused on the baby that she hadn't paid enough attention to her husband? And all that time she'd been so incredibly sad after her mother died – had he just had enough of having a miserable wife?

She forced herself to stand again, put one foot in front of the other. Her cheeks were iced by the breeze hitting the tears on her face. At the end of the street she was hit by a billboard, which mocked her with a huge photograph of a husband with his arms around a wife who had her arms around a child. She wanted to scratch it down with her fingernails. But even if she could have reached it, they were bitten down too far to be any use at all. Instead, she held onto the railings, torturing herself by staring at that expression of the male model as he gazed down lovingly at his family.

How could this be true? How could Mark be having an affair? How would she cope if he ever left?

FOURTEEN

SOPHIA

The wide white marble stairs – which had been one of her biggest joys when they moved into the apartment – were a treacherous gauntlet now that Sophia couldn't see her feet on the way down. Holding onto the shiny wooden banister, she took each step slowly, bringing the second foot in line with the first before venturing again. Though she'd promised Megan she'd stay home, the four walls of the flat were starting to become oppressive. It would be May by the end of this week and she'd barely enjoyed the spring sunshine. A walk to the end of the street and back couldn't hurt.

She was on the final flight when the heavy front door opened to the sight of Alex's back with a large bag of fresh vegetables and bread on either side. 'Hello, neighbour.'

He jumped, turned around, then grinned when he saw it was her. As he backed away out of her path, he held the shopping aloft like trophies. 'Hi. Look, you've inspired me.'

From her vantage point, three steps from the bottom, she made a show of peering over at his groceries. 'I'm glad. Did you buy fresh pasta?'

He shook his head. 'Making my own.'

Now it was her turn to grin. 'I'm impressed. Give me a shout if you want any help making the sauce. I could give you my number and handhold you through it?'

It was a perfectly innocent suggestion, so she had no idea why the offer made her face blush. Damn hormones again. Thankfully, he didn't react the same way. 'That would be great, actually. If only to hear another human voice in that place.' He rested the shopping bags against the wall and slid his phone from the pocket of his jeans. She pulled her eyes away from the tightness of them. What was wrong with her?

She'd been feeling really – was there a less icky word than horny? – for the last week. Richard didn't want to have sex any longer and who could blame him? She was a whale. It wasn't just the sex, he barely touched her at the moment. Preferring to go for long walks – and long showers – instead. Was it any wonder she found herself staring at Alex like a teenager with a crush?

Once he'd typed in her number, Alex took a step even further back. 'Do you want to go out first rather than me pass you on the stairs?'

She was a little embarrassed to recommence her tentative old lady shuffle downwards. And was also reluctant to let him go yet. Conversation with Alex was so easy compared to the other people in her newly constricted existence. 'Actually, do you have a minute? There was something I wanted to ask you?'

Other than her physical needs, she'd been thinking about something else a lot that week. TV news was showing overflowing hospitals and some frightening statistics. The thought of taking herself there in a few weeks was frankly terrifying. She'd begun to wonder whether it was the best idea in the circumstances. 'I wanted to ask you what you know about home births.'

He didn't look surprised, which was somewhat of a relief in itself. 'Quite a lot actually. My mother was a midwife who married a paediatrician—' he held out his hands '—so medicine runs through these veins.'

That was encouraging. 'I've been thinking that it might be an option for me. With everything that's going on out there.'

He nodded. 'I can see why you'd think that. There's no reason you can't have the baby at home. Has your pregnancy been straightforward?'

'Other than the conception? Yes. The hospital in England said that everything should run as if it was a normal pregnancy. I didn't even have morning sickness for very long. I've felt great, actually.' The weeks before the scan had been the worst. Waiting to see if the pregnancy would take. After that, it'd felt easy.

'Well, then. A lot of women are opting for home births now. You'd need to arrange it with the hospital to have a midwife come, which may or may not be easy at the moment. Then they would have a backup plan should anything complicated arise and you need to go into hospital.'

Anything complicated? For the first time, she felt the smallest trickle of fear about the birth. Surely she was in the safe stage now that they'd got this far? 'What kind of thing?'

He shrugged. 'I don't want to frighten you. But the baby could be in the wrong position, or your pelvis might be tilted, lots of unknowns until labour starts.'

She would have looked at her pelvis if there wasn't a huge mound of belly in the way. 'My pelvis?'

He frowned at her. 'Have you still not watched that film your sister sent you? But you have done some reading? Attended an online antenatal class?'

She felt that blush again. Megan had been on to her to do all of those things but she'd felt it was best not to know. It was too late now, after all. Still, he was looking at her as if she was a crazy woman. 'Well, I was going to do those things when I went back to England. You know, with my sister.'

Though he smiled, he pretended to accept the lie. 'Of course. Well, if that's not going to happen, maybe you need to start doing some research of your own. I can send you some links about a home birth? The kind of things you need to have at home. Videos of home births.'

He waved his phone at her and she almost blanched. The thought of watching another woman give birth made her feel a little sick. She was definitely of the 'I'll deal with it when it happens' brigade. Unlike Megan who could probably qualify as a midwife with all the research she'd done. 'Maybe.'

He laughed. 'Would you like me to talk you through it? I'll use the nice words?'

That made her grin, too. 'Do you have flashcards?'

'I'll knock some up while I'm waiting for the pasta to boil.'

'Thanks. Good bartering. I'll teach you to make pasta, you can teach me how to make a baby.'

Make? *Idiot*. She'd meant to say birth. Now her face was aflame. Either he was a gentleman or he hadn't noticed the slip. She prayed it was the latter.

* * *

'A home birth?'

Megan's reaction was akin to Sophia saying she wanted to give birth on top of the Leaning Tower of Pisa. 'I'm just thinking about it. The hospitals here are overflowing and it feels as if I'd be walking into the eye of the storm.'

There was silence at the other end. Poor Megan. It must be difficult for her being so far away. So out of control of the situation. Control was her middle name. When her response came, it was a weighted whisper. 'But what if something goes wrong?'

First Alex, now Megan. Why were they so obsessed with negative outcomes? 'Chances are it's going to be fine, Meg.

Women have been doing this for centuries, haven't they? It's the most natural thing in the world.'

Megan's voice cut through her optimism like a pessimistic blade. 'And women frequently died in childbirth less than a century ago.'

She deserved that. As soon as the words were out, she wished she could bite them back. Was there anything more insensitive to say to an infertile woman than how having a baby was 'natural'? 'What I mean is, I'm healthy and the pregnancy has been absolutely fine. Alex says that there's no reason it shouldn't go well.'

Megan's frown deepened with suspicion. 'Who's Alex?'

Idiot. Obviously, she should have led with him. What could be more reassuring than an Alex? 'He lives on the floor above us. He's a doctor. Well, he was a doctor. His mother was a midwife. He's delivered babies before.'

Predictably, Megan honed in on the negative. 'What do you mean *was*? How old is he?'

'He's young. Well, my age, I guess. He was a doctor in the UK but the conditions were too much. He left. He's a novelist now.'

Megan's laugh at the other end was not kind. 'So a failed doctor-cum-writer is going to deliver the baby of a forty-one-year-old woman during a global pandemic in a foreign country in a tiny apartment up three flights of stairs. I mean, what could possibly go wrong?'

Why was she being so nasty all of a sudden? Sophia's sympathy only extended so far. And her apartment was not tiny. 'These are not the conditions I would have chosen either, Megan.'

There was a big sigh on the other end. 'I'm sorry. That was uncalled for. I'm just... struggling a bit at the moment.'

Even without Megan's history, these circumstances would be enough to make anyone worry. Knowing what she did about the anorexia made it even more concerning. 'It's understand-able. This is tough on everyone. But it'll be okay, Megs. One day, this will just be a plot twist in the story you tell your little girl about how she was born.'

For a moment, she thought she'd said the wrong thing again, that Megan was employing one of her characteristic disap-pointed silences. It took a couple of beats before she realised that, actually, Megan was trying really hard not to cry. If she could've reached down the line to hug her she would have done. 'Oh, Meg. I'm so sorry.'

'Don't you be sorry,' Megan sniffed at the other end. 'You're doing this wonderful thing for me. I'm just... It's really rubbish being here on my own.'

But she wasn't on her own. 'Mark is there with you, isn't he?'

There was another pause as she dabbed at her eyes with a tissue and blew her nose. Her expensive eye make-up hadn't smudged a millimetre out of place. 'Yes. He's here. But he works a lot and I've just got too much time to think about everything.'

That was concerning. Sophia didn't know very much about eating disorders, but overthinking couldn't be good. Megan needed to keep herself busy. 'Aren't you working, too?'

'I am. But Bethany has brought her sister on board ready to help out when I'm on maternity leave. Between the two of them, and the fact that lots of our clients are still sussing out how to navigate the Covid landscape, there isn't a great deal for me to do. There's only so much disinfecting I can do.'

The tilt of her head and tentative smile was evidence that she was mocking herself. When she was last there, Sophia had wondered aloud whether her sister had shares in Dettol antibac-terial spray. Her self-deprecation made Sophia strangely protec-tive. 'You need to tell Mark how you're feeling. He works in a family business, for goodness' sake. Surely he can take some time in the day to see his wife?'

Like a window being slammed, Megan's face changed. 'No. He can't. And I wouldn't ask him to.'

That was strange. What was going on with Mark's job that Megan reacted like that? And surely Mark could see that his wife was struggling? 'You need something to keep your mind occupied, though.'

Megan's face crumpled in front of her eyes and her bottom lip wobbled as she spoke. 'I just wish you'd stayed here.'

The last six words were heavy with such need that Sophia's eyes pricked with tears. Had her sister ever said that to her? Even when their mother was ill, it had been more about her needing help that just wanting her company. 'I wish I'd stayed there, too.'

She surprised herself by realising that she meant it. So far, she'd been able to take everything one day at a time, live in the moment. Talking about the home birth with Alex had made it all feel more real. She was actually going to be giving birth in about a month's time. Not in a hospital in London with her sister by her side, holding her hand and talking her through it. But here, in Italy, on her own. And that was starting to feel pretty scary.

FIFTEEN

MEGAN

Although it was only ten minutes from Canary Wharf, Limehouse Road was a quiet residential street even in the middle of the day. When Megan and Mark had first moved there, his father having presented them with the deposit as long as they lived within strolling distance of the family home, it was one of the things they'd most liked about it. Today, that quietness was eerie. Megan had seen no one since she'd closed the front door behind her and embarked on her government-sanctioned daily exercise. After stretching, she crossed the road to avoid the cool shadows on this side of the street. The sun, at least, made the day bright and it was good to be outside.

It'd been almost two weeks since she'd overheard the conversation between Mark and whoever that was on the computer screen. So many times she'd tried to frame the question she wanted to ask but she was terrified of the answer. Analysing every word or movement looking for evidence that she didn't want to be there. When he'd come in from his run this morning, he hadn't looked as red as he normally did. Had he actually been running or was he meeting someone?

Running made her body feel better, but the release wasn't reaching her head. Like ticker tape, there'd been a constant stream of thought as she tried to rearrange the evidence in her head until it made sense. Or, better, had a more innocent explanation than the one she had in mind. *There are none so blind as those who will not see.*

She picked up her pace. What she really wanted to do was go to the gym, desperate for that cathartic burn in her muscles like never before. All of the facts were there in front of her, but she still couldn't believe that Mark would do this. He was a good man. He was Mark. Her loving, dependable, kind, thoughtful, Mark.

Tears that were becoming a daily occurrence welled in her eyes and she let them fall as she ran. *I need more time.* That's what he'd said to the face on the screen. What else could that possibly mean? He was leaving her for another woman and he didn't want to do it before the baby came. That's why he wasn't allowing himself to get attached to her. Not because of the surrogacy, but because he wasn't planning to be around to bring her up. The pain in her chest had nothing to do with the exercise.

At the corner, Megan jogged on the spot for a few moments, deciding whether to take the long or the short route round and back to the house, before turning towards the High Street. It didn't matter how many times she thought about this, she couldn't make it make sense. Mark was her safe place, her home. Yes, things had been a little tricky the last few months, but what marriages didn't go through tough times? Even on the news last night they'd talked about relationships in crisis during lockdown. She couldn't even begin to conceive of her life without Mark in it.

Mark had been her first serious boyfriend. She hadn't been interested in dating widely; he'd made her feel safe. They'd settled down early and been happy. Had that been the right thing? Had Mark grown bored of her? Had they outgrown one another? Real-life relationships couldn't sustain hearts and flowers all the time, could they? Passion was for the beginning stages; later it was more important to have friendship. And they were friends. Best friends. She was always there for him, and he did the same for her. Although, maybe they'd lost sight of that in the last couple of years. Maybe she'd let him down. Maybe he wanted, needed, more than she could give him.

She'd reached the small high street of shops, their dark windows bleak and sad. She stopped running when she got to the end, head down, catching her breath.

Sophia had dated a string of different men in the same time Megan had been with Mark. During her mother's last weeks, they'd sat in her room with cups of tea, catching up on everything she'd done and Megan had noticed how often men seemed to be the catalyst for change.

'So you had a different boyfriend in every country?'

Sophia had laughed. 'It wasn't quite like that. But, yes. I've had a few romances.'

She wasn't kidding. She told them about Ben, the photographer, who'd taken her to Alaska. And Finn who'd been an engineer of some kind who'd worked in the Middle East. And so many others over the years. Sophia portrayed herself as independent and adventurous. But, from what Megan could see, all she ever did was follow behind her latest boyfriend and whatever his passion was.

'Didn't you ever want to settle down in one place? With one person?'

Sophia had looked at her as if she was crazy. 'Goodness, no. Eventually, it stops working and I need to move on.'

That night in bed, she'd hugged Mark close. Grateful for the stability he'd given her. Now she felt as if he'd pulled that rug from beneath her. She couldn't live without him. How could she make him see that? She couldn't be alone. She bent over double and threw up into the gutter.

As soon as she got home, she got in the shower, then took her time blow-drying her hair straight, applying her make-up and choosing a dress that she knew Mark liked. If they were going to have this conversation, she wanted to look as good as she could for him. Turning to the side in the mirror, she knew that she didn't wear it as well as she used to, but that was age, wasn't it? No one looked as good in their thirties as they did in their twenties. If you loved someone, you accepted that, didn't you?

This time, she knocked on the bedroom door. Still, when she opened it, he jumped. He was wearing his stupidly large headphones and a guilty look on his face. On the screen: the same woman as before.

Due to the headphones, she couldn't hear what she said to Mark, but it was something about speaking later. As the window on the screen disappeared, it left a screensaver of Megan and Mark on holiday in Greece three years ago. When had they last smiled like that?

He pulled the headphones from his ears. 'Did you want me? I thought you were out for your run?'

'I came back. We need to talk.'

Ten minutes later, they were both in the sitting room; her on the sofa, holding a pillow in front of her like shield; him in the armchair, with his hands on his knees as if he was in a job interview. 'What do you want to talk about?'

Where should she even begin? Though she'd tried to rehearse her words on the run home, she still couldn't bring herself to accuse him of being unfaithful. 'I know there's something wrong, Mark. I just don't know what it is.'

He frowned. 'What do you mean?'

It was easier to think about this when he wasn't in front of her. Seeing the confusion on his familiar face made it even more difficult to believe what she suspected. She tried again. 'Between us. Things are strange. Ever since we started with the surrogacy, you've been distant. I know that you weren't keen on it to start with, but then you agreed. You said you were behind it.'

Did he look relieved? 'I know. And I was.' He paused. 'I thought I was.'

All she could hear was the ticking of the clock, the traffic in the distance, the wind rushing through her ears. She could barely get the question out of her mouth. 'Thought?'

Mark swallowed. Coughed. Swallowed again before looking at her. 'I knew how important it was to you to have a baby and I wanted that for you.'

Nausea lapped at her stomach. She tried to stay calm. 'I thought you wanted a child too? We'd always said that we'd have a family.' All the fertility treatment, all the pain. Surely he wouldn't have gone through all of that unless he really wanted a child?

He dropped his head into his hands. Beneath his floppy blond fringe, his voice sounded like it was coming from a mile away. 'I know. I know. I did want it. I wanted it all to work.'

The nausea was getting worse. How long had he been feeling like this? Letting her go on and on about the baby and the birth and the surrogacy and not wanting any of it? And they hadn't even touched on the subject of the other woman. She couldn't bear to have this dragged out any longer. She needed to know everything and she needed to know now. 'Mark. You need to be honest with me. What is going on?'

When he looked up, his face was full of fear. 'I'm trying, Megan. I really am. But this is difficult for me.'

She put a hand to the base of her throat and squeezed. Difficult for him? How the hell did he think she was feeling?

'We're having a baby together, Mark. How can you do this to me?'

He clenched his fists in his lap. 'I know that. I know we're having a baby. That's what... I can't do this, Megan.'

She was getting more terrified with each evasive sentence that came from him. Despite her shock at seeing that woman again, she'd still held a tiny hope that he wasn't actually having an affair. This was Mark. Dependable, dutiful Mark. He loved her. Why would he do this? But he clearly was. And if he wasn't going to say it, she would. 'I know that you're having an affair. I just want to know who it is and how long it's been going on.'

Did either of those things make a difference? Was she more likely to forgive him if it had been short-lived and with a stranger?

But Mark raised his head in surprise, then shook it slowly from side to side. His face contorted in an agony she'd never seen in him before. 'I'm not having an affair.'

Why was he still holding back? Couldn't he see that she *knew*? The sickness in her stomach was turning sour, acidic, hot, angry. She didn't deserve this. She'd been a good wife. He owed her the truth. 'I heard you. Speaking to that woman about me. I'm not proud of myself, but I had to know. I stayed and listened. You telling her that you couldn't speak to me about it. Well, you can tell me now. I'm all ears.'

His head dropped to his chest. 'I'm not having an affair. Anita isn't my girlfriend. She's my therapist. I've been having counselling.'

Was this real? The ticker tape of possibilities kept feeding through her brain. 'Counselling? For what? What is it that you can't tell me?'

He sighed and ran his fingers through his hair. 'I don't even know where to start. There's so much.'

She shivered. Somehow she knew that this was going to be worse. Much worse. 'Is it me? Is there a problem with me?'

Mark's face flooded with a wave of love that made her heart ache even more. 'Oh, Megan. There's nothing wrong with you. There's never been anything wrong with you. You are beautiful and kind and the most wonderful human being I know.'

Though every inch of her wanted to collapse into his arms, to be told that everything was going to be okay, she could almost see the 'but' hanging in the air like a guillotine. 'Tell me, Mark. Not knowing is so much worse.'

He sighed like a dying man. 'I need to start at the very beginning.'

Whenever Mark told a story about work or something he'd done, he would drag it out with every tiny detail until she'd roll her eyes and beg him to get to the point. Interrupting him now wasn't going to get her anywhere, though, so she merely nodded.

'When we first met, we were so young.'

'Oh please, no.' She groaned in pain as she doubled up over the cushion. There was no way in which this ended well. She couldn't hear it, she couldn't. It was too hard.

Mark looked genuinely distressed, trying to reach out to her. 'Megan, please. I don't want to hurt you. I can't bear it.'

This had to be over now. All in one painful hit. Not death by a thousand cuts. 'You don't love me, do you? Who is she? Tell me.'

He was speaking so slowly, so carefully, she wanted to shake the information out of him. When she refused to let him take her hands, he didn't seem to know what to with his own. 'There is no she. This is not about another woman.'

He was clearly lying. This hadn't come out of nowhere. 'What is it about, then?'

The fingers of his right hand twisted the wedding ring on

his left. It was platinum; engraved with their wedding date, it matched her own. 'This is about me, Megan. About who I am.'

They were going around and around in circles and not getting anywhere. 'You're not making any sense.'

He closed his eyes, held his breath for a moment and then spoke the words that spun her world around on its axis.

'Megan. I think I'm gay.'

SIXTEEN

SOPHIA

With the spring sun gaining strength and the dew of the night almost dried from the grass, mid-morning had become Sophia's favourite time of day to be in the garden. No one else must be taking advantage of this space because everything was still set up for them: she on the fold-up chair, Alex on the upturned flower pot. This time she had a notepad and pencil, and she was poised for him to begin.

He leaned his forearms on his knees, reading from the phone in his hand. 'First thing you need is a large plastic sheet.'

Sophia screwed up her face. 'Do I even want to ask what that is for?'

'I would've thought that's pretty obvious.'

Alex made a whooshing motion with his hands which left nothing to the imagination. 'Wow. You're really romanticising this for me.'

'Sorry. Is that what you wanted? Okay.' Alex pushed his glasses up his nose and tilted his head, holding his hands together as if he was talking to a small child. 'You'll need to make sure you leave the door unlocked when you got to bed so the stork can fly in with your baby.'

She poked out her tongue. 'Very funny. What else do I need?'

Alex returned to his phone where he'd been scrolling through the list he'd made. 'A bucket in case you're sick.'

She poised with her pen over the notebook. 'Seriously?'

Alex was laughing at her face. 'Did you watch *any* of the birthing video I sent to you?'

She'd almost watched it a couple of times but hadn't got up the nerve. 'I meant to.'

He wagged his finger at her. 'You are a very bad student.'

Even doing all this was pushing her out of her comfort zone. When she'd offered to carry Megan's baby, she really hadn't given the birth itself much thought. Once they were through the first few months, and even more since the baby had started to kick, she'd given herself up to the moment. Now, the reality was coming home to roost.

From nowhere, heavy drops of rain blurred the ink on her notepad. She closed it quickly, stuffing it under her thin t-shirt to keep it dry. Alex followed her inside, but when they got to the top of the third-floor stairs he hesitated.

'Just come in. It'll be fine. Richard's out, anyway.'

He took the chair that Richard usually used, and she opened her notebook again, rewrote the words that had been smudged. 'Did you really mean it about the bucket?'

He nodded. 'I'm afraid so. It's pretty possible that you'll be sick, although it's not always the case. And there's the other end, too.'

'Stop!' She held up her hand. Alex had been very easy to get to know, and she was very relaxed in his company, and he was trained as a doctor, but this was going too far.

'Okay. Okay. Let's talk about the nice things. A lot of women like to make the environment comfortable. It's one of the top reasons they choose to give birth at home. Low lighting. Maybe candles. Massage oils. A hot water bottle.'

She scribbled away as he listed them. 'Now this sounds a lot better.' She paused and looked at him. 'Be honest. How bad is it?'

'Giving birth? I haven't actually done it.'

She pretended to hit him with her notebook. 'I mean, in the births you've attended. What do the women say? How is it?'

His face was serious. 'Every birth is different. Some labours are over in minutes. Others are hours. Or days.'

Surely, he didn't mean that. 'Days?'

'It really isn't worth worrying about now. Just prepare the best you can and be flexible. Your midwife will guide you through the whole thing.'

Sophia had met her midwife last week. A kind but efficient woman who nodded along to Sophia's enthusiastic Italian as if she was indulging a chatty child. Strangely, it'd been comforting. 'So we just call her as soon as I go into labour?'

'Yes. But she won't necessarily come straight away. You'll need to keep her updated on how the labour is progressing. Remember about timing your contractions?'

She scribbled that down, too. 'Won't you be here?'

For the first time, he looked wrong-footed. 'Me?'

She felt silly now for having expected it. But she had. The whole time they'd been talking and planning, she'd just assumed he'd be there. 'I just thought... I mean, I might need some support.'

'But you'll have Richard there. And the midwife. I'll just get in the way.'

They looked at each other for a few breaths, before there was a scratch of the key in the door and Richard fell into the room, his arms full of produce from the market. An apple tumbled from the top of the bag and rolled to Alex's feet. He bent and picked it up.

Richard's voice was sharp. 'What are you doing here? You're not supposed to be inside here.'

He'd not been so hot on the lockdown rules when he wanted to open up his dig again. 'Alex is helping me to prepare for the home birth. And he lives on his own, so I'm pretty sure it's okay.'

This wasn't going to be a subject that improved his mood. Richard's lips tightened and he strode across the sitting room, slamming the kitchen door behind him.

Alex held the apple out to Sophia. 'I think that's my cue to go.'

'I'm sorry. He just...'

'It's fine. I completely understand. He's right. It's against the rules.'

'But you don't see anyone else. It's safe.'

'Still. I'll send you the list. And you might want to think about getting some clothes for the baby if you haven't already.'

As soon as Alex had gone, Sophia opened the kitchen door. 'That was rude.'

'Not as rude as chatting up my girlfriend when I'm not here.'

'Now you're being ridiculous.'

'Am I? I can see the way he looks at you.'

She felt her cheeks warm. 'Yes, you are being ridiculous. We were talking about all the things we need to get for the home birth.' She held out her notebook. 'You can read it for yourself. I've made a list.'

He raised his eyebrows. '*We* need to get?'

Time for another deep cleansing breath. 'I was hoping you would help.'

'Why are you doing this? Why can't you just go into hospital like everyone else?'

It was important to stay calm. 'I don't know if you've noticed, but the hospital is rather busy right now.'

'Which means we have to turn our apartment into a labour ward? You promised, Sophia. When you started on this ridiculous idea, you promised that it would not affect me, affect *us*. And it has. It *is*.'

On reflection, that had been a rather naive promise. 'I know. But I had to do it, Richard. I told you that.'

He shook his head and took the wine glass and bottle away with him to the bedroom.

She was done. As soon as this lockdown was over, she and Richard would be parting company. A long time ago, she'd promised herself that she wouldn't take this kind of behaviour from a man. In fact, if she hadn't been pregnant, she might have left already. She'd seen first hand how it ground you down staying with a man who treated you badly.

Her mother had been a different person before and after 6.30 p.m.: the time her father got home from work. Before then – after Sophia and Megan got home from their schools – she was full of smiles. She'd have snacks ready for them as soon as they got in and the three of them would watch TV together on the sofa before she had to get the dinner on. Sometimes Sophia would do impressions of her teachers to make Megan giggle, other times Mum would buy some new pens or paper and they'd draw together at the kitchen table while she prepped vegetables.

One of Megan's favourite dolls was a rag doll Cinderella. One half of the doll was Cinders in rags, but if you turned her upside down and pulled up her brown patched skirt, there was another Cinderella underneath, dressed in blue satin for the prince's ball. Their mother had been like that: two different people. As soon as her father arrived home, she would change from their smiling happy mother to a weaker version of herself who let him talk to her like she was nothing and did anything he said.

As Sophia had got older, she couldn't stand to watch. Staying out longer and as late as she could get away with. When her father shouted at her – and she'd give it back to him – her mother would shoo her up to her room. In front of their father, she'd be reduced to a weak-willed mouse, doing anything she could to keep the peace.

Sophia sank onto a kitchen stool, picked up one of the carrots Richard had been peeling and bit into it. One of the last times she'd seen her mother, she'd tried to speak to her about it. The kind doctor who'd visited hadn't been able to tell them how much longer their mother had, but she'd said the time was coming closer. It had been Sophia's turn to bring her dinner – if you could call the tiny portion of chicken and carrots a complete meal. Her mother's face had been drained of colour, but her eyes were still bright when they'd opened as Sophia had entered the room. 'Hello, sweetheart.'

'Hi, Mum. Megan has sent me with your dinner.'

Her mother had turned her face to the side as if to avoid even the faint aroma from the plate. 'I'm sorry. I'm just not hungry.'

She'd expected this. 'I know. But Megan is going to kill me if you don't eat something. I've had strict instructions.'

Her smile had been weak, but it was there. 'She's a good girl.'

Even now, there was a twinge of jealousy. 'She is. Bossy, though.'

The smile was stronger now. 'She's always looked after me.'

Guilt had prickled at Sophia. 'I know.'

Balancing the plate on her lap as she'd sat in the chair beside her mother, she'd reached for her hand. It was slight and papery, more like the wing of a fragile bird. 'Why did you put up with it, Mum? Why did you stay with him?'

In those final days, they'd slipped in and out of serious conversation so often that her mother had answered without a hint of surprise. 'He was my husband, Sophia. And he was your father.'

She'd heard that line so many times twenty years ago. 'But

your life would've been better without him. Our lives would've been better without him.'

Her mother's eyes had been watery as she'd looked at Sophia. 'I'm so sorry that I let you down.'

She shouldn't have started this conversation. Who knew how many breaths her mother had left? She didn't want her to waste them apologising. 'It's over, Mum. I'm okay.'

A tear had slid down her pale cheek onto the pillow. 'I'm glad. And I'm so glad you're here with your sister. You're all each other has got once I go.'

A lump had risen in Sophia's throat. She hadn't wanted to talk about this. 'Megan has Mark. She doesn't need me.'

Her mother had squeezed her hand. 'She does need you. Promise me, Sophia. Promise me that when I'm gone, you'll be there for her. She's not as strong as you.'

Had her mother got them confused? Megan was the capable one. The sensible one. The one with her life together. But the last thing she'd wanted to do was upset her mother now. 'Of course, I will, Mum. She's my sister.'

Three days later, her mother had passed away. Sophia had kept her promise to look after Megan. When the baby was born, she and Mark would have the family she craved.

Sophia wriggled off of the stool and scraped the carrot peelings into the bin. She would also keep her promise to herself: to never be the kind of weak woman who allowed a man to rule her life. Once lockdown was over, and the baby was safely in England, she would leave Richard and start again somewhere else. But where? And with whom?

SEVENTEEN

MEGAN

When Megan woke up, for a few blissful moments she forgot the conversation of the night before. Then it came over her in waves and everything Mark had said threatened to drag her under.

'I think I'm gay.'

Mark's face when he'd said those words had been so full of anguish that it'd taken her breath. 'How... What... You can't be?'

'I know it's a shock. For you, I mean. I think I've always known. Just thought I could, you know, ignore it.'

She hadn't known anything. Her entire world was being turned upside down. Nothing made sense anymore. 'You've always known? Our entire marriage?'

He'd reached out to touch her, but her body had stayed stiff and cold. How often had she lain awake next to him in bed, willing him to take her in his arms? And now she recoiled at his mere touch.

Mark had put his hand to his mouth; she'd seen that he was struggling, too, but she'd felt numb as she'd listened to his explanation. 'We were so young when we met, Megan. Babies, really. And you were exactly what I needed in my life. You were kind and sensitive and you just, well, you just *got* me like no one else ever had. Not my parents, or my friends. No one.'

This was a twist on a cliche: my wife is the only one who understands me. 'I remember.'

Hadn't she felt the same about him? The drama club had been a respite for her from all that was going on at home and in her head. Being someone else for a while was like shedding a heavy coat and replacing it with a diaphanous drape that allowed her to fly. And Mark had been the best part. From the first time they were paired up, he'd been her partner, her safe space, her familiar. His would be the face she'd search out as soon as she'd arrived each week. Relief making them both smile when she'd see him wave from across the room.

'For a long time, I wasn't sure if what we had was a friendship or something else. I'd had feelings for other people – boys and girls – but there'd been no one like you. No one that I'd connected with so quickly.'

Again, she could relate. Her bony frame had not been something that attracted teenage boys who were far more interested in the girls whose breasts and hips had developed. Mark had only had eyes for her and that'd been mesmerising. 'Go on.'

He'd swallowed. 'You know what my parents are like. My father. The expectations he had – still has – for me. With the business. With life.'

She knew all too well how important the family firm was in all their lives. Her father-in-law had inherited it from his own father and was determined it would be passed down to his descendants. It was one of the reasons she'd felt so pressured to produce a child and, ideally, a boy. It was like being related to Henry VIII. But this had seemed irrelevant to what they were talking about. 'But your parents liked me. They welcomed me.'

He'd nodded. 'I know. I think my dad had an inkling; maybe before I did. Once, I heard him refer to me as "sensitive" to my mother. I knew what he meant by that. When I brought you home, they couldn't get me married off to you quickly enough.'

Megan had closed her eyes as she'd remembered it. They *had* been super welcoming to her. Inviting her to a family wedding only the second time she met them. They would quiz her about her plans for a career, where she wanted to live, whether she wanted children someday. Mark used to find it irritating; she'd found it frightening. Viewed from a different angle, it was even more terrifying. 'Are you telling me that you married me to distract your parents from the fact that you were homosexual? That you've been gay this whole time? For the whole of our marriage? It's all been a lie?'

Memories had flicked through her mind like a movie reel. Birthdays, romantic weekends away, their engagement, exchanging gifts beside the Christmas tree, punting in Cambridge, dinners in fancy restaurants, their *wedding*: all of these memories were now coloured by this new history that he was writing in front of her. She'd slid her arms down her thighs and dug her fingers into the skin. How could this be true?

Silent tears had coursed down Mark's cheeks and he'd brushed them away with the back of his hand. 'No, not a lie. Never a lie. Being with you has been the most wonderful part of my life, Megan. You are so different to my family. Genuine. Caring. Thoughtful. It was the easiest thing in the world to fall in love with you. And I did – I do – love you.'

How could she believe that? 'But you're just not passionate about me?'

He'd whimpered like a hurt animal. 'Please, Megan. Don't be like that.'

What had he expected? 'Like what? I'm trying, Mark. But this is pretty difficult to process. Tell me the truth. Did you know? When you asked me to marry you, did you know then that you were gay?'

She'd held her breath waiting for his answer and he'd looked her so deep in the eye that she'd known he was telling her the truth. 'I think I always knew. But I thought it didn't matter. Because I loved you so much, I honestly believed that what we had would be enough. And it was good. It was enough. But then you wanted to have a baby so much and... that's when it got more and more difficult.'

She remembered how he'd been. How he'd struggled with each part of the process. But she hadn't for a second guessed that this was the reason why. 'You said you wanted a baby, too.'

He'd taken another deep breath, wiped his face dry and nodded. 'I did. That wasn't a lie. I did want to be a father and I knew that you would make such a fantastic mother. But when we found out that it wasn't possible, I also felt relief.'

Relief? The word had hit her like a slap. That was possibly the most painful thing he'd told her. The final meeting at the fertility clinic, when the doctor had told them that there was no point continuing with the treatment, had been one of the darkest days of her entire life. And he'd felt relief? 'Why didn't you tell me?'

His face had creased with the weight of emotion. 'How could I? I knew how you felt. How much you wanted to be a mother. How could I deny you that?'

Megan's head had hurt. At any moment, she'd kept thinking that she was going to wake up or Mark would tell her that none of this was true. How could she not have realised? How could he have kept this from her? And why was he telling her now?

'So what's changed, Mark? You've lied to me all this time, why tell the truth now?'

He'd winced at her tone, her emphasis on the word 'lied'. 'During the fertility treatment, I think we were both struggling, weren't we? Then we had to think about what to do next and I was just, overwhelmed, I suppose. When Sophia offered to be a surrogate, I never thought you'd agree. I mean, you hadn't even seen her in twenty years. That's why I didn't put up any resistance. I never thought you'd do it.'

He'd made his feelings pretty clear at the time. But she'd been so desperate to have a baby that she'd grabbed at the opportunity with both hands. He hadn't stopped her. 'So this is my fault?'

His face had crumpled. 'No, Megan. It's no one's fault. That's what Anita has helped me to realise.'

'Anita?'

'My counsellor. The woman you saw on the screen. I've been having therapy for the last four months.'

Four months? He'd kept this a secret all that time? 'And what does this Anita think you should do?'

He'd straightened up, placed his splayed hands on his thighs, back to job-interview mode. 'She hasn't told me what to do. But we've talked a lot about being open and honest. I know that it's not fair to keep this from you. To live a lie.'

She'd wanted to laugh at his therapy speak. She'd spent enough time in counselling sessions to recognise the lingo. Right now, she'd settle for the lie to not have to face all of this. 'And this is where you start telling the truth. This is it? You don't want to be together any longer?'

Mark had pressed his palms together as if in prayer and brought them to his lips. 'No, I'm not saying that. I do love you. I love you so much. I don't want to leave you and I definitely don't want to hurt you.'

It'd been too difficult to make sense of it all. 'You're going to stay? And then what? We just continue to pretend that our marriage is okay?'

He'd wiped fresh tears from his eyes. 'I don't know, Megan. I don't know what to do. But I do know that we need to work something out.'

In the end, she'd been too exhausted to keep talking. She'd gone to bed alone and left him to sleep in his new 'office'.

Wide awake now, she checked the time on the phone beside her bed and saw she'd had a missed call from Sophia last night. It was unusual for her to be the one to call. The phone rang about seven times before Sophia picked up. 'Hi, Megan. How are you doing?'

She had no idea how to answer that question. 'I'm okay. You called me?'

'Oh, yes. It was nothing important. I was just speaking to Alex about preparing for the birth and I realised that I haven't bought any clothes for the baby yet. I didn't know if you wanted me to go ahead and get some things or if you already have stuff?'

Only her sister would need reminding to buy clothes for the baby. Megan thought of the tiny vests and sleepsuits she had in the drawers upstairs. 'I have clothes I can send you.'

'Okay, great. I mean I can get some, but I thought you might have a special outfit picked out for first photos.'

Megan pressed her fist hard into her breastbone where the pain was. Of course, she had one. She'd scrolled for hours to find the perfect sleepsuit for her baby's first photos: not too fussy, not too plain. But what was the point of that now? 'I'll send you some things. But maybe you'd better get a few vests just in case the package gets lost or anything.'

Sophia seemed blithely unaware of how devastating this was for her. 'Good idea. I have to get all the stuff for the home birth anyway. I'll add it to my list.'

The damn home birth again. The way in which Sophia had made such a dramatic flip of their plans was so infuriating. Megan's fist tightened and she slammed it into her pillow. Why was everyone changing their minds all of the time? 'For the love of God, Sophia, I thought you'd realise how stupid that idea was. You need to be in a hospital. A home birth was never part of the plan.'

Sophia's response was so flippant Megan could've thrown the phone across the room. 'Plans change.'

Everything changed apparently. Even husbands. But this was dangerous. 'You have no one there to support you. What if something goes wrong?'

Again, her nonchalance was incredible. 'If something goes wrong, someone will drive me to the hospital.'

How could she make her understand? This wasn't like deciding 'eat in or take out' on a Friday night. These decisions had huge consequences. She could hear her voice getting louder and she didn't care. 'But it might be too late, then. This is my baby, Sophia. My only chance. You can't risk this.'

The patronising sigh was more than she could take. 'It's not a risk.'

Megan wanted to scream. 'You say that about everything. Life's an adventure to you, isn't it? It's the rest of us that have to pick up the pieces when things go wrong.'

'What's that supposed to mean?'

It was as if the words were pushing their way out of her mouth; she no longer had control. Decades of resentment came pouring out. 'You know exactly what it means. Leaving me at home with Mum and Dad. Staying away when we needed you. Oh, I know you sent postcards. But you could have come and checked on us once, just once in twenty damn years! You just don't care about anyone except yourself!'

The silence at the other end was stony. 'I'm going to go now.'

'Of course you are. It's what you do best after all.'

When she hung up, Megan rolled over into a ball and hugged her legs tightly into her chest. What had she done?

EIGHTEEN

SOPHIA

Sophia wasn't given to fits of anger. Boredom, irritation, annoyance, yes. But she'd never been one to shout or even feel the surge of emotion that anger seemed to need.

Today, though, it coursed through her veins like lava. How dare Megan try to tell her what to do about the birth? This was her body, her health. She wasn't the one about to go through a – she was now realising – massive experience with very little help. Did she not stop and think for a minute that Sophia was actually pretty damned scared now the event was imminent? Where did she get off calling her selfish?

For the first time, the walls of her lovely apartment seemed too close together. She wanted to pace and shout get these feelings out of her. Even the garden didn't afford enough space for what she needed. She needed to walk and walk. To get as far away as possible from here, from her sister.

And where was Richard again? Considering he couldn't go to work, and they had plenty of food in the cupboards, he was spending a lot of time out of the apartment. While she was cooped up in here with these... feelings, like a dam about to burst. She knew what she'd promised Megan, but she had to get out.

The day was warm and she was carrying around her own central heating system, so there was no need for a coat. She tried to pull on a pair of trainers, straining around her stomach to push them onto her feet. Even that made her out of breath. But Megan had no consideration for that, did she? No idea of the cost this was having on Sophia's body. And no understanding of why she didn't want to risk herself – or the baby for goodness' sake! – by going into a hospital that would have people dying from the awful bloody virus.

When the trainers wouldn't go on her swollen feet, she fell back onto the sofa. Everything was against her. There were other shoes she could wear but the effort of trying to get the trainers on had beaten the urge to walk from her. Only a couple of weeks ago, she was still working. Now she was useless and exhausted. Her whole life, she'd been in control of where she went and what she did and how she did it. Now, she couldn't even put on the shoes she wanted.

How dare Megan accuse her of leaving her to all the responsibility? Her in her huge house with her rich husband. It wasn't as if she wanted for anything. She knew nothing about the real world. About having to be on her feet all day and getting paid a pittance. Hadn't she had the easy ride of it, going to university? Hadn't Mark's family even paid a huge deposit for their house? Not having a baby was the first thing in her life that hadn't gone her way and now she was kicking off about that. She was controlling and demanding and wanted everything her way. She always had. She remembered Richard's warning. *This is not going to end well.*

If she wasn't going out for walk, she'd need to find something else to do. She couldn't just sit here and wallow in her anger. There were vegetables in the kitchen which were on their last legs and she'd planned to cook them into a ratatouille for dinner. Until Richard appeared at home and she could rant at him, she might as well get on with it.

Even preparing food was getting more difficult now that she was too big to stand close to the counter. The tiny kitchen she'd thought was cute was now cramped and impractical. Even yesterday it'd been fine, but today everything was irritating her. She slammed the chopping board onto the counter and grabbed a couple of onions, chopping them into large chunks, the way she liked them, and poured a generous glug of olive oil into the pan with the garlic. Then she started on the peppers. Ordinarily, cooking was soothing. Now she felt almost violent with the knife in her hand, coming down with force onto the thick wooden chopping board.

As soon as she sliced into the courgette, she knew what she'd done. Then the pain came and then the blood. 'No. No. No.'

She held her index finger under the tap until the cold water iced the sharp pain. Then she inspected the cut, it was small but deep and the blood wasn't stopping. She grabbed a clean towel and pressed it to her finger, looking for plasters. Nothing anywhere. She started to laugh. Oh, the irony of all the medical preparations she'd been making and there wasn't even a plaster or bandage for a small cut. Pretty quickly, the laughter turned into tears and sobs shook through her.

Despite all Richard's warnings, she really thought she was doing the right thing in having this baby. That this would help her and Megan to become close again. She'd promised her mum that she'd look after her sister, and she'd done just that. Offering herself up like some kind of human sacrifice. *Use my body*. How dare she call her selfish!

Breathe. What was she going to do about this cut that wouldn't stop bleeding? Alex would have a plaster. She scooped up her phone from the couch where she'd thrown it down and found his number with her thumb. When he answered, she barely gave him time to think. 'Have you got any plasters or bandages? I've cut my finger and it won't stop bleeding.'

'Of course. I'll bring you some. Just sit down and if you feel lightheaded, put your head between your legs.'

Lightheaded? She actually felt as if her blood was pumping around her body five times faster than usual. She couldn't sit down; her legs were restless and agitated. She opened the front door ready to meet him. She should've said she'd go up to his flat. In fact, she might as well go now.

Maybe it was her agitated state, or the pain in her finger, but she was halfway up the flight of stairs when she heard Alex open his door. As she called out to him, 'I'm on the way up,' she lifted her head and missed her footing on the next step.

The marble was slippery and the extra weight she was carrying at the front of her body made it difficult to regain her balance. Somehow – maternal instinct? – she managed to twist her body so that she fell onto her back rather than her stomach. Hard and cold, the sharp steps bit into her as she lay there, unsure of how much damage she'd done.

'Sophia!' Alex was next to her in a second. 'Are you okay? Does anything hurt?'

What hurt? She didn't know. Her heart was beating fast, she was terrified about what might have happened. Could she have hurt the baby? 'I think I'm okay.'

His voice was professionally calm and measured. 'I don't want to frighten you but there's blood on the front of your shirt. I'm going to call an ambulance.'

She followed his eyes to the trail of blood across the blue and white stripes of her shirt. Then shook her head. 'That's my finger. The blood is from my finger.'

He breathed out in relief. 'Okay. I should have realised that. I still think we need to get you checked out. Can you stand?'

She accepted his arm as he held it out to her. She was okay. 'I just want to go back to my apartment.'

'Okay. But take these steps slowly. Hold onto the handrail.'

As they got to the door of the apartment, Richard appeared, whistling to himself. When he saw Alex, though, he scowled. 'Again? You're here again?'

'I fell over, Richard. Alex was helping me.'

At least he had the decency to look embarrassed. Then concerned. 'Are you okay? Let me help you.'

But as soon as he reached for her, she felt a deep cramp across the bottom of her stomach. So intense, that she bent double. 'Oh my God.'

When she righted herself, Richard looked stricken. 'What's going on? Are you okay?'

If Richard was hot and panicked, Alex was cool and calm. 'Let's get you inside so that I can check you over.'

She'd been squeamish about the details of the labour, but now she didn't care. 'The baby's okay, isn't she? Please tell me she's going to be okay, Alex?'

'It seems as if you're having contractions. This could be it. It's happening.'

'But it's too early. I'm only at thirty-seven weeks. I'm not ready.'

Alex's voice was as soothing as a glass of warm milk. 'Well, your baby didn't get that memo. She wants to come now.'

Not my baby. She wanted to say. Had she risked the baby by that fall? Was Megan right about her? Was she selfish? Unthinking? 'It's too soon. Take me to hospital. Make it stop. I can't lose this baby, Alex. I can't lose her.'

His arms were strong and supportive as he guided her back into her apartment. 'It's only three weeks early. The baby will be fine. You need to calm down. We can go to the hospital if you want to, or we can call the midwife.'

She was still worried that going into the hospital was another level of risk. 'I don't know. I don't know. Call the midwife, see what she thinks.' She couldn't be trusted with this decision. What was the right thing to do?

Alex nodded, his voice still calm. 'Good idea. Richard, can you call the midwife and let her know? The number is stored on Sophia's phone. Tell her to come as soon as she can.'

Richard hurried away as if relieved to be given something tangible to do. 'No problem. Where's your phone, Soph?'

'It's in the kitchen.' She thought of something. 'And Megan. You need to call Megan. She needs to be on FaceTime so that she can be part of this.'

Alex was arranging pillows behind her so that she was propped up in the bed. 'We need to worry about you first. Let's get the midwife here and check you out and you can worry about your sister later.'

She could feel another contraction coming. This was all happening too fast. While she could still breathe, she grabbed at Richard's arm. However she'd felt about her sister mere minutes ago, there were some things that were more important. 'You have to get her on the phone, Richard. She can't miss this. She can't.'

NINETEEN

MEGAN

When Richard called, Megan had been sitting on the small armchair in the nursery. Looking around the room now – the changing table, the small wardrobe, the beautiful wooden cot – it felt ghostly. As if it was made for a child who would never come. Had she tempted fate by her excitement at getting everything ready?

On her lap, a tiny sleepsuit covered in pink roses. The only clothing they'd bought for the baby had been white vests and sleepsuits. But once she knew that she was expecting a girl she hadn't been able to resist. The day after the 4D scan, she'd visited a baby boutique and chosen this for her daughter's first outfit. The one she'd be in for her first photographs before it would be kept in a memory box for the rest of her life.

She peeled the sleepsuit from her lap and draped it on her chest before wrapping her arms around it. As she closed her eyes, its emptiness made her weep; tears squeezing under her lashes. By the time the baby was here with her, this newborn sleepsuit would be too small. She felt as useless as it was.

Because she'd left her mobile downstairs, it took her three or four rings to get downstairs and another two to find it on the kitchen counter. When she saw Sophia's name displayed, and the fact it was a FaceTime call, she wiped the tears away with the back of her hand and took a deep breath before she answered.

But it wasn't Sophia's face on the screen; it was the side of a less familiar face that she thought was Sophia's boyfriend Richard. 'Hello.'

He stopped talking to someone off screen and turned his face back to look at her. 'It's happening. The labour has started.'

He sounded so clinical – like a technician on mission control – that it took her a few moments to understand what he was saying. 'Sorry?'

Again she was speaking to the side of his face. He was talking to someone. He looked agitated when he came back to her. 'The baby is coming. Sophia has gone into labour.'

She grabbed the side of the kitchen worktop, not trusting her legs to hold her up. 'But she can't be. The baby isn't due for another three weeks.'

He spoke to her slowly, like she was a small child. 'I know. She had a fall on the steps. More of a slip really. Maybe that started things going.'

Megan gripped the phone tightly in her hand. 'Is she okay? Is the baby going to be okay?'

In the background, she heard Sophia's voice. 'Bring her here. Let me see her.'

The room turned upside down on the camera as Richard did as Sophia requested. Then – thank God – she saw Sophia's face. 'Hi. I'm fine. We're fine.'

'What happened? Are you sure you're not hurt?'

Guiltily, she was more worried about the baby, but she couldn't say that. Sophia shook her head. 'It was stupid. I just slipped on the last step and fell onto my back. I'm fine. Alex has checked me over. I think the baby decided she wouldn't take her chances on me doing it again, though.'

Megan couldn't bear to think about how much worse that could've been. What if it had been the top step? And she'd fallen forward? It was terrifying. 'I'm so sorry for what I said. I was cruel and ungrateful and—'

'It's okay. I know that... hold on.'

She watched a look of intense concentration seize her sister's face, her eyes staring down the pain of the contraction. She wanted to reach inside the screen and hold her hand, wipe the sweat from her face. They'd planned the whole thing, or rather she had and Sophia had nodded and said, 'Whatever you want.' She and Mark were going to be in the room with her the whole time. Mark! He was out for a run. She should call him.

The contraction seemed to be over. Sophia smiled weakly. 'Well, *they're* no walk in the park, I can tell you.'

It didn't matter how painful it was, Megan would have taken her place in a heartbeat. 'Have you got any pain relief?'

'Only paracetamol at the moment, which is like trying to mend a broken leg with a sticking plaster. We're waiting for the midwife to come. Meet Alex.'

She nodded at Richard to move the phone and now there was another man in shot. Blond and slim with the kind of glasses that made people look clever, he smiled warily at the camera and gave a self-conscious wave. 'Hi. I'm the stand-in midwife.'

She didn't care who he was, at the moment he was the only person there with any medical knowledge. 'Is she okay? And the baby?'

She could hear groaning off camera. Alex glanced over to where Sophia must be having another contraction. That must've been only a couple of minutes since the last one. When he spoke, he didn't bring his eyes back to her. 'As far as I can tell, the fall didn't hurt her. I don't want to move her now she's in labour, though. We're hoping the midwife will be here soon.'

'And if she's not?'

Contraction over, Richard moved the camera back to Sophia, she looked even less comfortable this time. 'Then we'll have to do it ourselves. It'll be okay.'

This time she sounded irritated. Megan didn't want to make this even more difficult. 'You're amazing, Sophia. You can do this. You are so incredible.'

Was that fear in her sister's face? She'd never seen that expression before. 'I hope you're right. Are you going to stay on the line and watch?'

Where else in the world would she want to be? 'Of course, I...'

She stopped speaking when she saw another rigid expression on her sister's face. Another contraction. They were coming fast now. Was that normal? She heard Alex's voice off screen. 'Okay, Sophia. They're coming quicker now. Maybe this baby wants to come and meet you sooner than we thought.'

Sophia's head fell back onto the pillow. Out of breath, she managed to speak. 'Have you decided on a name yet? She needs a name before she comes.'

Naming the baby had been the last thing she'd had on her list for Mark. She would go with the name she wanted. 'Millie. Her name is Millie.'

Richard was still holding the phone so that she could see what was going on, but now he pointed the screen at his face. 'I need to put you down for a minute. I need to get the phone stand.'

Now she was staring at the ceiling of their apartment. It was agonising not being able to see what was going on. Sophia had mentioned that Richard had a phone stand that he used for zoom calls which she planned to set up for the birth. That must be what he was doing. But why did he have to take so long about it? 'I'm still here, Sophia. Are you okay?'

'She's fine.' Was that Alex's voice again? 'She just needs to catch her breath now. Where's that damn midwife?'

The last sentence was much quieter and probably not intended for her ears. Where was that midwife? Did they not know that it was getting urgent? 'Can I call them for you? Chase them up?'

She was desperate to do something, anything, to help.

'How's your Italian?' Alex called. Did Sophia just laugh? Where was Richard with the bloody phone stand?

The screen moved again. He must be setting it up. Then she could see a wider angle of the bed and her sister on it. There was a thin sheet covering her from the waist and she was wearing a pale-blue top, propped up against two or three pillows. Her head rested backward and her eyes closed, she looked feverish. Something didn't look right. 'Is she okay? Is Sophia okay?'

Alex was in the camera view too and he nodded. 'She's fine. Just resting between contractions.'

For the next few hours, Megan watched helplessly as Sophia's contractions got further apart and then closer together. Mark was out and she couldn't tear herself away from the screen. Sophia was incredible.

Finally, she heard Alex telling Sophia that she was getting close. 'You're nearly at ten centimetres. You might be ready to push soon.'

Ready to push? She'd read that some women have really short labours but this was moving so quickly. Was that bad? Megan needed to get Mark. Whatever was going on between them, it wasn't fair to let him miss this. But she wasn't about to risk cutting off this call by calling his phone. What could she do?

Taking the phone with her, she walked to the front door and looked out. Should she risk walking down the road to find him? Then she had another idea. Elsie.

When she knocked, it took Elsie a while to come to the door. Probably doing her Pilates again, because she was out of breath. 'Sorry, love, I was—'

'Have you got your phone?' She didn't have time for niceties or small talk. 'I need you to call Mark. He needs to come home right now. The baby is coming.'

Elsie's eyes widened. 'I'll get it. Hold on.'

It seemed to take forever for Elsie to come back. In the meantime, Megan's eyes were glued to the screen. No one was talking to her now. Richard was holding Sophia's hand and Alex was checking her over. She wanted to ask what was happening, but she'd just be a nuisance. If only she could be there and be a part of this. She could help. She could soothe Sophia's pain.

Elsie was even more out of breath when she reappeared. 'Okay. Give me the number.'

She reeled off Mark's number and Elsie plugged it into her phone. But she shook her head. 'It's engaged.'

Engaged? Who was he calling on his run? She didn't care right now. She just wanted him here. 'Can you keep calling him, please? When he answers, tell him the baby is coming and he has to come home right now.'

'Of course. I will. I'm redialling right now.'

Megan left her and returned to the house, to the sitting room. Mark had mentioned last week that there might be a way to cast her phone to the television so that she could watch the baby born on a bigger screen. But he hadn't got round to sorting it out and now it was too late. They thought they'd had time. Another three weeks at least. *Please let her be okay.*

'Okay, Sophia. When you're ready, it's time to push.'

Alex sounded so calm, so certain. But everything in Megan wanted to tell him to wait until the midwife came. She was still terrified that something was going to go wrong. On screen, Alex was directing Richard to move closer to Sophia and support her.

She saw Sophia grab on to his arm as if she was drowning. *Come on, Sophia, you can do this.*

The front door banged open and Mark shouted down the hall. 'Megan? Where are you?'

'I'm in here. The sitting room.'

Hot and sweaty, he slipped in beside her and reached for her hand. 'It's really happening.'

His tone of voice held not a trace of excitement. In fact, it sounded more like dread. She tried not to rise to it. *He'll be different when the baby is here.*

They sat in silence. Watching as Sophia pushed and rested. Pushed and rested. Everyone in the room had forgotten that they were there, which was even more evident when Alex pushed the sheet higher and they got a more intimate view.

Mark almost recoiled. 'This doesn't feel right, Megan. I don't think we should be watching like this. I definitely don't think that I should. She's your sister.'

'But you were going to be there. That was always the plan, that you would be at the birth, too.'

'Yes, but I could have stayed more in the background. I mean, she's pretty much naked and—'

'And you can't bear a naked woman anymore?'

She knew she was being cruel, and he looked hurt. 'I'm here, but I can't watch. I'll sit over at the dining table.'

Now she was really angry. Was it not bad enough that she was watching through a screen? Now he wanted her to experience the whole thing on her own? 'Then you might as well go. I don't want you here if you're staring in the opposite direction.'

If she'd thought her anger would make him realise that he was needed, she was much mistaken. All she wanted was to see this baby born and now it was like watching it on television. She's going to miss out on the most miraculous moment of her child's life. Did that not mean anything to him at all?

'Hold on. Don't push, Sophia. Don't push. There's something... hold on... Richard, can you...'

Whatever he asked Richard to do, he moved so fast that he
must have knocked the phone to the ground. She could see
nothing at all. All she could hear were muffled voices and
Sophia's guttural groans. What was happening? Was there a
problem?

She'd never felt so utterly powerless in her whole life. What
if the baby didn't survive?

TWENTY

SOPHIA

One minute she was talking to Megan between contractions, the next she was so deep inside herself, it was as if nothing and no one else existed. There was just her and the pain. It built and built until she almost lost herself and then ebbed like a tide.

'You're doing really well, Sophia.'

Was that Alex? Someone had her hand and her elbow. Was that Richard?

Another wave and then something new. A deep primeval urge to bear down and push.

'Do you want to change position? We can help you move?'

Strong arms, either side, holding the weight of her as she turned until she was on all fours. Another wave of pain as if fingers were squeezing, pulling, tearing at her. She groaned as the urge to push came again. She had no control over any of it. Her body took over and all she could do was respond.

'That's brilliant. You're doing so great.'

'You're amazing. This is incredible.'

Who was speaking? It was as if she was in a dark tunnel. Even if she'd wanted to communicate with the men in the room, she couldn't. Every ounce of her was focused on her body. On

the contractions that pulled her into them and didn't let go.
Richard was there. And Alex. But they weren't *here*. Not where
she was. Where the baby was. Nothing had prepared her for
this.

There was barely time to breathe between the contractions.
Was that Megan's voice calling her name? She wanted her here.
She wanted their mother. She wanted her mum here, she
needed her. She wanted to go home. 'I can't do this. It's too
hard. I can't do it. Please, I can't do it.'

Then Alex's face was close to her. 'You can do it. You're
nearly there, Sophia. You're so close. She's nearly here, just a
little bit longer.'

Tears spilled over her face as she pushed again. Every cell in
her body focused on pushing pushing pushing. The pain was
coming and receding. There was nothing in between. Why had
she done this? Why did no one tell her? Why was this so much
agony?

'Wait, just breathe now. Don't push. Richard, help with her
breathing.'

Now Richard was beside her. 'You need to stop pushing
now, Soph. Alex says you need to wait.'

Wait? Wait? Every part of her wanted to push, to get this
over with, to get to the finish, to have this over. But she trusted
Alex, she waited for him, she kept breathing. Tried not to focus
on the burning pain and the overwhelming need to push.

'Okay. You can push again. You're nearly there.'

The sound that came from her was that of a wild animal.
Nothing could stop this now. It was coming. It was coming.

'I can see the head!' Was that Richard? She needed Alex.
Where was he?

Then she heard his calm voice. 'One more, Sophia. A really
big push. You can do this.'

Her body was so weak, she was so tired, it was too hard. 'I
can't. I can't.'

He was there again, at her side. 'Yes, you can. Just one more and she'll be here.'

Teeth clenched, she pushed her elbows deep into the mattress. One more push. One more. It started in her chest, her heart and rolled down her body to the depths of her. Everything was dark, and tight, and she growled as it left her body in a whoosh.

For a few moments, there was silence, every inch of her was spent, done, empty. What was happening? Where was the baby?

And then she heard her cry.

Was there ever a sound so beautiful? Soft yet sharp, her tiny bleat reached inside Sophia and pierced her heart. Her whole body responded. 'Is she okay? Is she okay?'

Alex moved beside her and lifted a tiny, scrunched bundle onto Sophia's chest. She was warm and sticky and, oh, so breathtakingly beautiful. Her tiny pink screwed-up face snuffled against Sophia's chest. She couldn't stop staring. She was here. She was actually here. And she *knew* her. She knew that face. Her voice came thick and sore. 'Hey, baby girl. There you are. I've got you.'

It was as if someone had pulled her from the depths of hell and given her a slice of heaven. Arms, legs, nose, ears: every part of this baby was perfection. Her forehead was warm and soft under Sophia's lips. She only stopped kissing her so that she could look at her. How had something so beautiful come from something so violent?

A tumult of feelings coursed through every part of Sophia – pain, exhaustion, wonder; like tributaries, they flowed together until all she felt was love. Pure, powerful, perfect love. No one else spoke as she whispered between kisses. 'You're so beautiful. I love you, little girl.'

She hadn't been intending to breastfeed, but Millie knew what she wanted. She wriggled herself into position and suckled immediately. Like a little kitten. This time the pain was sharper and sweeter. All she could do was stare at this tiny human. 'Welcome to the world, beautiful girl.'

Alex smiled at her but kept a respectful distance. Even Richard looked flushed with it all. 'You were amazing, Soph. It was... incredible. I can't believe what I've just seen. You're a warrior.'

He bent down close and kissed her cheek. She smiled but didn't take her eyes from Millie's rosebud mouth. 'Isn't she beautiful?'

He kept his face next to hers, his cheeks wet with tears. 'She is. She really is. Just like her auntie.'

Grief sent a bolt through her chest. For a split second, she'd thought he was about to say *just like her mother*.

It took a moment to recover as reality seeped in. She was being ridiculous. Of course she was Millie's auntie. She tore her eyes from her and towards Richard. 'Is Megan there? Is she still on the line?'

From his confused reaction, Richard had clearly forgotten all about Megan on the other end, but when he retrieved the phone from where it'd been knocked to the floor, her face – white and pinched – was still on the screen. 'Are you okay? Are you both okay?'

Richard held the phone so that she could see better. Sophia forced a smile for the camera. 'We're both great. Meet your daughter.'

She held Millie close to the camera. Megan gasped. Then started to cry. 'Oh, Sophia. She's beautiful. She's so beautiful. Hello, my gorgeous girl. I'm your mummy and I can't wait to meet you and hold you.'

Tears began to fall down Sophia's face. This was so much. Too many emotions to hold at once. Too many to even name. 'She is beautiful, isn't she?'

Megan was sobbing now. 'I don't know how I will ever

thank you, Sophia. She's just perfect. I can't believe you had to do it all on your own.'

'Well, I wasn't completely on my own.'

Richard circled his arm around her back. 'She was a complete warrior. I have no idea how she did it.'

She hadn't meant him. 'Alex was incredible, too.' She wanted to make sure he knew how grateful she was.

He was gathering together the towels that were soaked from the birth. 'I'm just relieved it all worked out. When the midwife gets here, she'll need to check you both over.'

As if he'd summoned her with his words, the apartment buzzer sounded. Richard kissed Sophia's knuckle before he let go of her hand. 'I'll run down and bring her up.'

He handed the phone to Sophia so that she could continue to speak to Megan. All she wanted to do was sleep. Or eat. And look at Millie.

Megan still looked concerned. 'Are you sure you're okay? Richard said you'd had a fall. Did you hurt yourself?'

The fall seemed to have happened days ago. 'I don't think so. I mean, I'm pretty sore down there and I'm exhausted. But I think we got through it together.'

She'd meant all of them, but she couldn't help but look down at Millie, who was now sleeping as if she'd been living out in the open for days. Alex reached over with a blanket and tucked it around her. Her little arms and legs curled in tightly to her body.

Now Megan spoke to Alex. 'Have you checked all her reflexes and everything? The Apgar scale?'

He nodded. 'Yes. She passed her first test with flying colours.'

'Of course she did.' Sophia pressed her lips to the dark hair on the top of Millie's head. 'She's a genius.'

Megan started to cry again. This time it seemed more like relief. 'Thank you, Alex. For being there and for... everything.'

The door to the apartment opened behind them and the midwife bustled in, followed by Richard carrying a large bag. Sophia smiled when Alex saluted the phone. 'It's absolutely fine. But I'm pretty glad to be handing over now.'

Richard took the phone from Sophia and spoke to Megan. 'I think the midwife needs to get to work on checking them over. Shall we call you back later?'

The midwife was thorough in her checks with Sophia and baby Millie and pronounced them both in perfect health. There was no need to go into the hospital. She seemed to think it would be better for them to stay away from there completely. She waited to see that Millie was feeding well and that Sophia was confident in what she needed before leaving with the promise to return the next morning.

Alex offered to help the midwife downstairs with her bags, but she shooed away his attempts to help. Sophia had a sneaking suspicion that she'd assumed that he was the father of the baby. Once she'd gone, though, he took his leave. 'I'll leave you both to it. But you can call me anytime you need me. Really, even in the middle of the night.'

More tears spilled from Sophia's eyes; they seemed to be endless. 'I don't know how I'll be able to repay you. You were amazing.'

Even Richard held out his hand to shake Alex's, a look of awe on his usually cynical face. 'Yes, thanks, man. You were incredible. I'm glad you were with her.'

Alex flushed and accepted his hand. 'Yeah, well. Me, too. It was a privilege.'

Sophia's throat tightened with the camaraderie between them. It felt as if they'd all come through a battle together. It would be a long time before she could get her head around this experience. She wanted to pull Alex into an embrace, but she settled for accepting his chaste kiss on her cheek. 'Well done. You did great.'

Richard left her alone to see Alex out and she looked down at the baby asleep in her arms. It really was a miracle. Even though she'd felt her kicking for the last few weeks, it still felt unbelievable that this tiny creature had been inside her all that time.

And how was it possible that she felt as if she loved her already? She knew it must be the hormones released during the birth. It was biological, wasn't it? These alien feelings – were they maternal? – would disappear when she gave the baby to Megan. She should call her again now, so that she wasn't missing out on any of these precious first moments.

Maybe she'd just give it five minutes more and then she'd call. Five minutes wouldn't matter, would it? Megan would have the rest of her life with Millie. Surely she wouldn't begrudge Sophia just a few moments alone?

'It's just you and me, at last.' She kissed Millie's soft dark hair and breathed in the warm, musky scent of her. How had she been so certain that she didn't want this? Those thoughts belonged to another lifetime. Before. When she was different. When Millie wasn't here.

Squeezing her close, she tried not to think about the moment she would have to let her go.

TWENTY-ONE

MEGAN

When the midwife arrived – and Richard terminated the call – Megan sat for a while in silence, trying to let her emotions settle. Fear, excitement, loneliness, desperation, joy: it was a heady cocktail. Over everything, though, was the knowledge that she was finally a mother. In the quiet of the sitting room, she held a cushion close to her chest, dropped her face onto it and sobbed.

There was no one in her life who'd understood how hard it'd been these last few years. Every appointment, every test, every month was further evidence of her failure. Of her body's failure. Maybe people assumed you got used to it, came to expect it. But that wasn't the case. However hard she'd tried, it was impossible not to allow a little hope to creep in. Then, like water in the cracks, it froze and broke you apart. After a while, people stopped even asking. Instead, they would shut down conversations about children so as not to hurt her. Kind, but devastatingly painful.

Wiping her eyes, she realised now that she hadn't actually allowed herself to imagine that it was all going to work out this time. Maybe she might've started to believe if Sophia had been home with her for the last few weeks of the pregnancy, but the lockdown had put paid to that and, with it, any emotion as dangerous as faith and hope.

But there was no mistaking that she was here now. Once they were through the terror of those last moments – when the screen had been tipped onto the floor – she'd seen her with her own eyes. Was there a more perfect gorgeous baby in the entire world?

Mark must have heard her crying, because he pushed open the door to the lounge and was next to her in three steps. 'Are you okay? What's happened?'

She lifted her tear-stained face. 'We have a daughter. She's here and she's beautiful, Mark.'

Now he began to cry, too. But his reaction seemed even more complicated than hers. 'I'm sorry I couldn't stay. I'm so sorry, Megs.'

She couldn't process anything else than the birth right now. Despite it all, he was still Mark, her Mark, and she needed this moment. She reached out for him, let him hold her close as she whispered over and over, 'She's here. She's really here.'

It seemed to take a really long time for the midwife to do everything that was needed, and Megan was beginning to worry that there was something wrong. Had they been taken into hospital after all? Finally, the call came and then she sat with her hand in Mark's as Sophia introduced him to his daughter. 'Here she is.'

This time, Mark couldn't take his eyes from the screen. 'I can't believe she's real.'

Hadn't she thought the same when she'd seen her for the first time? But there was something in Mark's tone that wasn't quite the same as the way she'd felt about it.

It was also strange to see the baby in Sophia's arms. Especially when Richard had his arm around her, kissing the top of her head. Telling Mark how incredible she'd been. It didn't take a genius to work out why it made Megan feel so strange: they looked like a family. But she needed to put that out of her head. Millie was her child: hers and Mark's.

She reached out to touch the screen, wishing with every inch of her she could stroke their daughter's cheek for real. 'Isn't she beautiful, Mark?'

She wanted him to really see her, fall in love with her. Despite everything they were going through right now, she'd desperately wanted him with her for the birth. It was bad enough that she couldn't be in the room at the beginning of her daughter's life. But to have to watch alone had been unnecessarily cruel. When she'd seen Millie for the first time, her hand had reached for his on the sofa, but he'd gone. If only he'd stayed in the room to see her born, she knew he'd feel more connected to her. That should be them with their arms around their child.

He reached for her hand now, though. 'She is. She really is. Where did all that dark hair come from?'

No one said it, but it was obvious to all of them that the baby's hair was the same colour as Sophia's. Had Mark also noticed how it made them look even more like a happy family of three?

The next morning, by the time she called up to Mark to ask if he wanted breakfast, Megan had already sent three WhatsApp messages to Sophia and been rewarded with a clutch of photographs of a sleeping Millie. She'd pored over them, trying to see a likeness for her or Mark. Her dark hair was likely to change as she grew; lots of babies are born with dark hair. She should've asked what colour eyes she had – the pictures were no help in that department.

When she called Sophia, there was no answer and Mark still hadn't come down, so she made a drink for them both and took it upstairs, knocking on the door to his makeshift office and waiting to be called in. 'I made you a coffee.'

'Oh, thanks. I was going to come down in a minute.'

'I've been trying to get through to Sophia. Once I do, we'll be able to see Millie again.'

Half of his face was hidden with the coffee mug. 'Great.'

She sat down on the edge of the bed, the bed that should have been Sophia's. How much easier this would all have been if things had gone to plan. Maybe Mark would never have even said those things to her. It could all just be a huge mistake, a moment of madness. They needed to talk about this. Properly. 'Why don't you come down and have some breakfast?'

When they got downstairs, she swept her hands in front of the fruit and pastries on the kitchen island like a hostess on a game show. 'I have bacon and eggs, too, if you want them?'

Mark looked as if what he wanted was to turn around and go back to his office. 'No, a croissant would be great. That coffee smells good. Thanks for putting all this effort in. Are you eating, too?'

She'd merely opened the packet and washed a few blueberries. Why were they speaking to each other like strangers? 'Yes, I'll have something. But I want to talk. Properly.'

He took a deep breath. Nodded. 'You're right.'

Five minutes later, they sat opposite one another at the kitchen table. Megan fought to keep the emotion from her voice as she spoke. 'We can do this, Mark. Raise this baby. All those things you said the other night about feeling that things weren't right, I don't think it's true. We've had a tough couple of years, but it's just a blip. All marriages go through them. When the baby comes home, it will be different.'

Mark was pulling a croissant apart and avoiding her eyes as

he spoke. 'It's not a blip. And this is not something that only happened in the last couple of years.'

The pain au chocolat on Megan's plate was more for decoration than anything else. With her finger, she dabbed at the greasy flakes of pastry that had fallen onto the white china plate. 'How can you be so sure?'

He looked up. 'That I'm gay?'

Every time he said it, she wanted to hold her hands to her ears. But she needed to deal with this and it needed to be now. 'Are you not bisexual? I mean, we did used to have sex.'

Mark continued to tear at the croissant. 'I don't know. I'm still figuring it all out.' He took a deep breath. 'I know that I don't find any other women attractive. Except for you.'

That wasn't surprising. Hadn't she always been quietly smug that he never reacted to another woman the way some of her friends' husbands did? That he'd only ever had eyes for her? She could cry for her naivety. 'So what's changed? I'm not enough any longer?' Something else occurred to her. 'Have you been... exploring elsewhere?'

She'd expected the answer to be a resounding no, so her heart dropped further when he hung his head. 'I have been to a few gay clubs. It wasn't really my scene. I just felt I needed to... see for myself. But nothing has happened. I would never cheat on you, Meg. Never.'

She believed him. It gave her just the smallest sliver of hope. 'So you might not really know for sure?'

He looked as if he might cry. 'I know.'

His tone was as firm as a slammed door. It was so difficult to reconcile the Mark she'd known so well with the man sitting opposite her. She held on to the edge of the breakfast bar. How could this be happening? It couldn't be. 'So where do we go from here? Do you want to see men? Do you want to get divorced? What are we going to do?'

Mark rested his forearms on the table, the way she'd seen

him do a thousand times when – even though she always asked him not to – he discussed business with his father over dinner. 'I've been talking it through with Anita, my therapist. She said she's happy to do some sessions with us together. So we can try and find a way forward.'

If her stomach hadn't been empty, Megan would have been sick. Years of therapy for her eating disorder meant she knew the good of it, but why the heck did she and Mark need someone there just to listen to them talk to one another? For a *way forward*? *No. No. No.* 'What does that mean? Be honest with me, Mark. What are you planning to do?'

'I'm trying to be completely open, Megan. But I've lied to myself for so long that it's really hard. I want to be honest. I want to tell you the truth. I don't want to hide anymore. If this awful bloody virus has shown us anything, it's that we don't have forever to make our minds up what we want out of life.'

He couldn't have winded her more if he'd punched her in the throat. Trying to breathe, she brought her hand to her collarbone, felt the thud of her heart beneath her wrist. It took her a few moments before she trusted herself to speak and, even then, she could only manage a whisper. 'I already know what I want out of life. I've always known. I want us and Millie. I want our family.'

Tears filled his eyes as he spoke. 'I'm so sorry I've done this to you, Megan. You have to believe me. I've never wanted to hurt you. Ever.'

Did it matter? Whether he meant to hurt her or not, he was tearing her fragile world apart. The hand on her chest rounded into a hard fist, the knuckles grinding into her breastbone. Fear and grief distorted into anger. 'It's not just me, is it? Millie is barely in the world and you've abandoned her already.'

He leaned forward in his seat, fear in his eyes. 'No, I won't ever do that. Whatever happens, I'll support you and the baby,

Megan. Financially, of course, but in other ways, too. I would never leave you to do that on your own.'

Whatever happens? What did that mean? Was he planning on leaving her? She couldn't take this any longer. Couldn't sit here while he rained more and more pain onto her. When she stood, the chair scraped across the kitchen floor. 'I need to get some fresh air.'

The newly bloomed brightness of the flowers in the garden mocked her as she walked the gravel path. Neatly bordered grass and thoughtfully spaced splashes of crocuses, daffodils and hyacinths. In the far corner, the rose bush that Mark's parents had bought them for their tenth anniversary was still bare. *The Forever Rose.* What a joke.

She still didn't have it clear in her head what Mark was planning to do. If he hadn't even been with a man, maybe this was all some kind of midlife crisis? There was a huge difference between fantasy and reality. Between attraction and physical touch. Was it possible that this was merely a reaction to impending fatherhood? A good friend of hers had waited out an affair between her husband and his PA. Pretended she didn't know. Sat it out until it fizzled. It was a cliche, but they were still together, weren't they? Their children both lived in blissful ignorance with both parents under the same roof. Was this like that? Could she do the same?

It wasn't often that she was in the garden at this time of the morning. Closing her eyes, she focused on the sound of the birds, the rustling of the leaves, trying to regain the joy of yesterday. With any luck, Elsie would be out soon and she could tell her that Millie was here. She was desperate to tell someone; make it real. Forcing Mark's revelations from her mind, she tried to focus on the image of her daughter that was already etched onto her brain. She wouldn't let this pain colour the most important day of her life; she wouldn't.

If only her mum was there to tell. Just the thought of

presenting her with Millie – making her a grandmother – strengthened the ache of loss she carried. Her mum would never know her granddaughter. And Millie would never know the kind, creative, generous grandmother she could have had in her life. After her mum's shattering diagnosis, Megan had been so determined to have a baby while she was still here, overwhelmed by the need to have even a few months, or weeks, with both her mother and her child.

But her mother had lied to her, too. All those years when she didn't tell her that Sophia had tried to get in touch. If only she could've asked her when she was alive. Why did she keep them apart? Why did everyone she loved keep secrets? Sophia had persuaded her that their mum had done it because she thought it was the right thing to do and Megan *had* to believe that. To think otherwise would bring down every good memory she'd ever had. Losing her mother from her life had been the hardest thing that had ever happened to her. Not having her here to meet her daughter was agony.

Elsie's French doors opened onto a patio and she frequently brought her morning cup of tea out there, so Megan didn't have long to wait before she made her way out into her garden. 'Morning, Elsie.'

She watched her neighbour put her hand to her heart dramatically. 'Oh, you gave me a fright. What are you doing up so early?'

Megan forced a smile and held out her hands: this was one of the moments she'd imagined and she was going to enjoy it. 'The baby's here. She was born last night.'

Elsie beamed. 'Well, that's marvellous. I'm absolutely thrilled. What did she weigh?'

That was another question that she hadn't thought to ask. 'I'm not sure.'

Elsie waved away her own question as she picked her way across the grass from the patio to the fence. 'Ignore me. It's a stupid question. I have no idea why we are all so obsessed with asking. More importantly, what's her name?'

'Millie. Millie Rose.'

Elsie's hand fluttered to her chest. 'Well, that's lovely. Rose for your mother?'

Megan nodded, not trusting that she could speak over the huge lump in her throat.

Elsie's face was so warm, so gentle, that Megan wished she could hug her. 'She'd be very proud of you, love. And your sister. Goodness, that baby has so much love around her, doesn't she?'

It was a fight not to let tears overwhelm her again. She pushed Mark's reaction from her mind. 'I'm just desperate to see her. In real life.'

'Of course, you are. There's nothing like that new baby smell.'

Elsie didn't mean it, but her words made Megan realise what else she was missing out on in these first few days. She'd tried not to be jealous of Sophia breastfeeding – if it was the best thing for the baby then she wanted it, of course – but it was difficult to see them connected like that. If things had gone to plan, she would've held Millie as soon as she was born. She'd even planned to hold her to her bare skin and bond straight away. Each tiny part of the process was being lost. But she had a daughter. She had to focus on that. 'I was going to call her again. Would you like to meet her? On camera, I mean.'

Eagerly, Elsie stepped closer to the fence. 'I'd love that.'

But when Megan called Sophia's number, there was still no answer. She tried again twice more, but no response. Tears pricked the back of her eyes. 'Sorry, I can't seem to get through.'

Elsie's smile was kind. 'Don't you worry, love. Your sister is probably changing a nappy or trying to get the baby down for a nap. It's relentless in the first few days.'

Now the tears really were likely to fall. She needed to get

back inside before she ruined this moment. 'I'm going to have to go and speak to Mark.'

Elsie raised her tea cup. 'Okay. I'll speak to you tomorrow. Congratulations again, love. I can't wait to meet little Millie Rose.'

In the kitchen, Megan tried calling again, but there was still no answer from Sophia. Upstairs, she could hear Mark already on a work call. Was this really the end of the road for the two of them? She'd wanted a baby more than anything else in the world, but she never thought she'd have to raise her on her own. Was that what was going to happen *going forward*?

And if it was, could she do it?

TWENTY-TWO

SOPHIA

Considering that all Sophia did all day was feed, change and care for Millie, it was amazing how quickly the hours disappeared. Partly, it was due to the fog of exhaustion: continual broken sleep wasn't fun, it had to be said. Even so, there was something magical about being alone with Millie in the early hours of the morning. Sometimes, while she was feeding her, she'd open the window blinds and look out on the silence and darkness tucked around the town. It was as if they were the only people awake in the world. Then, once she'd placed her gently back into her crib, she'd watch her little chest rise and fall, marvelling at how a body as tiny as that could contain all the organs that made it work. During the day, she could spend an hour at a time just watching Millie in her arms, the way her nose twitched in her sleep was positively hypnotic.

Before Millie was born, she'd spotted a soft yellow scrapbook in a local stationer and planned to create a baby book for Megan. At the time, she could never have guessed that Megan wouldn't have been here to see Millie for herself. When Richard was out, she'd used his printer to print the photographs she'd taken on her phone and, with Millie asleep on the rug beside her, she had them spread around her. Each one so perfect, it was difficult to choose.

At a week old, Millie had changed immeasurably. Gone was the scrunched up red bundle and, in her place, a porcelain doll with cornflower eyes and dark hair. Each time she FaceTimed Megan – usually about three times a day – there was a change in her. She was opening her eyes wider, grasping onto things more tightly, focusing her attention for longer. That morning, she would have sworn in court that she was trying to hold up her head. It was a tightrope talking to Megan about these things. A fine line between making sure she didn't miss out and drawing her attention to the fact that that was exactly what was happening.

'She really seems to be looking at me.' There was so much hope in Megan's voice that she went with it.

'I think she is. Talk to her.'

'Hey, baby. It's Mummy here. I miss you so much and I can't wait to see you. Are you having fun with Auntie Sophia?'

Auntie Sophia. It conjured up memories of their own kind but distant Auntie Marie who lived in Cornwall. Nothing like the connections she had with Millie. Sophia snipped at the coloured paper she'd bought to back the photographs. Yellow – Megan's favourite colour – to match the book, purple for contrast. This was the first creative project she'd started in a while: it was fun. Not quite the kind of project she would've done as part of a fine art degree, but a way to utilise her artistic skills a little. One of the photographs she'd printed from her phone was of her holding Millie minutes after she was born. Sophia looked horrendous – red cheeks, hair plastered to her head, exhaustion in the creases by her eyes – yet there was a joy in her eyes that she'd never seen in any picture of herself. She brought it closer. Yes. There it was. Pure unadulterated happiness. Should she include this in Megan's book? She wasn't sure how she would feel about it. But this was the first ever photograph of Millie. Should she cut herself out?

Her feelings for the tiny bundle in her arms were far stronger than she could've imagined. At night, after Millie had fallen asleep, the tiny 'o' of her mouth still twitching as if feeding from an imaginary nipple, Sophia would lift her close to her face, breathe in the warm milky freshness of her. Her skin was so soft, her hair so fine. Closing her eyes, Sophia would try to imprint the feel of her on her memory; never to be forgotten. These were stolen moments, she knew that. If they had been at home in England, it would be Megan getting up for the night feeds, Megan who would dress and change and hold the baby close. In the original plan, they'd agreed that she'd stay with them for the first two weeks after the birth, would express milk for the first week at least. But now Sophia wondered whether Megan would've wanted her around that long. Whether she would feel – as Sophia felt now – a jealous need to be the one to provide everything the baby needed? And would she herself have wanted to stay around and see Megan take control?

Last night, after the night feed, she'd sat up for a while with Millie asleep in her arms. Really she should've put her straight into her cot as soon as the feed was over, but these moments were too precious. Other mothers would see weeks and months of these night feeds stretching into a seeming infinity of exhaustion. For her, there was a time limit on all of it.

She shook her head. That's because she wasn't a mother, of course. She wasn't doing herself any favours by thinking of herself like that. With a firm press, she glued the photographs to the backing paper and started to trim them into shape. Millie in her crib, on her playmat, even in Alex's arms.

Sometimes Mark would join Megan on the call, sometimes he wouldn't. Even when he was there, there was an awkwardness about him. It was as if he didn't know how to act around her or the baby and Megan would go into overdrive, trying to bridge the gap between them. This morning, she'd decided it was time to ask Megan what was going on.

'How are things with you and Mark? You said there were issues.'

'We're fine.'

It was the most obvious lie she'd ever heard. 'Come on, Megan. I'm not stupid. You can talk to me about it. What's going on?'

Megan's shoulders drooped. 'He's going through some stuff. To be honest, I thought he was having an affair because he's been so distant. But then I discover he's been having therapy.'

'Oh?' That in itself wasn't a bad sign. Lots of people were being more proactive about their mental health these days. 'Is it work stress?'

She shook her head. Her face twitched. 'No, it's not work.'

This was like pulling teeth. 'So, what is it? Lockdown?'

She could see her sister wrestling with herself, her fingers tapped her lips as if she was debating whether to let the words out. When she did speak, it nearly knocked Sophia from her seat. 'He says he might be gay.'

Gay? Mark? 'What?'

Megan smoothed her hand down her neck until it rested on her chest. 'Yep. Your face is pretty much my reaction too.'

Mark and Megan must've been married for almost fifteen years. This didn't make any sense. 'And why is it "might be"? How can he not know at his age?'

Megan looked broken, as if her face was carrying the weight of her heart. 'I think he does know. But he's trying not to hurt me.'

This still made no sense. 'Surely you can't suddenly just become gay? I mean, how long has he known? Did you suspect anything?'

She shouldn't be firing questions like this: Megan flinched

at each one. 'No. Or, maybe yes? I don't know. If I think back, we haven't been close for a while. Not *physically*, I mean.'

She stuttered through the explanation, blushing at her allusion to their sex life. Maybe other sisters talked about things that happened in their bedrooms, but they'd never had that kind of relationship. Sophia tried to be gentle. 'Well, that doesn't necessarily mean he's gay. Sometimes men lose their sex drive.'

She was out of her depth on this one. None of her relationships had lasted long enough to get to that stage. A single tear made its way down Megan's face and she brushed it away. 'It's more than that. He's pretty certain. But he says he still loves me, so that's something.'

It was *something*, but it wasn't enough, was it? Sophia didn't know Mark that well. He seemed like a decent guy, but he was always 'busy working'. Even when she'd stayed there that last month when her mother was dying, Mark had been a benign but background presence. She'd wondered what Megan had seen in him, to be honest. She also wondered now whether his 'work trips' had been something else. 'What does it mean for you both? What are you going to do?'

Megan looked exhausted as she rubbed her temples with her finger and thumb. Sophia burned with the injustice that Mark was making her feel like this. Why did he have to dump this on her now? If he'd known for years, then why did he wait until Millie was born to throw their life into chaos?

The depth of her sister's sigh almost broke Sophia's heart. 'I just don't know. We've talked but I'm still not sure what he wants. He says he's not leaving. He'll make sure I'm okay. We'll have to find a way through, I suppose.'

Sophia couldn't believe what she was hearing: it sounded horrendous. Like a loveless marriage in a Thomas Hardy novel. Megan deserved so much more. What about what *she* wanted? 'You can't do that. This is your life, Megan. You can't just accept that... I mean, will he—' she struggled to phrase this tactfully '—will he be exploring that side of himself while he's still married to you?'

Megan's grimace made it clear what she thought about sharing him with someone else. 'I don't know. I don't want to think about it, to be honest. At the moment, we're just tiptoeing around each other, trying not to start another row.'

Sophia had been doing something similar with Richard before Millie was born, but this was on a whole other level. They were married and they had a child. Who was her other big concern in all this. 'And what about Millie? How is she going to fit into this arrangement?'

Megan straightened her back. 'We both love her. Mark isn't going anywhere. We'll make sure she has everything she needs. This doesn't have to affect her at all. She'll have both of us. Always.'

Whatever she thought now, Sophia knew that wasn't going to work out. 'And what about you? What about what *you* need?'

Megan stuck out her chin in the way she used to every time Sophia would suggest doing something differently when they were children. 'I need to be Millie's mother. That's all I want. I just want to have my baby home and hold her close. I can cope with anything else if she's here. Can I see her again?'

Sophia tilted the camera and her arms so that Megan could see the whole of Millie, from her dark hair to her tiny pink feet. It was heartbreaking to see Megan like this. Not only was she separated from her child, and still grieving their mother, she was being cruelly abandoned by her husband. How lonely must she feel right now? 'Can you see your mummy, Millie?'

Megan's eyes were bright and her throat was thick with emotion when she spoke to her daughter. 'Look at your little toes, baby girl. I can't wait to kiss those toes when I come to get you.'

But even though she felt sorry for her sister, this was not an ideal situation for any of them. Despite her belief that they would be able to be good parents, Sophia could see that Mark didn't seem to want to be involved as much as she'd imagined.

Tears were falling down Megan's cheeks now. 'Your mummy can't wait to give you a big cuddle. I love you so much, little Millie.'

You'd have to be made of stone not to feel for Megan right now. And there was something else to consider. 'Are you looking after yourself? I mean...'

'What do you mean? Of course, I'm looking after myself. Myself is the only person I'm able to look after right now.'

After the softness with which she'd spoken to Millie, Megan's voice cut through the air. Sophia kept her own tone light. Megan really didn't look like she had a handle on things. What if she was ill again? What if this sent her down a spiral that she couldn't come back from? Mum wasn't there to pick her up again. Did Mark even know what had happened before? Should she call him and ask or was that a betrayal to both her sister's and her mother's confidence? 'Well, maybe take the opportunity to do something nice for yourself. I mean, I know it's all a bit tough right now but—'

'A bit tough? There's a global pandemic, my husband is gay and can't even meet my own daughter. I think there are other words for it.'

The volume of her outburst made Sophia jump which, in turn, made Millie cry. She lifted her onto her shoulder and rubbed her back. 'Shush, shush, Millie. It's okay. Everything's okay.'

Megan had looked as if she were about to smash the screen or burst into tears. Now she just looked devastated. 'I'm so sorry, Millie. Mummy didn't mean to shout. I'm so sorry.'

Sophia could understand her reaction. But this situation didn't just affect Megan, did it? Much as she loved Millie, getting up in the middle of the night, constant feeding and nappy changing wasn't exactly a walk in the park. And she didn't have all the stress that Megan was going through. Or the medical history. How was she going to cope? 'I'm just going to lay Millie down in her crib, Meg. She feels a bit warm.' It was a lie to get out of this conversation. She chose the wrong one.

Megan sat up, on high alert. 'What do you mean, she's hot? Is she running a fever? Do you need to get a doctor? Maybe strip off some of her clothes?'

She looked frantic, wild. 'No, no. She's fine. I just meant that I'm getting hot with her laying on me and I'm worried that will make her too hot. It's better to lay her down in the cot anyway. That's what the book said that you sent me.'

She was lying about that, too. She'd only read about ten pages of that awful book. Even though the smiling woman on the cover looked like everyone's favourite grandmother, her advice wouldn't have been out of place in a handbook for prison instructors.

This lie had a more desired effect. 'Okay. Fine. But can you check her temperature every hour and let me know? And make sure that you give her enough fluids.'

She needed to get off this call. 'Will do, I'll call you later. Take care.'

Though she hadn't planned to, she did lay Millie down in her crib, where she yawned and stretched her arms and legs. Sophia looked down at her. 'You and me both. That conversation was like a straitjacket.'

Still in shock, she watched Millie twitch as she fell asleep. What if this situation proved to be too much for Megan? What if she couldn't cope? She'd said she was desperate to have Millie with her, but what if she was saying that because she felt she had to? Eating disorders were exacerbated by stress. What if this made her ill again?

And, if Mark's news had been a shock, Megan's response to it was bewildering. It seemed as if she was just going to accept the situation, live a lie, focus on what Millie needed – and what

Mark wanted – at the cost to herself. During their conversation, Megan had reminded her of someone and now she knew who it was: their mother. Like their mother, she was putting her own happiness behind her husband's. Like their mother, she was accepting this situation instead of fighting for what she needed. Like their mother, she was weak.

Sophia shivered. When she'd needed her mother the most – at nineteen, lost and afraid – she'd let her down. Through her weakness, she'd failed to be the mother she should have been. And that had changed the course of Sophia's life. Maybe, all their lives. Could she really stand by and watch Megan's weakness ruin Millie's life in the same way?

A thought whispered through Sophia. Would it be better if she kept Millie here with her? At least until Megan and Mark had sorted themselves out? She'd promised their mother that she'd look out for her sister. What if doing that meant that she had to make this decision for her own good?

TWENTY-THREE

MEGAN

The next morning, Megan woke up with the horrors. That hideous feeling that she'd done or said something she shouldn't. Telling Sophia about Mark had been a mistake. For a start, it made the whole awful mess of it more real. Plus, it was further confirmation of how much of an utter failure she was. Not only could she not conceive a child, but even her husband didn't want her. Not only was Sophia beautiful, but her body was strong and fertile and – judging by the little she'd heard about Alex – she had two men over there who seemed to be in love with her.

It was no longer a surprise to find the other side of the bed empty. She forced herself up and in front of the long mirror so she could really look at herself. Despite the running she was doing every day, her flesh felt loose. Ignoring the pallor of her cheeks and the dark circles beneath her lashes, she looked herself in the eye. 'This is difficult, but you can do it. You are strong. You are enough.'

When she'd been really poorly, in her mid and late teens, it'd been her mum who'd said these words to her and, somewhere deep inside, she could still hear her voice. 'You're so beautiful, Megan. You're my beautiful girl.' Dealing with it all had been hard for her mum. Sophia thought their mum was weak, but she'd been Megan's strength when she'd had none of her own. Now, looking at her own daughter she knew that she had to get through this. Had to keep well. Though her mum may not be here, her words were stamped on Megan's heart. 'This is difficult, but you can do it. You are strong. You are enough.'

In the kitchen, she poured herself a small glass of orange juice and, for want of anything better to do, called Bethany.

'Hi, Beth. It's me. Just checking in. How's things? Can I do anything?'

'Hi, Meg. Nope, nothing really to do. Petra's been working the socials, doing a bit of research on the accounts that are using humorous posts to grow their followers. Once she's got something concrete to tell us, I'll let you know. More importantly, how's that baby doing? Is she still completely gorgeous?'

She'd already forwarded a photograph to Beth and enjoyed hearing her gush about how beautiful Millie was. 'She's a week old today and is getting even more beautiful if that's possible. And yes, she's doing really well.'

'I think you're doing really well, too, Meg. This can't be easy for you.'

A lump swelled in Megan's throat and she swallowed it down. 'It's pretty tough. But not as bad as some people have it right now.'

'I know but that doesn't mean you don't have the right to feel sad.' She paused. 'What about your sister? I know you said she wasn't very maternal. It must be strange for her.'

'Weirdly, she seems to be taking it in her stride.' As she said the words, it struck her again how natural Sophia looked with a baby in her arms. Considering how she'd always laughed in the face of anyone who asked if she had children, this shouldn't have been the case.

'Well, that's good. At least you know she's looking after her well.'

Megan had known Bethany a long time. They'd shared many conversations over the years about some of their deepest secrets and fears. She could trust her not to judge. 'She is looking after her well, but she's not doing things the way we agreed.'

'What do you mean? Like what?'

'Like getting her into a routine with eating and sleeping. And she's still breastfeeding. I mean, I know I'm asking a lot, expecting her to express and bottle feed when I'm sure it's a lot more work than just getting it straight from the source, but it's just not what we agreed.' She didn't say that she was worried that each day of breastfeeding was creating another link in the bond between Sophia and Millie.

'I understand.'

'What would you do? Would you ask her to stop? Am I being completely unreasonable?'

Bethany sighed. 'I get it. I really do. When my mother-in-law looked after the kids when they were small, she would never do what I'd asked. If I asked her to make sure they stayed awake, she'd let them nap. If I told her they weren't to have a snack, that's exactly what they got. And I felt as if I couldn't complain about it because she was doing me a favour having them. But it would be me who had to stay up three hours later than usual trying to get them to sleep that night.'

'So I'm not being a controlling psycho?'

Bethany laughed. 'Not this time, no.'

That was a relief. Sometimes she didn't know the boundary between normal behaviour and her own need to have everything just so. 'Thanks. I don't really know how to handle it.'

Bethany didn't know Sophia, except the snippets that Megan had told her over the last year or so. 'Is it out of character for her to go her own way and ignore what you've agreed?

Or is it something you can put down to the strange situation she's in?'

It was totally in character; Megan remembered laying at the top of the stairs at home when Sophia had come home later than curfew and she was rowing with their father about breaking his rules. Then the later, whispered, conversation with their mother where Sophia had begged her to 'just tell him to leave me alone.'

'She does have a tendency to go her own way with things.'

There was a pause at the other end of the phone. 'And how is she going to be when this is all over, do you think?'

Megan's heart thudded in her chest. She didn't want Bethany to voice the darkest fear that she had. But that was the anxiety talking. She didn't really believe that it was a possibility. For a start, Sophia had always been the least maternal person she knew. 'I think she'll be relieved. She's always said that she's too selfish to have a baby.'

Even quoting Sophia, Megan felt guilty for using the word selfish. How could she say that when she'd given up so much for her in the last few months?

After Bethany had rung off, she opened the fridge and looked inside. Nothing looked appetising, but she needed more calories than the orange juice. In the deep drawers at the bottom, she found a bunch of bananas – Mark had a weird liking for having them cold – so she tore one off and took it out into the garden.

She'd barely taken a bite when, on the other side of the fence, she heard a wheezing cough. 'Elsie? Is that you? Are you okay?'

'Sorry, love. You stay well back. I should be indoors but I needed to breathe, it's so stuffy in there.' The last word was lost to a cough.

Megan took a step back from the fence and raised her voice. 'You don't sound good at all. Have you taken a test?'

'Not yet. But it's probably the damn virus. I haven't got the energy to book a test or get myself to a test centre.'

'What has Peter said?' Peter was a good son; he often checked in on his mother. She'd seen him dropping food to her doorstep a few times already.

'I'm not telling Peter. I don't want him to—' this time the coughing went on for longer. 'I don't want him to worry.'

'Well, I'm worried. You need to call him or call your doctor. Do you want me to do it for you?'

'No, no, no. You've got enough on your plate. I'm going to take myself in for lay down. I'll be alright in the morning. It just feels like flu. I'll speak to you later, love.'

Fear fluttered in Megan's belly. 'Call me, Elsie. If you need anything, call me. And if you're not feeling better tomorrow, you must call Peter.'

'I will, I will.'

As she watched her walk towards her back door, shuffling like an elderly woman, a feeling of dread came over Megan. Should she call Peter anyway, even though Elsie wouldn't want that? She'd ask Mark what he thought; it would give her an excuse to speak to him, too.

On the other side of the bedroom door, however, she could hear Mark's father giving him chapter and verse on something he had or hadn't done; it wouldn't be a good time to interrupt. But she needed to talk to someone about Elsie.

Sophia answered on the first ring, her voice not much more than a whisper. 'Hi, Megan. Sorry, Millie's just gone to sleep. She had me up at horrific o'clock and I actually managed to slide her from my body into her crib, so I don't want to even breathe in her direction right now.'

Megan pushed down her envy. 'That's okay. It's you I wanted. I need some advice.'

'Really?' The surprise in Sophia's voice was palpable. 'Go ahead. Whatever you need.'

'It's my neighbour.' She explained the situation and her dilemma about whether to call her son behind her back.

'I wouldn't.' Sophia's voice was certain. 'If she's walking around the garden, she's more than capable of calling her son if she wants to. You can't interfere.'

Interfere sounded so negative. 'But what if something happens to her and no one knows?'

'By all means call to check on her. But you can't just take over. She's an adult.'

'But if it was my mum, I'd want to know.'

'But she's not your mum. And you can't take all the responsibility like you did with our mum.'

That rankled. 'What do you mean by that?'

'Oh, don't take offence, you know what I mean. Look, while we're on the subject of advice, I've been thinking about you and Mark. You can't do this. You can't sacrifice yourself so that he stays. There has to be another way.'

She definitely shouldn't have opened up to Sophia about this. It had been a moment of weakness. She could have predicted that Sophia would tell her what to do. And with her history of going through men like water, it was no surprise that her advice would be to throw Mark out and raise the baby alone. 'I don't want to be a single parent, Sophia. This will be fine.'

'How can it be fine? You'll be miserable.'

'I won't be miserable because I'll have Millie.'

It was impossible to make Sophia understand. She'd always wanted more from life than it could possibly give. That's why she flitted from place to place, job to job and man to man: she was always looking for something new.

'He's your husband, Megan. Not your flatmate. You can't live like that.'

Where did she get off telling Megan how she could live? 'He's also my best friend. It will be okay.'

'You're going to end up like Mum!'

For a second or two, Megan couldn't speak. 'What do you mean?'

'You know what I mean. Living half a life. Doing what Dad told her.' She lowered her voice. 'And she was weak. She let us down.'

Loyalty to their mum made Megan frown, that wasn't the way she saw it at all. 'She was a great mum. She always looked after me. You don't know what it was like after Dad left. You weren't there.'

'Really?' Sophia's voice had a hard edge to it. 'Or was it you who looked after her? Once Dad left, you stayed with her way longer than you should have. You even commuted to university so you didn't have to leave her. If you really love your children, you have to let them go, Megan.'

Anger flashed through Megan. What did Sophia know about raising children? And what did she know about what Megan and their mother had been through? 'You don't know what you're talking about!'

Behind Sophia, Millie woke up and her cry tugged at Megan's heart. Sophia reached into the crib to pick her up and lifted her close to her face. Megan was struck again by how similar their colouring was. Sophia soothed Millie in a gentle voice. 'Hey, baby girl. Are you waking up? Did you want to say hello to your mummy?'

She shifted the phone on its stand so that Millie was in close-up. She was so beautiful. Megan watched as her tiny hand gripped onto Sophia's finger. Looking to all the world as if they were a mother and child. They were bonding. Of course, they were. As far as Millie was concerned, Sophia was her mother. Had this been a mistake? Should they have gone for an anonymous surrogate? Someone who the baby would never see again. Were these bonds going so deep that, forever, she would have a connection to Sophia? What if she never felt that instinctive love for Megan? Had she made a terrible mistake?

Right at that moment, she made up her mind. She needed to get out there. Mark owed her this, at least. She wanted to get to her baby.

TWENTY-FOUR

SOPHIA

After his brief spell of wonderment at the miracle of birth, Richard had shown very little interest in the baby. In fact, that morning, while Sophia was changing her on the mat in the sitting room, he'd been positively insulting.

'Her arms and legs are so skinny. She looks a bit like an alien.'

Sophia had had to fight the urge not to kick him in the shins. 'No, she doesn't; she's gorgeous. That's how babies' legs are supposed to look.'

He'd laughed into his coffee cup on the way back to the bedroom to work. 'Alright, calm down, Tiger. I was only joking.'

She'd reached down and scooped Millie up from the mat, holding her close and rubbing her back. 'Don't listen to that mean man, Millie.'

Richard might have been joking about her being a tiger, but she did feel protective. She knew first hand how it felt having a mother who hadn't had her back; even when she'd begged her. It was also why she was so concerned about what was going on with Megan and Mark. However Megan tried to paint it, if Mark was actually gay, how were they going to stay together?

Already, she regretted being as firm about it as she was yesterday, but Megan needed to see sense. By the looks of her on the screen, she wasn't doing so great herself. Sophia wasn't running away this time; she was going to step up and help.

The bedroom door opened and Richard appeared, shrugging on a smart navy jacket. 'I'm just popping out.'

Even during the day – before the strict evening curfew kicked in – they were only supposed to leave their home to buy necessities. And hadn't he only just made himself a drink? 'I thought you were working?'

He was at the front door before she had pushed herself up to standing, Millie safely tucked into her shoulder.

'Yeah, but I need to think through some stuff and I do that better in the fresh air.'

That's the first time she'd ever heard him say that. 'I wanted to talk to you about something. I'm worried about Megan and Mark. They're not doing so great. And Mark...'

She didn't know how to finish that sentence. She'd barely seen Mark on screen since she'd returned to Italy, but when she did, he was distant and detached. It was obviously difficult to communicate with a newborn baby over FaceTime, but he was barely interested. Fidgety and furtive, it was as if he'd rather be anywhere in the world than on that call. Megan might have married their father's polar opposite in character, but that didn't mean he would be any better as a husband. Or a father.

Richard already had the front door open. 'There's not much point talking to me about it. I don't even know them. I've not even met them. I'll see you in an hour or so.'

The door banged shut and the framed photo of her and Richard on the back of it swung dangerously on the nail she'd hung it on.

It was telling, wasn't it, that she'd been with Richard for over a year and he'd never met her only real relative. She hadn't met anyone from his family either. They'd lived in a bubble, the two of them, their relationship separate from anything else in their lives. It'd never bothered her before – she had no interest in meeting his dusty work colleagues or introducing him to Natalia from the cafe – but her only sister might have been curious about the man she was with? On her trips back to England for the baby appointments, Megan had always said, 'Of course, Richard is welcome to come, too,' but he had always muttered about being too busy or having other plans. Without checking with Richard, she'd invited Megan to Italy, but Mark was always working on some vital project and Megan would never fly alone.

Millie had dozed off on her shoulder, so there was no excuse not to lay her in the Moses basket and get on with the mountain of laundry piling up in the corner of the bedroom. For such a small little body, she sure did generate a lot of washing. Sophia scooped it up in her arms and tried not to lose a stray vest on the way to the washing machine.

Already, she could see how looking after a baby was hard work. Richard might complain that she couldn't stay awake long enough to watch a film or that he was the one who had to cook the dinner every night now, but she was totally exhausted. If Mark wasn't fully on board with taking Millie – worse, if he wasn't around at all – could Megan do it on her own? If she wouldn't even get on a plane without Mark to hold her hand, how was she going to cope with solo parenting?

She stuffed in the last muslin and sleepsuit and pressed the door closed. She needed to talk to someone about all of this. Maybe Alex would be able to give her some advice.

Alex answered the phone on one ring. 'Are you calling to save me from throwing my laptop out of the window?'

She laughed. 'Not going well, then?'

'Worse than that. Not going at all. There's some Windows Update being installed and it keeps stopping and starting again. What can I do for you?'

'Lend me your ear for half an hour? In exchange for a coffee?'

'I'm on my way.'

Just seeing Alex's face made her smile. He was so much easier to talk to than Richard. Richard's Byronic intensity had been very attractive when she'd met him, but it was less attractive when you had to live with it day in, day out.

'Quick. Let me in before someone spots me.'

He moved his head and eyes from side to side as if he was a secret agent on a mission and she laughed. 'I think you're safe. Come in.'

He followed her through the sitting room, looking left and right. 'Where's Millie?'

'She's asleep in the bedroom. Richard's out.'

He raised an eyebrow at her. 'You're bossing the baby care. My brother's wife had to have my niece strapped to her twenty-four seven or she screamed the house down.'

The compliment was nice. 'Well, I'm lucky. She's an easy baby.'

'Your sister is going to love you when you hand over a fully trained baby.'

Her stomach clenched even thinking about that. 'That's kind of what I wanted to talk to you about. Let me put the coffee on first.'

Alex hovered at the entrance to the tiny kitchen and watched her fill the Moka pot with hot water and coffee. 'Proper Italian coffee, eh? I tried to use one of those when I first got here, but it got all clogged.'

Sophia screwed the pot onto the base. 'You're probably using fine grounds. The coarse ones work better.'

She turned on the gas and put the pot on the ring, handle out so it didn't get hot. She felt Alex's eyes on the back of her head as she laid the cool tea towel out ready. He pointed at it. 'What's that for?'

'You put the pot on there at the end. It stops it brewing. Otherwise, it can have a burned flavour.' She turned and stood with her back against the worktop. 'So, my sister. I'm not sure she's ready for the baby.'

Alex dragged his eyes from the Moka pot. 'Not *ready*? What do you mean?'

Alex didn't know Megan or was ever likely to meet her, so surely it was okay to be honest. Anyway, she had to talk to someone. 'There're problems between her and her husband.'

The water bubbled on the stove. Alex frowned. 'Irrevocable problems? As in, their marriage is in trouble?'

Telling him about Mark coming out seemed a step too far. 'I don't know for sure. But I get the impression that her husband isn't really... on board with having a baby. And my sister looks like she's struggling.'

Alex pushed his glasses closer to his eyes. 'And she says she wants you to keep the baby?'

She almost lied. 'No. She wants the baby, but I'm wondering if I should offer? If she's not well enough to look after her. Just for a while.'

The pot hissed as the steam was forced up through the grounds. Alex glanced at it, then back to her. 'I don't know your sister, obviously. But I'm assuming she's desperate to have her daughter as soon as possible. She's already missed out on the first ten days of her life. I know you're trying to look out for her, but I'm not sure that suggesting they are apart for longer will go down too well. I mean, Millie is her baby.'

He was right on one count; it wouldn't go down well with Megan. But, legally at least, Millie was actually Sophia's child.

When they'd sat down and talked about the surrogacy, Megan had been most particular to explain everything to Sophia about the legalities. She'd listened, but it hadn't seemed hugely important. She'd known that the baby was Megan and Mark's and she was going to hand it over as soon as it was born. Back then – before she'd met her – it had seemed to be merely a matter of the correct paperwork. Last night, Sophia had checked on the UK government website and it had confirmed what she thought she'd remembered. It was there in black and white at the very top of the page. *If you use a surrogate, they will be the child's legal parent at birth.*

The bubbling in the pot began to rumble as the rich dark coffee dribbled through the spout in the middle of the pot. 'The thing is, I have to think about Millie, too. According to UK law, I'm Millie's mother. To become her mother, Megan has to apply for a parental order – whatever that is – or adopt her.'

Alex's eyes widened. 'But that's crazy. Didn't you sign a contract or something?'

Megan would've loved that, Sophia was sure. 'Wouldn't have been legally binding. You can't do that in the UK.'

Alex shook his head. 'Wow. I didn't know that. I mean, it doesn't make any difference, though, does it? It's not as if you're going to try and keep her.'

The coffee started to spurt a little; she must have the temperature too high. Sophia grabbed another towel and moved the pot so that less of it was on the heat. There was no way of explaining this to him that didn't make her sound crazy. That she hadn't realised that she was going to feel like this. That she and Millie would have so much time on their own. She hadn't known how much she would love her and want to protect her. 'I know you're right. I'm just worried about her. About both of them. About how Megan is going to be able to cope. If her husband leaves... well, she's never been on her own, ever.'

She turned her back as she rested the hot Moka pot onto the cool towel, wrapping it slightly to bring it off the boil.

Behind her, Alex's voice was gentle. 'I know this must be difficult, Sophia. Neither of you knew that this would happen; this pandemic has ruined lives in so many ways. But you're her

aunt, not her mother. It's not your decision to make. You really
need to talk to your sister about your concerns.'

Tears burned at the back of her eyes. How could he possibly
understand? He hadn't experienced what she had. It was time
to change the subject before the tears spilled over. 'I'm having
my coffee black. Do you want cream?'

'Black is good for me.'

They were silent for the few moments it took to pour the
coffee into two espresso cups, and it was enough time for her to
regain control of her emotions and be ready to turn to him with
a smile painted on. 'Let's sit.'

There was an awkwardness between them now, which
made her regret talking to him about this. Was he judging her
for wanting to keep Millie safe? But there seemed to be something else on his mind. 'Look, Sophia, I wasn't sure whether it
was my place to tell you this but, I can't not.'

Her stomach prickled at the look on his face. 'What is it?'

He took a deep breath. 'Okay, yesterday I—'

'Well, fancy seeing you here again.'

Sophia jumped. She hadn't even heard Richard's key in the
door. 'You're back quickly.'

Richard crossed his arms and raised an eyebrow at Alex.
'Not a moment too soon, it seems.'

Alex slid his cup back onto the coffee table and moved
towards the door, which Richard hadn't yet closed. 'I'd better
get back to my laptop. Thanks for the coffee, Sophia.'

There was something decidedly strange in the way both
men were behaving. As soon as Alex had closed the door behind
him, she turned to Richard. 'What was that all about?'

Richard laughed. 'Just a bit of fun. I think Dr Alex might
have a bit of a crush.'

She hated when he was patronising. 'You're being
ridiculous.'

Millie must have been woken by the door closing because

she started to cry. Leaving Richard standing in the sitting room, she went to rescue her from the crib. 'I'm here, baby girl,' she whispered as she scooped her up. 'Everything's going to be okay. I'm here.'

As she held Millie close, she felt again that urge to keep her safe, whatever the cost to anyone else. She'd hoped that Alex might understand, might help her. But if he wasn't going to, then she would be forced to try again with Richard. To persuade him to let Millie live with them.

TWENTY-FIVE

MEGAN

Through the half-open blinds, blue flashing lights lit up the sitting room and drew Megan to the window. For a moment, she thought the ambulance was going to stop at the end of her path, but it drew forward until it was outside Elsie's house. Was the ambulance for her? *Oh no.*

Two paramedics wearing protective clothing jumped out of the front of the ambulance, one of them carrying a box of equipment. By now, Megan could see that the neighbours in the other houses were at their front windows, waiting to see what was going on.

How long had it been since Elsie had first felt unwell? One day seemed to merge into another. Though she'd spoken to her over the fence each day since, she hadn't seen her out there at all today; she'd been too preoccupied to check on her. Of course, she couldn't have gone in, but she could have knocked on the door or, at the very least, called her on the phone.

The paramedics had disappeared around the side of the house, probably to let themselves in the back door. Had Elsie called them? Though she hated being a voyeur, Megan couldn't tear herself away from the window until she knew that Elsie was going to be okay.

Yesterday, on the phone to Bethany, she'd complained about how awful it was to be separated from Millie. Her words came back to haunt her now as she watched and waited for sight of Elsie. This bloody virus was ruining her first days and weeks as a mother, but she'd cope with that as long as Elsie was okay. Ever since they'd lived in that house, she'd been a kind and thoughtful presence in their lives. Since losing her mother, Elsie had been even more than a neighbour to her. She couldn't imagine not having her there.

The coffee Megan had made herself five minutes before the ambulance arrived was now cold in her hands. Watching and waiting was driving her crazy. It was as if she were destined to be a mere spectator in all areas of her life right now. Why hadn't she called Elsie to check on her? There was movement in Elsie's front garden. One paramedic was through the front door. Behind him, he pulled a stretcher on a trolley with a very frail-looking Elsie under a sheet, an oxygen mask on her face. Without thinking, Megan ran to the front door, pushed it open and called out. 'Is she okay?'

One of the paramedics looked up at her. It was hard to see her face behind the Perspex mask. 'Please stay inside.'

Megan took a step backwards. 'Is she okay, though? Elsie? We're friends. Please tell me she's okay.'

'We're taking her in. If you know her family, perhaps you'd like to call them?'

Was there something ominous in their tone or was she imagining it? 'I will. I'll call her son now.'

She closed the door behind her and found Elsie's son's number. Elsie had given it to her months ago when she'd gone on holiday to Spain with her sister. 'I'll give you Peter's number in case anything happens at the house while I'm away.'

He answered on the second ring. 'Hello?'

'Peter, it's Megan. Your mum's neighbour.'

'Is she okay? What's happened?' It was a sign of the times that his first thought was bad news.

'An ambulance has just taken her to the hospital. They wouldn't tell me anything, but I can only assume her Covid has worsened.'

There was silence on the other end for a couple of beats. Then his voice was a whisper. 'She didn't tell me she had Covid.'

She should have guessed that. Independent and stoic, Elsie would have preferred to deal with it herself. 'She probably didn't want to worry you, Peter.'

At the other end, a stifled sob made her heart squeeze, then he must have composed himself. 'Thank you for calling, Megan. I'll call the hospital now.'

'Will you let me know how she is?'

'Of course. Thank you.'

Without realising, she'd been pacing up and down the sitting room the whole time she'd been speaking to him. Sinking onto the sofa, she let the phone drop beside her and stared at it. That bond between a mother and a child was unbreakable, however old they both grew. Elsie had tried to protect her son from the worry of her being ill; he was brought immediately to tears at the very thought of losing her.

How soon did that bond form? She remembered Bethany's words about Sophia. *How is she going to be when this is all over?* Each time she called, though, it became clear that Sophia was falling in love with Millie. Her face lit up when she spoke about something she'd done, or a noise she'd made that had caused them to laugh. Right now, Megan was too raw and vulnerable – too worried about Elsie and confused about Mark – that she just didn't have the courage to speak to Sophia about her feelings for

Millie. Tomorrow, she would call her and make sure that what she'd told Bethany was still true. That Sophia didn't want a baby. Somehow, she'd work out how likely it was that she'd struggle to give the baby up.

* * *

Sure enough, when she spoke to her the next day, Sophia was a picture of maternal bliss. Megan couldn't help the sarcastic tone to her voice. 'You seem to have got this childcare stuff off pat.'

Sophia shrugged. 'I don't know about that, but, yes. I guess we're getting the hang of it.'

'We? Is Richard getting involved?' Somehow, that made things worse. The thought of them playing happy families with her child made Megan nauseous.

'No, I meant me and Millie. I've been reading some really interesting things on some of those links Alex gave me. There's one with some great recipes for Millie when she gets to the weaning stage.'

Megan's throat tightened. Weaning? 'But that's not for months yet. She's not even two weeks old until tomorrow and babies don't start solid food until they're at least four months old.'

Sophia's tone was so gratingly superior. 'Actually, that's not necessarily the case. Different cultures approach it differently. Some experts believe you should let the baby lead you when they're ready. You just need to be vigilant for the signs. It's the same with potty training. Do you know, in China, they—'

'Millie won't be weaned until at least four months and she'll be back with me by then.' She hadn't meant to snap but she couldn't listen to Sophia's hippy-dippy airy-fairy research for a moment longer.

'Of course. I'm not trying to tell you what to do. I've just had time to do some research while I've been stuck in here.'

'And I've been researching for the last five years, so you don't need to worry.' It was actually a lot longer than that. She'd wanted a baby since she and Mark had got married. He'd been the one to say they needed to get their careers off the ground first, then find the house, decorate it the way they wanted it, encouraged her to start a business. Now she thought about it, he'd been putting barriers in the way of starting a family for years.

After a pause, Sophia's voice was annoyingly calm and caring. 'I'm a little bit worried, to be honest. You don't seem yourself, Megan.'

She wanted to ask what she thought Megan being herself would look like but wasn't sure she'd like the answer. 'I'm fine. My neighbour was taken into hospital yesterday. I'm worried about her.'

Sophia's voice softened. 'I'm sorry to hear that. And you've got all this with Mark, too. How is that going?'

She wasn't in the mood to talk about that again. 'Actually, it's fine.'

'Really? Because you don't seem fine to me. I just wonder whether having a baby on top of all that is going to be too much for you?'

There it was. She'd been right. Sophia didn't want to give the baby up. She wanted to keep her for herself. 'Are you trying to suggest that you keep Millie?'

Sophia looked as if she'd slapped her, but she soon righted herself and reinstated her supercilious tone. 'I'm not saying anything right now, I'm just saying that I'm here for you. If everything is too much for you, then you don't need to take this on, too. I can look after her. I *am* looking after her. There's no rush for you to take over as soon as the lockdown is lifted. You can take your time.'

Her words fell inside Megan like a stone. 'How dare you.'

Sophia pressed her lips together, looking as if she was

weighing her words before she spoke. But Megan was not ready for what she said next. 'I know about the anorexia, Meg. Mum told me. And I'm so sorry I wasn't there for you, but I'm worried that all of this will just – I don't know – bring it all back.'

She couldn't breathe. Her mother had told Sophia? She'd known this whole time? As if she were frozen, Megan couldn't formulate a response. How could she just throw that into the conversation as if it were nothing? Sophia was worried the anorexia would 'come back'? What did she think it was? Chickenpox? 'I can't believe you've just said that. You are using that as a reason so that you can take my child? You are unbelievable.'

Sophia didn't look remotely ashamed of herself. 'Don't jump down my throat. You're not listening. I'm trying to help you here.'

Megan's laugh bordered on hysteria. 'Help me? Help yourself more like. I should've known it. I should have known this would never work out. When have you actually done anything for anyone except yourself?'

Sophia closed her eyes as if Megan was the unreasonable one. 'Let's not do this again. I let you shout at me before, because I know you're going through a lot. But I'm not having it again.'

'You don't have anything you don't want, do you? That's why you don't stick around for long, why your relationships never last. If you don't like the way something's going, you just walk away.'

That one hit home. Sophia flushed with anger. 'Because that's madness? Leaving a situation that's not working? No. Far better to stay put even when you're miserable. When you're making other people miserable.'

'What's that supposed to mean?'

'Oh, come on, Megan. You living with Mum all that time. Saint Megan sacrificing her place at Durham and going to UEL instead so that she could stay with her mother.'

'But I had to stay with her. I couldn't leave her alone.'

'Why not? She was a grown woman. Mum was just an excuse.'

'Oh, I see what this is. You're trying to put this one on me so that you don't feel bad for all the years you spent hundreds of miles away. Is that what this is? You think sending a few post-cards was enough? You made no effort with the family you had, but now you think you might like to have a go at a family yourself?'

'I was there for the last weeks with Mum. When she needed me, I came.'

'You came because I asked you to. Because I was able to put you up in my house. The house that I'd taken Mum into when she had nowhere else to go. And even then, you left everything up to me.' She held up a hand to stop Sophia's interruption. 'Oh, I know that you sat in Mum's room for hours talking to her. But I was the one who had to plan and cook her meals, work out the medication, liaise with the hospital for her appointments. Don't you think I would've liked to just sit and chat?'

'I couldn't get involved in those things because you'd just taken it all over. We all had to do it your way.'

'It wasn't my way. Do you think I wanted to be the nurse for my mother? But someone has to do these things and it's always me. I had to take over everything because you weren't there. You can't be relied upon. Ever.'

'You can't rely on me? If that's true, why did you let me be your surrogate?'

'Because I was desperate, Sophia. I wanted a baby so much that I'd even trust you. My last possible resort in all other things. I wanted to be a mother so badly that I took a risk on you.'

'Well, maybe you shouldn't have.'

Silence fell like a shutter at a window. There it was. The truth. Sophia wanted to keep Millie. Megan felt the fire of rage in the pit of her stomach erupting faster than she could control it. 'I'm coming for my baby, Sophia. As soon as lockdown is lifted, I'm getting on a plane and coming for my daughter. And you'd better not try and stop me.'

TWENTY-SIX

SOPHIA

For a few moments, Sophia sat staring at her phone screen. What had just happened? Megan was off the scale. She wasn't well. Should she call Mark?

A cry from the bedroom meant Millie was awake. In her crib, she looked so tiny, waving her arms in front of her, her tiny legs tucked up. 'Hey, baby girl. Are you awake? I'm here, I've got you.' She picked her up, enjoying the weight of her in her arms. Cradling the back of her head in one hand, she slipped the other underneath her, resting her cheek to the side of her face. 'Oh, Millie. What shall I do? How am I going to work this out?'

It had bowled her over, these feelings she had for Millie. She was starting to understand the obsession that some women seemed to have with their babies. It was pretty consuming. Last night, she'd lain awake and watched Millie's little chest moving up and down as she breathed. So fragile, so beautiful.

How could she hand over this precious vulnerable child when Megan was behaving like this? It wouldn't be fair to either of them. Megan needed to focus on her and Mark and how they were going to sort that out. A loveless marriage? What kind of

environment was that for a baby to grow up in? What kind of
life would Millie have with Megan as a mother? She'd promised
her own mother she'd look out for Megan, but maybe this was
the way to do it. To take care of her child.

Could she do it? Keep Millie here with her? It was going to
be a pretty difficult conversation with Richard. Maybe, if she
could make him understand that Megan wasn't in a good place,
he might agree to let her stay. As far as their own relationship
went, she'd have to do what she had to do for now.

Her stomach churned at the thought of asking him. Ordinarily, she didn't get nervous. She'd always been confident in
any situation she came across. Her mother used to tell stories
about her when she was young girl who would happily waltz up
to complete strangers and make them her best friends. But she
knew that this conversation with Richard about keeping the
baby was important to get right. She needed to give it her absolute best shot.

At least he'd been in a good mood when he'd left earlier.
He'd spent the morning locked in the bedroom with his laptop,
firing off emails like bullets. Whatever he was cooking up, he
looked pretty pleased with himself. Just before her conversation
with Megan, he'd swept through the living room and announced
that he was going out to get the ingredients for a new recipe. She
could only hope his good mood would last until he got back.

First thing she did was tidy away all the baby paraphernalia.
It irritated him that their once spartan apartment was now deco-
rated with muslins and the jungle-design playmat and piles of
toys and washing and an overspilling changing bag. Millie made
it clear – pretty emphatically – that she didn't want to be put
down, so Sophia had to scoop things up in her right arm while
cradling Millie in her left.

Next step was to make Millie look as adorable as possible: a
very easy task. She sorted through the clothes in the drawer.

There were a few outfits that Megan had sent, but it felt inappropriate to use those for this purpose. In the end, she settled for a mustard yellow sundress with a delicate frill on the sleeves. 'Who could say no to you in that dress, Millie? This will be a breeze.'

It really was a surprise how much she was enjoying caring for a baby. It was as if this part of herself had been dormant and waiting for this moment. Or maybe it was just Millie. She really was an easy, happy child. Laying on the bed, kicking her little white socks, she gurgled to herself and jammed her fist in her mouth. Sophia leaned down and blew on her neck, which was guaranteed to make her wriggle.

She glanced at her watch. How much longer did she have until Richard returned? Did she have time to put on a dress? Some make-up? Then there was a knock on the door. Had he forgotten his key?

But it wasn't Richard; it was Alex. 'Is Richard here?'

That was a surprise. 'No. What do want him for?'

'No, I don't... I mean, I wanted to talk to you.'

She'd forgotten about whatever it was he'd started to tell her. But this wasn't great timing; Richard was going to be back any minute. 'Actually, could I give you a call later? I just really need to get something done.'

He looked uncertain. 'Can I tell you quickly? I've been wrestling with myself about coming to tell you this, but—'

Footsteps on the stairs interrupted them. Was Richard singing?

He was clearly in a good mood as he didn't even baulk at Alex being at the door. 'Have you heard the news?'

Alex looked as confused as she felt. 'No. What news?'

'The lockdown. It's over. We are free to be out of the house.' He held up a bottle of wine. 'We're celebrating.'

This was wonderful news, so why wasn't Sophia feeling

celebratory? She knew, of course. This meant that Megan would come.

Richard reached over and held Millie's hand. He smelled as if he'd already had more than a glass of wine. 'You're free, little Millie, we're all free. Put that in her scrapbook, Sophia. Nineteenth of May, lockdown is over.' He nodded to Alex and sidled past Sophia in the direction of their small kitchen, carrying bags full of food, still singing to himself.

She smiled at Alex. 'What was it you wanted to say?'

'It doesn't matter. I'll catch you tomorrow. Looks like you're celebrating.'

Her natural curiosity would normally have made her squeeze the information out of him, but she wanted to capitalise on Richard's good mood. Plus, it sounded as if speed might be of the essence now. 'Okay. Let's catch up soon with a coffee in the garden?'

Alex was already backing away towards his apartment. 'Yeah. Great.'

Unpacking the shopping, Richard was practically dancing around the kitchen. It made her smile to see him like this, the grumpy, belligerent Richard of lockdown had been far less attractive. 'You're in a very good mood.'

'Of course, I am. And we're celebrating.' He pulled what looked like a very good bottle of Prosecco from one of the bags.

'Wow. You are celebrating.' She wasn't really drinking at the moment because of the breastfeeding, but a glass or two wouldn't hurt.

His face was full of mischief. 'Ask me why.'

Surely that was obvious? 'I'm assuming the end of lockdown?'

'Yes. But something else.'

It had to be about his work. 'They're reopening the dig?'

'Yes. But something else. I've got a new job. A far more prestigious dig. In Oman!' He popped the cork from the bottle, quickly moving it over the sink when the Prosecco spilled over the sides.

'In Oman? The Middle East?'

He seemed to read her confusion as admiration. 'I know. It's so exciting. The job comes with accommodation and they're going to pay for our flights. They want me soon, so I'm going to fly over next week, but you can come whenever you're ready.'

This was definite. There was no discussion. No consideration for what she might want to do. And what about his work here? 'How will they feel about you walking away from the project here?'

She couldn't see his face, because he had the cupboard door open, searching for wine glasses. 'What? Oh, they were pretty relieved, I think. We're over budget and behind schedule. They need to save money. My wages will help.'

He'd already told them? Where was she in the pecking order of finding out? She swallowed. Baby steps. 'This is quite a surprise. I mean, we love it here. And I have a job.'

The glasses chinked as he set them down on the side and poured the wine. 'Don't worry. They must have coffee shops in Oman.'

His patronising tone stung. 'But I'm happy here. This apartment, the people we know.'

He passed her a glass and held his up for a toast. 'We'll meet new people. Here's to an exciting new opportunity.'

The Prosecco wasn't as cold as she liked it and it felt thick and perfumed at the back of her throat. 'Also, I don't want to take Millie somewhere like that yet. She's so tiny and it'll be so hot for her.'

Richard frowned. 'Lockdown is over. You can drop the baby off with your sister and then join me. There's no rush. We have to give a month's notice on this apartment anyway.'

She took a deep breath. 'I'm not sure if my sister is up to

having the baby with her yet. There's a lot going on for her at home.'

Richard frowned. 'Well, we've only got this apartment for a month. Will she be ready by then?'

This was the moment. *Here goes nothing.* 'The thing is, I was wondering... whether I should keep the baby. Forever. Raise her myself.'

For a moment, he froze. Then he started laughing. 'You're joking, right?'

'No. I thought... I mean, you've got used to having her around, haven't you? And she's such a good baby, so I thought maybe you wouldn't mind if...'

She trailed off as he shook his head. 'No, Sophia. This is your sister's baby. I don't want to live with your sister's baby. I don't want my own baby. We've talked about this. I thought you felt the same?'

They hadn't really talked about it. Not properly. But she did know that he didn't want children. She just hadn't realised until now that she did. 'But she's—'

He held up his hand. 'I don't dislike children. I just don't want one of my own. I never will, Sophia.'

'I see.'

He reached out and put a hand on her shoulder. 'This next place will be amazing. Living in the Middle East! What an experience for us both. Not having kids means you're free to do whatever you want. That's good, right?'

He planted a kiss on her cheek before taking his glass into the sitting room, whistling a tuneless melody. As far as he was concerned, the conversation was over. He was leaving to live in Oman and just assumed she'd go with him.

You're free to do whatever you want. Her freedom to fly from place to place *had* been good. But now? What if she didn't want that any longer? Where did that leave her?

TWENTY-SEVEN

MEGAN

Shock gave way to absolute rage after Megan's conversation with Sophia. How dare she suggest that Megan wasn't in the right place to look after her baby? She'd been in that place for so long that she'd forgotten what it was like to not be yearning for her own child.

After knocking loudly on Mark's office door, she pushed it open. 'We need to talk. It's urgent.'

Mark's father Chris filled his computer screen, his thick grey hair and equally thick Yorkshire burr more familiar to her than her vague memories of her own father. They must be in the middle of one of the plethora of 'discussions' he demanded each day. 'Hello, Megan, love. Everything okay?'

Mark didn't ask for much from her, but hiding anything of consequence from his parents was one of them. There was no way he'd have shared their current issues with his father. 'I'm fine, Chris. Just need your son for a moment.'

True to form, he ignored her. 'This is a rum turnout all this lockdown stuff, isn't it? Sounds like the prime minister is finally going to let us out and about again. How are you faring with your business?'

Her work was pretty much all she ever spoke to Chris about. Mark's mother would be the one to do the house and family chat. They had their roles and topics of conversation and they stuck to them. 'We're okay. Bethany is doing a lot of it. She has her sister helping her.' She realised that she hadn't done any work herself in days. Not that she could muster up the energy needed to care.

Mark must have seen the look in her eyes, because he took the rare step of cutting off his father just as he opened his mouth to reply. 'I need to go, Dad. I'll get those figures together and send them over to you by the end of the day.'

'Goodbye, Chris.' She waved at the screen and left the room.

Downstairs, she waited on the couch for Mark to join her. Eventually, they might have to tell his parents what was going on with the baby. Although she hoped it wouldn't come to it, they might need to take legal action to get Millie back.

Mark sat opposite her on the armchair as she told him about her conversation with Sophia. At no point did he interrupt or express an emotion. She wanted to shake him. It was all very well being easy-going, but sometimes you needed to get angry. When she'd finished, she pushed herself back in the sofa and looked at him. 'Well?'

His face was so passive, that she wasn't sure what he was going to say. But it certainly wasn't what came out of his mouth. 'I know this is going to sound... terrible, but do you think it might be the best thing if Sophia *does* keep the baby?'

Her stomach started to squeeze. She might actually be sick right here on the carpet. 'What?'

He shifted in his seat, leaned forward, palms turned upwards. He reminded her of a dog rolling over on its back in supplication. 'Give me a minute to explain. This is a really difficult situation right now. Between us. We've got a lot to work out and... bringing a baby into that does make it really difficult.'

'Difficult?' she nearly spat with the word. 'Difficult?'

Now he turned his hands over and waved them downwards as if he was calming a wild animal. Had he learned this body language in business school? He was also keeping his voice excruciatingly calm. 'I know this might sound shocking, after everything we've been through to get to this point.'

We've been through? *We*? It was her who'd had all the invasive examinations, taken the mood-altering hormones, ridden the rollercoaster of hope and devastation month after month, year after year. When people had stopped even asking her how things were going. Looked at her with pity instead. Changed the conversation away from babies out of a well-intentioned tact that actually had the opposite effect and made her feel even more isolated and different. And now, when she was so close, he wanted her to just let their baby go? 'Millie is our biological child. Both of us.'

'I know that. But she's clearly happy with Sophia. Wouldn't it be selfish to tear her away from her now?'

Selfish? She couldn't believe what she was hearing. Surely, he couldn't mean this? 'I thought you wanted a baby?'

'*You* wanted a baby, and I wanted you to be happy. I already felt awful about the way I was feeling.'

Prior to the last few weeks, they'd barely had a cross word in their marriage. Now, it felt as if they were yelling on a daily basis. At least she was. 'So you let me have a baby out of guilt? And now you've realised that you have to be involved and you want out?'

The face she'd always thought of as gentle, now looked weak and afraid.

'Look. I'm not saying this is a definite thing. I'm just suggesting that we think about it. This hasn't worked out the way we planned, has it? Sophia was supposed to be here so that you could take the baby straight away. But now she's been living with her for the last fortnight, bonding with her, being her mother.'

Megan wrapped her arms around herself. This was a nightmare. It had to be. She was going to wake up in a minute and find that none of this was true. 'I'm her mother.'

It was even worse when he put an arm around her as if he was doing this for the best. 'If Sophia and Richard want to keep the baby, and she's happy there with them, maybe we should at least consider it. I'm worried about you, Megs.'

She shrugged off his arm, couldn't bear for him to touch her. 'Not you, too? Worried about me? Think I'm going to stop eating again? Concerned the anorexic can't be trusted with a daughter, is that it?'

He flinched with each word as if she were throwing shrapnel in his face. How dare he and Sophia bring that up to punish her? Did they not think that she had worried about this herself? Especially when she'd found out the baby was a girl. But she looked after herself now. She wouldn't slip down that slope again. She wouldn't.

He knit his hands together and leaned forward as if in prayer. 'Please, Megs. Stay calm. I'm just worried about you, and it sounds as if Sophia feels the same. We both want to make sure that we do the right thing for you and the baby.'

The baby. She realised that Mark had never once used her name. To him, she was an issue to be resolved. Did he even think of her as his flesh and blood? What had happened to him? He had always been her strength. Living with him had kept her safe. Had she not known him at all? 'I'm going for a run.'

He reached for her arm. 'Megan, please. We need to talk about this.'

She turned on him, fury erupting from her. '*Now* we need to talk? When it's something you want to talk about? Not the last, who knows how many years when you've been living some kind of secret life. No, Mark. I do not want to talk about this. Millie is my baby and I will never give her up.'

As she got to the hallway, he called out to her. 'Please, Megan. Just think about it.'

How she *hated* that word. *Just* accept it. *Just* eat. *Just* relax. If she could *just* do any of those things, did people not think that she would?

Since lockdown began, she'd started living in leggings and t-shirts, so all she had to do was shove her feet into trainers and slam the front door behind her. How she wished Elsie was next door for her to talk to; how she missed her mother. Hot tears burned her cheeks as she pounded down the road. She needed to be anywhere but with him. She just kept going and going, paying no attention until she found herself at the park.

In trying to outrun the pain, she'd pushed her body too far. Her lungs were on fire, she couldn't go on. Hands on the back of a bench to prevent her legs from buckling, she couldn't move another step. She had to stop, breathe, recover. When a young mother dragged her pram from across the asphalt and sat directly in front of her, she froze, transfixed by the tenderness with which the woman lifted the tiny baby from the pushchair.

The damp wood of the bench filled the underneath of her fingernails. Still, she couldn't tear her eyes away from the beauty of the two of them, their love. The fire in her chest spread to her belly. It was so easy for this woman, her child now cupped in her elbow, her face turned towards her baby. It was so easy for all of these women, at the bottom of slides, pushing swings, hovering by roundabouts. But not for her. Not for Megan. She couldn't have these things.

The heat of her anger subsided into smouldering ashes. Should she be this shocked that Mark had no feeling of connection to Millie? Hadn't he been reluctant from the beginning to let Sophia be their surrogate? Yet, he'd rolled over so easily that she'd assumed he was on board. Or was it, rather, that she'd wanted it so badly that she didn't even care? Because he'd always given her what she wanted, hadn't he? He liked to keep people happy.

Now she thought back even further, had he married her just to keep his parents happy? His own parents had married young, had him – their only child – shortly afterwards. When he'd taken Megan home, they'd welcomed her with open arms, invited her on family holidays, started to refer to her as their daughter-in-law long before they were even engaged.

Was Mark right that they'd guessed? Had he only married her because she was a way for him to hide what he couldn't tell them? What he hadn't really reconciled with himself?

She bent forward with a groan. The pain inside her was physical. A knot of grief and anger. How had she not realised that he was never in love with her? Not in the way she wanted. Not in passionate, romantic, desperate love.

But there was a small voice at the back of her brain that wondered if she had been just as much to blame. When you grow up with very little, it's easy to be seduced by safety. Mark's family were wealthy, his upbringing was privileged. A different kind of life had been laid out before her. One in which she didn't need to worry about money for bills or food. Had she really fallen in love with him? Or had she been in love with the security and care he brought to her life?

And did any of this even matter now? This wasn't a theoretical moral discussion about a fictitious baby. Millie was real. She was here in the world and she was their baby. Hers and Mark's. Though she'd never forgive him, she'd let him walk away if that's what he wanted to do. But she was going to do anything she had to in order to get Millie home. Anything. Even if it meant bringing legal action against her only sister.

TWENTY-EIGHT

SOPHIA

The next day, Sophia was absolutely exhausted. For some reason, known only to herself, Millie had been up three times in the night and had been really difficult to settle. Even once she'd gone back to sleep, Sophia had lain awake going over her conversation with Megan.

Whatever the outcome between Mark and Megan, her sister wasn't coping at all. This was worrying. Stress like that might be all that was needed to trigger a relapse in her anorexia. And how would it be if they added a newborn into the situation?

The way she'd snapped at Sophia yesterday had taken her breath away. She'd always known that her sister didn't approve of the way she lived her life, but she'd never spoken to her like that before. Ordinarily, she was the queen of passive aggression. When she'd stayed at her house for that month before they lost their mother, Megan had almost driven her crazy with the way she washed up her cup the minute she'd finished her coffee or rearranged her shoes on the rack so that they were paired up and facing front. She never actually said that Sophia's natural untidiness was unacceptable to her, but she might as well have done.

But then, of course, her mother had told her about the anorexia and it had made her see things a little differently. Made her understand a little more Megan's need to control her world.

When Millie woke for the fourth time at 6 a.m. Sophia decided to give in and get up. 'Honeymoon period is well and truly over, isn't it?'

The second time she'd got up in the night, Richard had complained about being woken and stomped off to sleep on the sofa. He wasn't there now, though. Was it too much to hope that he'd appear shortly with coffee and cornetto? She hadn't spoken to him again about the move to Oman. Was there any way she could persuade him to stay? If he left, she wouldn't be able to afford to live in Italy and pay for childcare for Millie. What was the solution?

After another feed – how much did this child want? – Millie dozed off again, but Sophia couldn't go back to sleep with everything buzzing in her head. Richard was still out, but she'd awoken the cornetto monster and had a craving for the sweet pastry. Lockdown was over now, so maybe she could take Millie out in her pram?

Natalia had dropped off a pram for her shortly after Millie was born. Even the thought of using it gave her a fizz of excitement. This would be Millie's first trip out into the world. She dressed her warmly in a little pram jacket and tiny mittens, which would probably be off in seconds. But it wasn't until she opened the door to their apartment that she realised that getting the pram down the stairs would be no mean feat. She was hovering in the doorway, with Millie in the crook of her left arm and the handle of the pram in her right hand, when she heard – then saw – Alex coming down the stairs.

'Look, Millie, it's our knight in shining armour.'

He stopped at the bottom step and grinned at her. 'If it's not my two favourite damsels in distress. What can I do for you, fair ones?'

'I want to go for a walk and I need to get the pram downstairs. I should have asked Richard, but I don't know where he's gone and I'm desperate for pastries.'

She felt pathetic even asking, but Alex didn't miss a beat. 'Your wish is my command.'

She frowned. 'I think you've changed character there, Knight Alex. Isn't that the genie and the lamp?'

He stopped halfway down the next flight and turned to look at her. 'Who's the writer here? And, more importantly, who's the person who needs a favour?'

'Good point. Ignore me.'

She followed him down, gripping the banister with the hand that wasn't holding tightly to Millie. She wasn't about to risk slipping over with this precious cargo.

Once the pram was at the bottom of the staircase, and Millie was tucked safely inside. Alex leaned over the pram and pulled faces at her. She was transfixed.

Sophia was pretty transfixed, too. Though she'd tried to ignore it, she did love being with Alex. He made her feel better about life. 'Richard has got a job in Oman. He's leaving in a few days.'

Alex swivelled around to face her. 'Ah, I see. That explains things. I'm so sorry. Are you okay?'

Explains what things? 'What do you mean?'

Alex flushed. 'Sorry. Ignore me. I just presumed... I shouldn't have.'

'Alex, what are you talking about?'

He sighed and stood up. 'That thing I kept wanting to speak to you about? I'd seen Richard with another woman and I thought that you should know.'

That had come from nowhere. 'Are you sure?'

Alex screwed up his face as if it was him who'd been unfaithful. 'I'm sorry, yes. I walked past them a second time to make sure.'

Suddenly, it all made sense. The times he'd disappeared every day. The conversations where he'd kept the door to the room firmly closed. How had she not realised? 'I'm an idiot.'

'No, you're not. He's the idiot here.'

She looked up into Alex's eyes and recognised what she saw there. Her stomach fluttered. Maybe staying here was a good idea after all. 'It doesn't matter, anyway. I don't want to go with him to Oman.'

'So will you stay here?'

That was one of a million questions at the moment. 'I don't know yet.'

For a few moments, they looked at one another. Then Alex held the door open for her. 'Enjoy your pastries.'

'Why don't you come with us? After keeping me up half the night, this one is likely to sleep through our breakfast date. Unless you were off somewhere?'

'No, just out to get coffee myself.'

'Great, let's go.'

Having spent so much time together, it should've felt natural to walk and talk, but it didn't. Being outside in the real world was different.

'So, Millie kept you awake all night? At least you won't have that once she goes home to your sister.'

She'd lay awake every night of her life if she could keep Millie. 'I guess so.'

They walked a few more steps in silence. 'It'll be a pretty special moment when she meets Millie. You must be close, you and your sister? To be her surrogate, I mean.'

Had she made the decision too quickly? After her mother's request, and discovering that Megan had no idea about the post-cards she'd sent, she'd been actually looking out for ways she could help her sister. Seeing how much pain she was in over not being able to have a baby, it'd caught her by surprise how much she felt for her. Her mouth had made the offer before her mind had caught up. 'The thing is, I kind of made a promise to my mother, just before she died, that I'd help Megan. She struggles with her mental health. She had anorexia in her late teens.'

They turned onto the road with the only open coffee bar and joined the queue stretching almost to the corner. 'That must've been tough for her. Forgive the doctor question, but was it the anorexia that caused her to be unable to have a child?'

Alex's question hit her like a slap. How had that never occurred to her? 'Is that likely?'

'I don't know about likely, but medically it's very possible. I mean, I don't know how dangerous her weight loss was.'

Nor did Sophia. Her mother hadn't been in a position to be pressed for details and – on her request – she'd never brought it up with Megan.

Before now. Guilt prickled in her stomach. If that was the case, how much worse might that have made Megan feel? On the night she'd made her surrogacy offer, Megan had said, 'It's my fault.' At the time, she'd assumed it was just a reaction to the bad news. Now she had to wonder whether or not Megan was carrying this unfair guilt alongside her sorrow about not being able to conceive. A cool breeze rippled along the queue and she shivered. 'That must be hard for her.'

'I would imagine it is.' Alex nodded towards the sleeping Millie. 'I bet she can't wait to see her daughter for the first time.'

He was right. But did that make it the best decision for Millie? And wasn't she the most important one in all of this? Was Sophia in a position where she had to hurt her sister to protect her child?

· · ·

Richard was home by the time she got back and he didn't even attempt to deny the other woman.

'She's just a friend. One of the researchers at the university. What was I supposed to do? You were pregnant and then you had the baby. I was just... out in the cold.'

She couldn't believe he was making this her fault. Or maybe she could. Didn't they all let you down in the end?

'I'm not coming with you to Oman. This is it for me.'

If she was honest with herself, it'd been over for a while; maybe even before lockdown started. Even so, it hurt when he merely shrugged. 'Okay. That's up to you. I'm going in a few days anyway.'

The apartment, though she loved it, was too small for them to circle each other for that long. 'Can you leave before then? If Megan comes, I'd rather you weren't here.'

He laughed. It wasn't kind. 'You're chucking me out of my own apartment? How dramatic. Fine. I can stay with one of the others.'

She didn't ask whether he'd be moving in with his researcher 'friend'. It was mildly surprising to realise that she didn't actually care. It took less than fifteen minutes for Richard to pack up his things. The apartment had been rented furnished, and his clothes fit into one large suitcase, so he left that night. Should it have shocked her that he had so few belongings, that he travelled so light? Hadn't she lived the same way?

Even knowing that he'd been unfaithful to her was a mere flesh wound now that she knew for certain that they wanted different things. Men always leave, she could live with that, but the thought of losing Millie was akin to losing a limb. She'd been inside her, she was part of her, she couldn't let her go. Richard said she had a month before she had to give up the apartment. She'd have to sort something out by then. Or, if Megan came, it might be sooner.

TWENTY-NINE

MEGAN

Megan had been trawling the Internet to find out her legal position. She knew that the baby was legally Sophia's until they got the parental order, but surely no court in the land would believe her feckless sister would be a better parent than her and Mark.

She was still furious with him, but she needed his help with this. Needed his strength and support. One of the many things he was good at was getting things done. Years of following the, sometimes illogical, demands of his father at work had trained him to be an excellent trouble-shooter. There were no problems he couldn't fix when she asked him.

A trickle of fear ran down her spine. What if there *was* no her and Mark any longer? They'd had no further conversations about where they went from here, but it was impossible for her to imagine a life without him. He was the one who'd brought her out of herself all those years ago, who'd made her feel as if she was beautiful in his eyes, who'd picked her up from the bathroom floor when yet another pregnancy test was negative, circled her in love when her mother died and told her that she'd never – ever – be alone. Even picturing his face made her want to cry. He was Mark, her Mark. How could she live without him?

Even though he'd suggested that Millie stay with Sophia, she couldn't imagine that he would actually support that. But what happened if he didn't support her getting the parental order? Would that change the strength of her legal position? Having read the rules meticulously, she knew that there were only six months in which to get the order signed; after that it would require an adoption. Millie wasn't adopted. She was her biological child. Surely the courts would recognise this?

She pushed her chair away from the laptop and rubbed at her eyes. Did she really want to start this? Sophia was her sister. And it wasn't the way she wanted to begin her life as a mother. Maybe there was still time to persuade Sophia that this was not the right way to go. If she could manage to get a damn flight, she could speak to her in person, but everyone and his wife seemed to be booking flights to Italy. The first one available left in five days' time and there was only one seat on the plane. Going without Mark filled her with absolute dread. Surely he could help her find a flight for both of them?

She pushed open the door to Mark's 'office' without knocking and he turned to her immediately. For the last two days, he'd treated her with hesitant attention as if she were a wild animal who might bite. She slid her phone onto his desk. 'I can't get two tickets on any flight to Sophia's airport. Can you look?'

He picked up her phone and scrolled through. 'I can try, but I don't think I'm going to find anything you can't.'

She knew that. She was just looking for him to do something to help her. 'I want to book for both of us to go.'

He kept his eyes on the phone screen. 'We can, but you might have to book a flight in a week or so.'

He might as well have said a year. 'I don't want to wait a minute longer than I have to.'

It might seem melodramatic, but Megan had visions of Sophia moving away with the baby to somewhere that she'd never find them. Unlike Megan, she'd travelled all over the world; she must have friends everywhere. How easy would it be for her to just disappear? Megan's stomach was in her mouth at the thought. Mark nodded, his voice careful. 'Then you'll have to go on your own.'

On her own? Didn't he know how impossible it was for her to travel without him? She'd never been abroad without his reassuring hand in hers. When she was young, there hadn't been the money – or the inclination – to be far from home. Since they'd married, they did everything together. But this was urgent. She needed to get to Millie as soon as possible. And Mark clearly didn't care. 'Are you sure you don't want to come?'

If anything, he looked relieved. 'It's fine. You go. But won't Millie need a passport to be able to bring her back? How do we do that?'

She could've kicked herself for not using her acres of empty time to work that out. 'Can you find out?'

He was as eager to please as a small puppy. 'Of course. Are you sure you want to go on your own? Especially if you can't bring Millie back yet? Wouldn't it be better to wait?'

Did he even need to ask? 'I want to see her as soon as I can.'

Downstairs again, she'd punched her credit card details in to book her flight and was looking for the easiest way to get from the airport to Sophia's apartment when there was a knock on the door. When Megan opened it, a well-dressed woman in a mask was on the doorstep. 'Hello?'

She moved the bag she was holding under her arm and squeezed one hand with the other. 'Are you Megan?'

There was something vaguely familiar about this woman, but it was difficult to place her when she could only see her eyes. 'Yes. I am.'

She looked relieved to have found her. 'I'm Susan, Elsie's

sister. I'm sorry to disturb you, love, but Peter wanted me to let you know. Elsie passed away yesterday. He was going to text you, but I was coming to the house to pick out her outfit for the funeral and I said I'd let you know. These things should be done in person, I think.'

Megan clutched the door frame for support, tears sprung to her eyes. Elsie was gone? But that couldn't be possible. She was so full of life. She did tai chi and Pilates. Painted and baked. How could she be gone? 'Oh no. I can't believe it.'

Matching tears filled Susan's eyes. 'Me neither, love. We wanted to thank you, the family, for being such a lovely neighbour to Elsie. She used to talk about you a lot. How kind you were. How thoughtful.'

They were being far too kind. Megan had never really done a lot for her: she hadn't needed it. All she'd done was pop in for a cup of tea once a week and very occasionally taken her shopping. Elsie had given her so much more. The week her mother died, she'd checked on her every single day. Made them a casserole for dinner one day, a chicken pie the next. Every time she'd seen Megan she would pull her in for a perfumed hug and tell her what a good daughter she'd been to her mum. 'She was a lovely neighbour to me. She always gave good advice.'

Susan pressed at her mouth beneath the mask. 'She did, didn't she? I don't know how I'm going to cope without her. She's my big sister. She's always been there. I've never known what it was to live without her.'

Pre-Covid, Megan would have held out her arms to hug this woman as she sniffed into her handkerchief, now she had to keep her distance. It was so very hard; it was inhuman not to reach out. 'I'll bet she was a lovely sister. Lots of fun.'

A little light crept into Susan's eyes. 'She really was. Growing up she used to get in all sorts of trouble with our mum. But she always looked out for me. Anything I needed, she was there. Anything.'

How lovely it must be to have that kind of relationship. That support. If only Sophia had been that kind of sister. Unfortunately, Megan knew exactly what it was like to live without her. She'd been absent for more of her life than she'd been part of. 'I can imagine it. She was always wonderful to me. I just can't believe that I'm not going to see her again.'

Elsie was always there: on her knees pruning the flowers in the front garden, over the back fence with a mug of tea. Since losing her mother, Elsie had been the most comforting presence in her life. A warm blanket on a cold day. She was going to miss her so much.

After a long blow of her nose, Susan tucked her handkerchief into her sleeve. 'Have you got a sister?'

She clearly wanted to talk, and even though she needed to make arrangements for Italy, Megan didn't have the heart to cut her off in the circumstances. 'I have. We're not as close as you and Elsie, though.'

The brightness of the afternoon sun shone through the edges of Susan's grey curls as she shook her head. 'That's a real shame. Sisters are important. Even when it's difficult, it's worth working at it. It's the longest relationship you'll have in your life, you know. No one will share the memories of your childhood like a sister will.'

The longest relationship of your life. Megan had never thought of it like that. There were plenty of times at home that they'd had fun before Sophia left. Private jokes, games they'd played, all the things that had left huge holes in Megan's life when Sophia left. And there had been other times more recently when Sophia had visited for hospital appointments, laughing about the good times. Because Sophia was the only other person alive that would remember those things from when they were young. 'You must have plenty of lovely memories of Elsie.'

Even beneath her mask, she could make out Susan's smile.

'Oh, I do. But plenty of memories of arguments, too. And not just when we were children and she didn't want her little sister hanging around with her friends. No, there's been plenty of humdingers over the years. Families are like that, aren't they? There was a spate of about eight Christmases where we had a row every year. It's a pressure cooker, isn't it? Getting everyone together like that. But that's the point of families. You can fall out and then, when you need each other, you're there in a trice.'

Her words squeezed Megan's heart. She *had* needed Sophia. Much as she'd tried to navigate the narrowing maze of options open to her in order to have a child, it had been Sophia who had offered. Sophia who had tried to make it work. She'd been there for her when no one else had. Her throat was tight when she spoke. 'My sister and I, we're having a bit of a falling out at the moment.'

Susan's nod was kind but firm. 'Then you need to sort it out, love. Whatever it is. Nothing is worth losing your sister over.'

Then her face crumpled into tears. Here was a woman who had lost her sister. Who would never get her back. Maybe she was right. Megan had a chance to make this right with Sophia. She didn't want a legal battle. They *were* sisters. There had to be a way to work this out. She would call Sophia and tell her that she was coming. They needed to meet and talk about this properly. Face to face. 'I'm really sorry you've lost your sister. Elsie was so special and I'll miss her very much. Will you ask Peter to let me know when the funeral is?'

Susan wiped at her eyes, the tissue almost disintegrating in her fingers. Her grief was so familiar. Megan might have lost her mother almost two years ago, but that pain was still close. 'I will ask him to let you know. But there's a cap on numbers. I don't think you'll be able to come, I'm so sorry, love.'

Of course. Another thing this damn virus had taken away from them. 'I understand. But I'd like to know. So that I can do something here for her.'

'Oh, you're starting me off again.' Susan gave up on the scrap in her hand and pulled another tissue from her pocket. 'Elsie was right about you. You're a lovely girl. I do hope you work it out with your sister.'

So did she. Because not working it out would be devastating on every level.

THIRTY

SOPHIA

For the first few minutes after waking the next day, Sophia had a strange feeling that she couldn't identify. Once she'd fed Millie, and squeezed in a quick shower while she slept, she realised what it was: relief.

With Richard gone, she didn't have to keep the baby quiet or stress about tidying things away. As the morning progressed, she found herself relaxing more and more into the rhythms of Millie's day. With no one to please but themselves, she felt a peace that had been missing. At some point, she'd need to think about work, where to live, childcare. But that was for the future. For now, she had savings in the bank and they could just... be.

'What shall we do today, Millie? Shall we walk to the park? Or go shopping? Let's get out of here.'

The pram now resided in the lobby, so it was easy to take outside. Though most people were still wearing face masks, they were walking differently: with more purpose to their stride. And they waved and nodded as they passed her. Things were beginning to get back to normal.

She passed other mothers, watching them closely for the first time. In the past, she'd dismissed them as having boring, predictable lives. Now she realised that each one of them might have a very different story. People that she passed – a workman sitting on a bench eating a sandwich, an elderly woman with her hand threaded through the elbow of her grandson, a mum chasing a toddler who'd slipped her grasp – they all smiled and nodded as she passed them with Millie in the pram. To them, she was a new mother out for a stroll with her baby. Was it weird how much she enjoyed that feeling?

Not many of the shops were open yet and Millie was a long way away from being ready for the children's playground that they passed. Could she still be here when she was big enough for the swings or the slide? Was that genuinely a possibility? Was she *really* thinking about keeping her sister's baby?

Around the next corner, the village church was set back from the road with a square green out front. At the back of the green, an empty bench beside a carob tree tempted her to rest a while. When they first moved here, she'd commented on this very tree and Richard had explained that it was also known as a 'survival tree' because of its ability to resist drought. She'd liked that almost as much as his other nugget of folklore that hidden treasures could be found beneath its roots.

The bench had seen better days and it faced the church rather than looking back to the street. Though she hadn't attended a service in years, Sophia liked church buildings: their coolness and their peace. When she was young, her mother had taken her and Megan to Sunday school at their local Methodist church at their father's behest. 'To make sure you know right from wrong.'

What would her mother say to her now about this decision? What was the right thing to do? Both Richard and Alex had been quick to remind her that Millie belonged to Megan and Mark. The embryo she'd come from was made from them, after all. But that was just biology. What about all the other parents –

adoptive parents – who are great mums and dads? And she had given birth to Millie. Surely that counted for something?

And her mother had also told her to look after her sister. The last few calls she'd had with Megan, she sounded as if she was unravelling. What if the stress of bringing up a child – alongside dealing with her marriage problems – became her undoing? Would keeping Millie safe in Italy make the situation better? Or worse?

'Sophia!'

She turned back in her seat towards Alex's voice. 'Hello.'

His long legs made it across the green in only a few steps. 'Are you thinking of going in?'

He nodded towards the church, but she shook her head. 'I don't think it's open yet. But anyway, I'm just resting my feet and having a bit of a think. Care to join me?'

He set himself down on the other end of the bench and stretched out his legs. 'It's a good place to sit and think. This is a lovely church. One of the reasons I came to this town was because the doctor I was researching is buried in the yard at the back. I do like a stroll around a nice graveyard.'

She laughed. 'That's an odd place for an ex-doctor to spend time.'

He twisted himself around so that he was looking at her. 'Actually, on that subject: I've got news.'

'Really? Is it about your book?' She'd forgotten to ask him about the novel he'd told her about when they first spoke. Though, in her defence, she'd had rather a lot going on.

He scratched behind his ear and screwed up his nose. 'Ah, no. I think that might've been a bit of a midlife crisis. Turns out it's not so easy to write a hundred thousand words, however great you think your idea is.'

She laughed at the comical expression on his face. 'I can imagine. So what's the news?'

'Well, it's kind of inspired by you, actually. And by what's happened here and in the rest of the world. I'm going to go back to medicine.'

She was thrilled for him. He'd been so brilliant during the birth. It was a waste of his talent to keep away. 'That's fantastic, Alex. You'll be an incredible doctor.'

He blushed. 'Well, that's very kind. I think all this business with Covid has made me realise how much I miss it.'

'It really is brilliant news. I'm sure it will be better this time.'

He frowned and dropped his gaze to his hands, picking at the nail of his thumb. 'There was something I didn't tell you before. Maybe I should have. I had a bad experience. A mother. During childbirth. She lost too much blood. Just minutes before, I'd been talking to her. I was just there to observe. Her and her husband were so full of joy; they'd just had a little boy. Then, from nowhere, she started to haemorrhage. They couldn't save her. The consultant on call was just... broken by it. And her husband...'

He didn't need to go on. She reached out and held his arm. 'That's awful, Alex. I'm so sorry.'

He swallowed. Then took a deep breath. 'That's why I was reticent about being there at Millie's birth. But obviously circumstances dictated and, actually, it helped me a lot. Made me realise that you have to show up sometimes, even when you're terrified.'

His eyes were so vulnerable, she wanted to hug him. 'I had no idea. I'm so sorry I put you through that.'

She still had her hand on his arm, and he put his hand over the top of it. 'No, don't apologise. You've helped me so much. More than you can know.'

He slipped her hand from his arm but kept hold of it. Familiar butterflies started in her stomach. She waited for him to say what she thought – hoped? – he was about to. A cool breeze whispered through the leaves behind them, carrying the laughter of a group of teens who were balancing on a low wall in front of the church. Everywhere, an air of possibility and hope of better days coming.

'I have a friend in Australia. She's on a really great training programme. She told me about it a couple of months ago, but I wasn't ready to listen. But I think I might go for it.'

It took a moment for her to realise what Alex had said. Australia? Not here, in Italy? Maybe his Italian wasn't good enough to study here. But... Australia? 'Wow. That's a pretty long way to go, isn't it?'

Her question didn't dent his enthusiasm. 'I know. But she was so enthusiastic about the hospital she's in. She knows how punishing it was in the UK and she said it's much better where she is.'

The fingers of the cool breeze crept into the back of her shirt and she shivered. Who was this woman that he'd never mentioned before and why was she taking him so far away? 'I see. Sounds great.'

Even she could hear the change in her tone. He frowned. 'You don't think it's a good idea?'

They'd only known each other a few weeks. It wasn't her place to have an opinion on what he did. Had she misread the signs? Been foolish to see this as anything more than friendship? Clearly, she had. 'If it's right for you, you should do it. Ignore me. I'm just thinking about my own situation. I'll need to find somewhere for me and Millie when the lease runs out on the apartment.'

'You and Millie? But she'll be going home soon, won't she?' His voice was far gentler than Richard's had been, but the message was the same.

'I don't know. There's no definite date yet, so I'm just playing it by ear.'

He looked her in the eye. 'I'm sure your sister will be

desperate to see her as soon as possible. Then you're free again. You can go wherever you want to.'

Free? That's what Richard had said. What did that even mean any longer? Free to do what? With whom? Where? Richard had gone, Alex was going, she was pretty sure she'd ruined her relationship with her sister for good. And why would she want to be free? Millie was her baby. She'd given birth to her, fed her, bonded with her. At forty-one, there were no guarantees that she'd be able to fall pregnant naturally again. Millie might be her only chance to have a baby. How could she give her up?

Before she could even begin to articulate this to Alex, her phone buzzed in her pocket. It was Megan. 'It's my sister. I need to take this.'

'Of course.' He stood up to go and then looked at her. 'I'm here whenever you need me, Sophia.'

As she watched him walk away, she picked up the phone. 'Hi, Megan.'

'Sophia, we need to talk about this. Properly. Face to face. I've booked a flight.'

At least it was on her turf. It wasn't as if Megan could snatch the baby and take her across an international border. 'You're right. We do. When are you coming?'

THIRTY-ONE

MEGAN

Megan had never flown alone.

An hour before she needed to be, Megan had been at the airport staring up at the departures board, willing her check-in desk to open. Still furious, she'd refused Mark's offer to bring her here, or even to help her to the Uber with her luggage. When she'd pulled her suitcase downstairs that morning, banging each step as she went, Mark was in the hallway looking up.

'That's a big case. How long are you planning on going for?'

'As long as it takes, Mark. One of us has to care about her.' Her stress about travelling alone was making her nasty; he'd looked as if she'd bitten him.

Now, with her bags checked in, all she had to do was go through the gate to departures. The long queue was spaced out and everyone was wearing masks, none of which helped her mounting anxiety.

It was a ridiculous thing to be nervous about. She and Mark had flown on holiday so many times since they'd been married. Such fond memories of their honeymoon, the beautiful beaches of the Maldives, the long afternoons laying on a sun lounger with a cocktail, the laughter in their private hot tub. Had all of that been an act? Had he pretended to be in love with her?

She shook her head. Now wasn't the time. She shuffled forward with everyone else in the queue, moving to the next sticker on the floor, each step a few inches closer to her daughter.

The plane was full and most passengers were speaking Italian. Were there any English passengers on there at all? Was she doing the wrong thing by flying to another country? Lockdown was lifted, but the virus was still out there. What if she inadvertently gave it to Sophia? To the baby? She'd tested before she left; she'd test again before she met her.

Across the aisle, a young mother was trying to entertain a toddler. The little boy had glossy dark curls and the longest eyelashes Megan had ever seen. He was arguing with his mother about something which was making her laugh and him increasingly irate.

The mother caught Megan watching them and she spoke to her in Italian.

'I'm sorry. I don't speak Italian.'

Effortlessly, she switched to English. 'He wants the last lollipop. I am telling him it's mine. He has eaten all the others.'

Megan smiled. 'I see.'

'Of course, I will give it to him. That's what we do, right?'

She tickled the boy until his frown turned into the most infectious giggle. The connection between the two of them was so clear, so lovely, so unbelievably painful.

Before switching her phone to airplane mode, she sent Mark a text: *All okay here. About to take off. Don't forget to find out about her passport.*

He replied almost immediately. *Will do. Good luck. Give her a kiss from me.*

If only he were here with her. He'd been her strength for so long. When her mother had died, she'd been unable to go into that bedroom for days afterwards, unable to bear the emptiness of that bed. Now her whole house was going to be empty. Loneliness clutched at her stomach like an iron fist.

Trying to distract herself, she scrolled through the photographs of Millie that Sophia had sent in the last two and a half weeks. Already she was changing, her eyes opening wider, her fingers less curled, her skin less red and crumpled. How important were these early days? She wouldn't remember them as she grew older, but maybe her body would. When adopted children were reunited with their biological mother as adults, did they not talk about 'knowing' them immediately? Recognising on some deep metabolic level that this person had given them life? Maybe it wasn't so crazy that the law recognised Sophia as Millie's mother. Maybe she was the crazy one for thinking that using her and Mark's embryo gave them any right at all to claim their daughter.

'Would you like any snacks or drinks?'

The flight attendant made her jump. 'No, I'm fine. Thank you.'

That was another thing. Mark had taken to watching her covertly at mealtimes. He hadn't known her when she was ill the first time, but she'd been honest with him about the anorexia, explained how important it was for her to go to the gym every day, eat at regular times. She couldn't blame him for being worried, but he could do with being more subtle about it.

Across the aisle, the little boy had won his lollipop and was leaning against his mother with his little fist around the stick. She was stroking his curls and whispering soothing words in his ear as the plane climbed into the sky. He trusted her, his other hand holding onto hers. He knew that, with his mother there, he was safe.

What if Millie never felt that about her? What if that bond never happened? It wasn't only the birth. Sophia had been breastfeeding her, forming a connection. Millie would be familiar with her touch, her smell, her voice. Megan would be a stranger to her. She had an awful image of tearing her from Sophia's arms and Millie screaming to be returned.

Was Mark right? Was the best thing for Millie to allow Sophia to claim her? Was she not the best person for it? Not her real mother? When she was small, at Sunday school, they'd been told a story about two mothers who'd claimed the same child. The King – was it Solomon? – had known the real mother as she was the one to sacrifice her own happiness to keep the child alive.

She looked over at the mother and her boy. She'd always been going to give him the lollipop because *That's what we do, right?*

That's what mothers do. They sacrifice what they want for the good of their child. She looked again at the photos of Millie on her phone.

She'd wanted a family for so long. But she wasn't bringing Millie back to be part of a family. Her mother was gone. Mark was going. She'd even lost Elsie next door. Was she really strong enough – *good* enough – to bring up a baby on her own?

And what if everyone was right to worry about the anorexia? What if she did get sick again? Who would look after Millie then?

When they'd had that terrible row, she'd called Sophia selfish. But what if she was the selfish one in taking Millie away from the person who would make a better mother than she would? No one could answer that question for her. Maybe, when she saw them together, she would know for sure.

THIRTY-TWO

SOPHIA

On the day Megan was due to arrive, Sophia couldn't settle to anything. She'd already dressed Millie, then redressed her in a nicer outfit, cleaned the kitchen and plumped all the sofa cushions within an inch of their lives. What was she trying to do? Prove to Megan that she was a wonderful homemaker? But she couldn't sit still doing nothing.

Alex had been round earlier with his bedding and toiletries. 'I feel like I'm going on a sleepover. Are we going to play on a PlayStation 'til midnight?'

It was strange to have him effectively move in with her, even if it was only for forty-eight hours. She'd moved in with people herself so many times, although she wasn't normally heading for the sofa.

'It's really good of you to do this. Give up your apartment for my sister.'

Megan had planned to isolate for two days in a hotel, but Alex had offered to let her stay at his place for the required time. It was a relief; she'd sounded wobbly on the phone at the prospect of even navigating a foreign airport alone. How strange it must be to need someone else to do the most straightforward things for you. It must be paralysing.

Alex shrugged. 'It's only two days.'

Two days. Only forty-eight hours and Megan would be here in this room, holding Millie. Sophia shook away the image. *One day at a time.*

Neither of them had had a sleeping bag, so he was tucking sheets into the cushions of the sofa with clinical precision. 'Are you going to be okay on there?' It seemed cruel to make him sleep on the sofa, but it wasn't as if she could invite him into her bed. Much as she'd like to, it wasn't as if there was any future for them. Plus, it would have been too weird to have him in her bed with Millie asleep in the crib.

'I can sleep anywhere. Once on a nightshift, I fell asleep propped up in the corner of the men's bathroom.'

Contrary to how she was feeling, his grin was infectious. 'Are you looking forward to it? Starting your training again, being back in a hospital?'

He paused with a pillow in his hands, giving her question more consideration than she'd expected. 'Yes. I am. But I'm mildly terrified, too.'

That, she understood. 'I felt a bit like that about having Millie.'

'And look how well that turned out.'

She looked down at the gorgeous bundle in her arms who had no idea that all this fuss was about her. 'She is pretty great, isn't she?'

'She is. But I meant you. This thing you've done for your sister. Bringing a life into the world. It's massive, Sophia. You're incredible.'

Her stomach lurched: she didn't feel incredible. Guilty, confused, terrified? Yes. Incredible? No. Facing Megan was going to be so difficult. It was as if the Sword of Damocles was hanging over her head. No matter what happened, someone was going to be hurt. 'I don't know how I'm going to do this with Megan today. And in the next few days.'

He frowned. 'Well, she'll be in my place for the next couple of days, but you've got the garden. She could see her from a distance.'

That wasn't what she'd meant, but the practical side was also an issue. 'You're sure it'll be safe for her to see her outside?'

He held out his hands. 'That's a decision the two of you have to make. But you've been taking her out in the pram. I don't see that it's much different from that if she keeps at a distance. And I can't imagine that your sister will be able to cope with being so close and not even seeing her.'

He was right. And Megan could retest as soon as she got to his apartment, too. 'But what about after that? When she can come into the apartment. Do you think she's expecting me to move out of the bedroom? Just hand her over? Do nothing for her any longer?'

Her heart beat faster with each thought. Couldn't he see how impossible this was? He'd seen her with Millie, he must know how much she adored her. How could she go from effectively being her mother one moment to a bystander the next? She couldn't do this. She couldn't.

Alex's voice was gentle. 'Don't think about it too much. Take it one step at a time. Take your lead from your sister and from Millie. Let it happen naturally.'

Naturally? Nothing about this felt natural. But how could she tell him that? How could she tell him that she was thinking about keeping her sister's child? 'Have you got any brothers or sisters?'

He flopped down onto the quilt he'd just shaken out on the couch. 'Two brothers, one sister.'

'Wow. That's a big family. Having gone through childbirth once, hats off to your mother for doing it four times.'

He laughed. 'Actually, it was twice. Me. Then twin boys. And my sister was adopted.'

Adopted? She stared at him. How had he never mentioned this before? 'Your mother clearly wanted a girl.'

'I know it seems like that, but actually it was more circumstance. Poppy was a foundling left outside a fire station in a large shopping bag. She was premature and they brought her into the special care baby unit where my mother was a consultant. She was in for a while and my mother says she fell in love with her, but we all tell Poppy it was just because she wanted someone on her team in the family.'

He grinned at her, but all she could think about was that tiny little baby who'd been abandoned by a mother who couldn't cope. His mother had stepped up and taken care of her. And *that* was incredible. 'Are you close?'

'I'm probably closest to Poppy, actually. The twins are their own thing, so we kind of banded together. Plus. she's the only other person in the family who doesn't work in a hospital, so she was really great when I decided to come away from all of that.'

How much better had Poppy's life been because she was adopted into Alex's family? She held the sleeping bundle in her arms a little closer. 'What does she do?'

'She's a primary school teacher. A really good one.'

The pride in his eyes as he talked about his sister made her heart warm to him even more. 'It's wonderful that you're so close. Megan and I used to be like that when we were younger.'

He raised an eyebrow. 'What happened?'

She didn't want to get into all of that with him right now. 'Life, I suppose. I moved away when she was only twelve. As adults, we're pretty different from each other.'

He looked interested. 'Different how?'

She could've given him a million examples. 'She's quite buttoned-up. Likes to be in control. Whereas I...'

'Don't like to be controlled?'

She laughed. 'Something like that.'

'But you're probably more alike than you realise.'

'We're really not. She'd be horrified if she heard you say that. I am most definitely not the older sister she wanted.' Or, she now realised, the sister she needed.

'And yet you're the one who's giving her a baby.'

His words sliced through her. She'd carried a baby for Megan, given birth to a baby for Megan. But the child in the crook of her left arm wasn't just a baby: she was Millie. Her Millie. How could she just give her away?

She picked up the pillow on his bed and gave it a shake. 'Could you see yourself doing what your parents did? Adopting a child?'

He looked at her with those eyes that reached deep inside her. 'With the right person, I could.'

If she hadn't been stressed enough before, now her heart was hammering in her chest. How could he say that to her when he was leaving to live on the other side of the world? 'And what might she be like?'

Alex shifted his position on the sofa so that he was facing her straight on and held out his hands as if he were about to deliver a speech. 'Okay. I've been wrestling with myself because I know this sounds crazy and you've got so much going on and you've just split up with Richard and we hardly know each other, but if I don't say this, I'll be kicking myself forever.'

He seemed to be looking for permission to continue; she could barely breathe. 'Go on.'

'I want you to come with me. To Australia. Once you've got everything sorted with Megan and Millie, obviously.'

She swallowed over the lump that was threatening to block her throat. Go to Australia with him? Did he mean it? And could this be exactly what she needed – a place to take Millie far away? 'Come with you? But what if I—'

A fuzzy crackle from the intercom stopped her mid-sentence. She pressed the button. 'Hello.'

The voice sounded out of place coming through the temperamental speaker. 'It's me. Megan. I'm outside.'

Sophia pushed down on the rising panic. 'Hi. I'll buzz you in. Alex's apartment is 3b. He's left the key under the doormat for you. Call me when you get inside.'

'Okay. Speak to you in a minute.'

A clatter at the other end and then silence. She turned to face Alex. 'I can't think about Australia right now. I've got to—'

He held up a hand to stop her. 'Of course. I'm sorry. It was terrible timing. We can talk about this another time.'

She nodded, took a breath. 'So, this is really happening. She's here.'

His face was that of a calm professional. He stood and slipped his arm around her shoulders. 'This is a good thing, Sophia. It's what you both planned.'

But a plan could be changed, couldn't it? If it wasn't a good plan any longer? Hadn't that been the way she'd lived her life; moving on when things didn't work out? 'What if I'm doing the wrong thing?'

He looked confused. 'Do you mean because of Covid? Putting Millie at risk?'

Again, it wasn't what she meant, but it would do for now. 'Yes. What if it's too soon?'

His arm still around her back, he rubbed her shoulder as if to soften the blow of his words. 'I get it, Soph. But I'm not sure if that's your decision to make. Megan is her mother.'

She almost groaned. Since Millie's birth, she'd been the one to decide whether she needed to be fed or changed or rocked in her arms. Whatever Megan had wanted from her end, she had been the one putting it into practice. And now, Megan would be expecting to take it from here. To make the decisions. To take Millie. She couldn't bear it. She couldn't.

Megan must have raced up those stairs and through the door because Sophia's phone was ringing already and, when she answered, Megan was out of breath. 'I'm here. I've done a test. It's negative. Can I see her? Outside maybe?'

It would be cruel to make her wait two days in that apartment without something. This was okay. Sophia would be the one holding Millie. Nothing was going to change for the next two days. 'Of course. There's a garden behind the building. Let me check that there's no one there and then I'll call you again. The door to get outside is opposite the one you came in.'

Was she still panting or crying at the other end? 'Okay. I'll wait here for your call. Please. Be as quick as you can.'

THIRTY-THREE

MEGAN

Though the courtyard was small, there was a mile between the two of them. Behind Sophia, warm Italian air rustled the newly minted leaves of tangled trees. They whispered something Megan strained to hear over the blood thumping in her ears.

Every inch of her itched to reach out towards the precious bundle in Sophia's arms. As children, it was always Megan who'd tended the plastic babies; Sophia was too old to be bothered with dolls. Yet, here she was the one with her arms around the soft blanket. 'Is she sleeping?'

'She's just this minute gone off. But I can wake her?' Sophia moved her arms to tilt her precious cargo in Megan's direction.

Megan held up her hand, 'No you don't need to... oh.'

Half of the blanket slipped from Sophia's arms and there she was. Not a doll. Not a toy they could share. A baby. A tiny perfect baby. Her daughter. Every inch of Megan's body pulled instinctively towards her, desperate to touch her, kiss her, know that she was real. *Can you feel my love? How much I want to hold you? To breathe you in. To feel the weight of you in my arms.*

Was anyone ever prepared for this moment? Meeting your

child for the very first time? Whether it was the blur of a frenetic delivery suite, coming round from a C-section anaesthetic, on the sofa of a kind foster family. That moment. Oh, that moment. How cruel that she was denied even this.

The evening was cool, but tears warmed her face. 'She's even more beautiful than she looks on the screen.'

Sophia looked down at the bundle in her arms, her love for Millie obvious. 'She is. Good genes, I guess.'

It was so difficult not to let jealousy taint this moment. 'She actually looks more like you than me.'

Over the fence, a door slammed and two young voices squabbled in Italian. The hollow leather thud of a football being kicked between two sets of feet. Laughter. More arguments. Then the rhythmic exchange from foot to foot.

Megan couldn't take her eyes from Millie. Hungrily, they searched every inch of her, the long legs, the soft little body and the tiny hands which clasped Sophia's finger. It was a physical wrench to pull her eyes away and look at Sophia. 'How are you? Are you keeping well?'

It was so artificial, this small talk. Had it only been two and a half months since they'd sat over a coffee in that cafe, looking at the pictures of Millie curled up inside Sophia? So often it was Sophia who drove the conversation, but she looked grateful to have something to answer. 'I'm fine. Thanks. How about you? What's happening with Mark? Why didn't he come?'

Her heart contracted at the mention of his name. Mark should be here. He should be seeing this. It would change everything. 'It was difficult to get a flight. I couldn't wait.'

Sophia persisted. 'So, he's coming tomorrow? The next day?'

Megan tore her gaze from Millie and shook her head. 'No. He's pretty busy. How's Richard?'

Sophia looked down at Millie, shifted her a little in her arms. 'Richard's gone.'

Gone? Did that mean she was on her own, too? Ironic that she'd questioned Megan's ability to look after a baby without Mark. 'I'm so sorry.'

'Don't be.' Sophia looked up as if she was challenging her not to sympathise. 'He was having an affair. And it was over between us anyway. This lockdown was the final knell. I don't need him here.'

Megan wondered if her bravado had anything to do with Alex. Had she already segued smoothly from one man to the next? How did she do that? 'Well, I'm sorry anyway. It can't have been easy looking after Millie on your own. Thank you.'

Her thanks seemed to be even more unwanted than her sympathy. 'It wasn't difficult. I've loved it being just the two of us.'

Megan's hand flew to her chest and pressed down hard. The 'us' stung. But she didn't want to argue with Sophia now. She didn't want to ruin this moment any further than it was already. Next door, the football banged against the fence so hard that it shuddered and it heralded a heated argument between the boys on the other side. 'How long will she sleep for, do you think?'

Sophia looked down at Millie, readjusted the blanket near her face, smiled at her. 'It's difficult to say. Sometimes two hours, sometimes ten minutes. You like to keep me on my toes, don't you, Millie?'

Megan had prepared herself for it to be difficult not to hold her baby, but this was agony. Her friends had had enough babies for her to know the feeling of their warm weight in her arms, the softness of their skin, the gentle sigh of their breath. It took every ounce of self-control she had not to sweep up to the end of the garden and take her baby in her arms. 'It must be strange. I guess you haven't been around many babies in the past?'

Sophia raised her head and an eyebrow. 'I was around you,

don't forget. I remember coming into the hospital with Dad when you were first born.'

Did she actually remember that? 'Really? You were only seven.'

'I know, but I do. I was so excited to meet you and Dad made me sit back on a chair with a pillow under each arm and he laid you on my lap. You were really heavy and your nappy was warm on my leg.'

An unexpected laugh came out like a cough. There was something about the detail which made it all the more poignant. Had they ever shared this memory before? 'Did I live up to your expectations?'

Sophia smiled. 'I think so. Mum said I used to tell everyone you were my baby.'

This, Megan remembered. 'Didn't you used to put me in your doll's pram when Mum wasn't looking?'

Sophia laughed. 'Apparently, I did. Then I used to cram all the teddy bears in there, too. There's a picture somewhere. Who'd have thought I'd be so maternal?'

The question hung between them on the air. Over the fence, the back door opened with a crash as one brother shouted at the other and then was slammed shut. Megan's heart squeezed in her chest and her voice broke as she spoke. 'I wish I could've been there when Millie was born.'

Sophia nodded. 'I know.'

In her arms, Millie coughed and then stretched out her arms. They emerged from the blanket, so tiny and fragile, her little fists battling with the air. Megan brushed away the tears in her eyes and made her voice as bright as she could. 'Hi, Millie. Are you waking up? Mummy's here, baby girl. I've come to see you.'

In response, Millie started to mewl like a kitten. Then a tiny foot encased in a yellow ribbed sock made its escape from the bottom of the blanket. Had her voice made her cry? Fear pricked in her belly. If only she could hold her, soothe her, rock her in her arms. Her hands itched to make this right.

Like an expert, Sophia moved Millie to her shoulder, cupping her with one hand as she rearranged the blanket. When she rocked gently, Megan almost echoed her, she was so transfixed by the movement.

The rocking and the shushing didn't seem to make any difference. Sophia sighed. 'I think she needs a feed, or a change. I'll have to take her inside.'

'Of course, yes.' Megan dusted her legs down with her hands as she stood; disappointment coursed through her that they were leaving. 'Please thank Alex for me. For letting me stay in his apartment.'

Millie's cries were getting more insistent. Sophia dipped up and down as well as from side to side. 'Will do. He said to tell you to help yourself to anything you want. There's a good bottle of Chianti on the kitchen worktop.'

It felt so artificial. This wasn't a social call. 'That's kind, but I don't think drinking alone is a good idea for me at the moment.'

She hadn't meant that as a ploy for sympathy, but Sophia tilted her head to the side in concern. How could she think about anything else when Millie was so upset? 'Look, why don't we meet down here again later? Once Millie's in bed? You can bring a glass of the Chianti and I'll bring a beer and we can talk.'

Listening to Millie's cry was actually tearing at Megan in tiny painful strips. Why didn't Sophia just go, change her, feed her, make her happy again? *Just go.* 'I'd like that. Thank you.'

'Okay. Do you want to go up first? I'll wait for you to get back to Alex's apartment before we make a move. I'll call when Millie's gone down tonight.'

Of course, Sophia wouldn't want to walk past her. She was an idiot. Megan bolted for the back door. 'Sorry, yes. I'll see you later.'

Once the door to Alex's apartment was closed, Megan pressed her back against it and gave in to the tears. Huge lumpy sobs that scraped her throat and shook her body. Not since her mother died had she felt this deep well of grief. She should be happy. She was two days away from holding her own baby and yet... it felt as if the dream of a family was still out of reach. To be so close – physically, figuratively – and still not be able to even stroke her daughter's cheek. It was so terribly hard.

In the mirror in Alex's bathroom, she searched her own blotchy red face. On the plane here, she'd doubted whether she could do this. But now, having seen Millie in the flesh, she would fight anyone to keep her. The first step was getting Mark on board.

Before FaceTiming Mark, she dug out her make-up bag and fixed her complexion, reapplied her mascara. Her heart was raw, but she was calm. He picked up on the first ring. 'Hi. Are you okay? Did you get there without any problems?'

For all her composure, just the sight of his face made tears gather in her eyes. 'Oh, Mark. She's so beautiful. It was so hard not to hold her, but she is perfect.'

His smile seemed genuine. 'I'm so happy you're happy. Really, I am. Once you left, and I was here on my own, I had time to think. And I can do it. I can be a husband and a father. Just forget what I said.'

Forget it? Did he mean that? Was it possible that they could raise Millie together as she'd planned? The temptation to try was overwhelming, but she needed to be sure. 'How can you just put all those feelings back in a box? If it was strong enough to tell me about it in the first place? Powerful enough to need therapy?'

He shrugged. 'We just need to work it out. How we can do it. We've managed this long and it's been okay, hasn't it?'

That same question had been haunting her for days. Ever

since his revelation. Maybe even before that. Had their marriage been okay? Had it been good?

Though it hadn't felt it at the time, they'd been pretty young when they got married. Twenty-three. Her own parents had been married younger than that; so had Mark's. Everyone had been keen to see them committed. Even Mark's father, who wasn't given to public displays of praise, had been telling everyone at the wedding how he was pleased that Mark had met 'such a nice girl'. Now she had to wonder if he was more pleased about the 'girl' than the 'nice'.

She'd been happy to be married, though. Their first home was a two-bedroom house on a new estate and she'd loved it so much. Choosing the colours for the walls, the blinds for the windows; she'd been like a child with her first doll's house. And Mark had been so gentle, so kind. Was it a passionate relationship? No, she couldn't say it had ever been that. But it was warm and loving and safe. With him, she felt as if all problems were kept at a distance. He wasn't the kind of husband who went drinking with friends after work or played golf all day on a Saturday or who pleaded for a 'weekend pass' for a boys' trip like some of her friends' husbands. He'd always been there. He was never going to leave her.

His familiar face was waiting for an answer, but all she had were questions. 'How would it even work? Will you still be sleeping in the same bed as me? Or would we be living parallel lives?'

To begin with, she'd been a little bit surprised, even relieved, that he hadn't wanted to sleep with her as often as she'd expected. When her friends would complain that their husbands 'take every hug as an opportunity', she'd laughed along with them and been grateful for Mark's unselfish affection. But it was difficult not to feel that it was her that wasn't attractive enough. Maybe he preferred a different kind of woman, a different kind of body. How ironic that felt now.

'I think it's best if we stick to what we're doing now. Separate rooms. Unless you think that will be strange for Millie as she grows up? Maybe we can just say that I snore? Or you do?'

His tremulous smile as he reached out for her with his eyes almost made her crumble. How hard it was when the person who was causing you pain was the exact same person you wanted to go to for solace. But if this meant she could have Millie... 'I don't know, Mark. Maybe?'

After the flight and seeing Millie, it was exhausting even thinking about it. Could she do this? Stay in a marriage where she knew that her husband was unhappy? That he wanted to be with someone else? What would be best for the baby?

He nodded. 'Let's talk about it when you get back. Just focus on Millie. I'll sort out all the passport stuff from this end and let you know what to do.'

There was the familiar wave of relief of him looking after her. This had been the pattern of their marriage since the beginning. He was more confident on the solid ground of bureaucracy and business. He knew what he was doing with that. And she was more than happy to have him do it. She didn't have the energy to think about any of this now. Working out their marriage would have to wait.

Once they'd said goodbye, she took in Alex's apartment for the first time. It was pretty bare for someone who'd lived here for weeks and so tidy she wondered if he even stayed here. Were he and Sophia an item? The way Sophia had been with Millie. The 'us' and the 'we' and the way that she looked at her. When – on the phone – she'd accused Sophia of trying to keep Millie, she'd just been angry and lashing out, but now? Was it really a possibility that Sophia – and maybe Alex – were planning to keep her baby?

Her body itched to walk or run after being folded up on the plane and then the taxi, but she had to stay here until her isolation was over. On the side was a note from Sophia – saying there was a pomodoro sauce for her in the fridge – alongside an addendum from Alex telling her where he kept his pasta. Her stomach was tight after the events of the day, but she had to eat. She had to be strong for Millie. After she'd eaten something, she'd try and close her eyes for an hour or so until she met Sophia in the garden tonight. Something told her she was going to need to be ready for that conversation.

THIRTY-FOUR

SOPHIA

Twilight made everything look different, draining colour from the grass, the flowers, the trees; everything was in contrast. Sophia had a glass of Chianti to match the one Megan had brought from Alex's apartment. Against the fresh scent of foliage, its dark velvety aroma was comforting.

In a reversal from earlier, Megan was curled up on the chair at the far end of the garden; Sophia was on the doorstep. Millie was asleep upstairs, and Alex had promised to call if she so much as whimpered. Sophia stretched her legs in front of her, unable to shake the feeling that she'd forgotten something. 'This is the furthest I've been from Millie since she was born.'

Megan stared at the glass in her hand. 'Lucky you.'

Sophia could have kicked herself for being so tactless. 'I know she's been in the world for over two weeks, but I still can't believe she's really here. Can you?'

Now Megan looked up at her. 'Until I saw her today, she still felt like an imaginary creature. Like a unicorn or something. Thank you for looking after her so well.'

It was uncomfortable, the way Megan was pushing this shifting of their roles. 'I've enjoyed it. I love her.'

Megan tipped the wine glass so quickly that only the merest slice of wine could have wet her top lip. 'Well, I hope I can do as well with her. I had a good role model, at least.'

Even knowing that she'd kept Sophia's postcards secret for over twenty years, Megan still idolised their mother. For Sophia, these last few weeks with Millie had actually reignited her anger at her mother's weakness. 'I'm not sure our mother is the best blueprint for motherhood.'

In the darkening evening, it was difficult to make out Megan's expression as she stared down into her wine glass. 'I know she made a mistake not telling me that you were trying to get into contact. But I also know she thought she was protecting me. You left once, Sophia. What was to stop you leaving again? And it was really tough for us, you know. When you left. She was so upset that you didn't even say goodbye. It was such a shock for her.'

Enough was enough. 'It wasn't a shock.'

Megan frowned. 'What do you mean?'

It was time for the truth. Maybe then, Megan would understand. 'Mum knew exactly why I left. I left because I was pregnant.'

Finding out she was pregnant had been an utter shock. She and Jed had been careful, but they must've done something wrong because the line on the test didn't lie.

She hadn't told him. There was no way he'd want a baby; his ticket to South America was already booked. He'd talked about nothing else. He was having a gap year before taking up his place at York. She would be in Manchester at the School of Art. They were going to make it work.

And then the pregnancy happened.

How she'd managed to sit her exam that morning, she still didn't know. Afterwards, her friends had planned to celebrate the end of their A levels with a trip to the pub. She'd feigned a headache and had come straight home.

Even in the half light, she could see Megan's face pale. 'Pregnant?'

Was it cruel to tell this story even now? But she'd started and now she needed to finish. 'Yes.'

After a week of little sleep and indecision, she'd gone to her mother for help. Once the whole thing had tumbled out of her, she'd begged her to help. 'I can't do this, Mum. I can't have a baby.'

Sitting on the edge of her bed, surrounded by posters of her favourite bands, her mother had held her close, her own tears falling into Sophia's hair. 'Oh, sweetheart. We'll sort this out. We'll find a solution.'

There was only one solution as far as Sophia could see. She'd only recently missed her period so she was only just pregnant. 'Mum, I can't have this baby.'

Her mother had stroked the tears from her face. 'That's a big decision, Sophia. You need to be sure. But I'll help you, love. Whatever you want.'

The relief had been overwhelming. This was going to be okay. 'And you can't tell Dad. I don't want him to know.'

'Can't tell Dad what?'

She'd frozen at the sound of his voice. How long had he been standing there? She'd wiped the tears from her eyes. 'Nothing. Just something about my exams.'

His laugh had been cruel. 'Don't lie to me. What's going on? Rose?'

He'd looked at her mother. So had Sophia, willing her to be strong. *Don't tell him. Don't tell him.*

But, of course, she had.

Megan's hands covered her face. Her eyes, above her fingertips, were dark and scared. She'd known what her father was like as well as Sophia did. 'What did he do?'

The fallout had been nuclear; the names her father had called her almost Shakespearean in their venom. And through it all, her mother had stayed silent: a shrine to weakness.

Sophia had tried to fight her corner. 'You don't need to worry about this. It's my problem. I'm going to sort it out.'

He'd sneered at her. 'Sort it out? I know what that means. Not in my house you won't. No child of mine is going to take the easy way out. You can give up that course of yours and stay here and face up to what you've done.'

Her mother had winced at that. Sophia had known how proud her mother was that she was going to university: the first person in their family on either side. Not proud enough to stick up for her in the face of her losing that place, though.

She didn't think her father had even cared about whether she'd had the baby or not. This had been just another way for him to control her life, make her miserable. Wasn't that the way he'd treated her mother all these years? Though it'd never been discussed, Sophia had been old enough to do the maths from her birth certificate and knew that her mother had been pregnant with her on their wedding day. He might've trapped her, but he wasn't going to get the chance to do the same to Sophia.

Two days later, she'd tried one more time with her mother, begging her to help. 'I can't, Sophia. Your father has made up his mind.' She'd reached for her hand. 'It'll be okay. I'll help you with the baby.'

Sophia had pulled her hand away. It was the last time she would feel her mother's touch for another twenty years. Three nights later, she'd kissed Megan goodbye and left.

Megan shook her head slowly. 'I remember that night so well. I had no idea what you were going through.'

Sophia gulped at her wine, swallowing hard over the lump in her throat. This was harder than she'd thought it would be. Aside from the conversation at her mother's bedside, she'd avoided thinking about this for many years. 'Why would you? You were only twelve, Megan. I wasn't going to tell you.'

Megan's face creased in sympathy or pain. 'And did you... I mean, where did... Did you have to...'

She couldn't even say the words; Sophia helped her out. 'Have a termination? No. I thought I wanted to. But then I couldn't go through with it. I already knew that the night I said goodbye to you.'

She could understand Megan's confusion. 'So, your plan was to have the baby?'

There'd been no plan. There'd just been the urge to run far away. 'I was nineteen, confused and alone. I had no idea what to do.'

'What happened?'

She'd miscarried the baby when they were in Brazil. The most traumatic experience in either her or Jed's young lives. When he'd discovered her on the floor of the bathroom of the cheap hotel they were staying in, he'd thought she was dying. When she'd told him the truth, they'd cried together and then he'd taken her to the hospital. Lying to his parents that it was he who'd been injured, they'd wired him the money to pay for her treatment.

Megan's hand fluttered to her mouth. 'Oh Sophia. That's so awful.'

Of anyone, Megan would know how that felt. Sophia didn't deserve her sympathy. 'It was my own fault. We'd been climbing that day. I hadn't been looking after myself. Jed didn't even know I was pregnant. Looking back, I think I wanted the decision to be made for me. I've felt guilty about that for a very long time.'

Megan reached out her hands, then let them drop to her sides. 'But, it's not your fault, Sophia. You were a child. I'm so sorry you had to go through that. I wish you'd told me. Later, I mean. When you came home.'

'When you were desperately trying to have a baby yourself? How could I tell you that I'd been unhappy to be pregnant?

That I'd lost a baby in those circumstances?' Watching Megan's pain and frustration at being unable to conceive had only compounded how guilty she'd felt about her accidental pregnancy. It was so unfair on her.

Megan screwed her eyes shut. 'I don't understand why Mum wouldn't stand by you. I mean, I know it was tough for her with Dad, but she loved us. It doesn't make sense.'

'She was weak, Megan. She wouldn't stand up to him. Not for me.'

Saying the words aloud didn't make them any less painful. As an adult, she'd learned about the paralysis that could come from years of emotional abuse, had understood a little more what made her mother react as she had, but it didn't stop her carrying that betrayal like a physical wound. That first day she'd returned to England and sat by her mother's bedside, she'd asked her why and she'd had no answer. All she could do was apologise.

Megan looked as if her world had turned on its axis. 'Is that why you didn't want children? Because of what happened?'

Years of pain and anger had been pressed down so deeply inside Sophia that, now they were starting to break up and float to the surface, she could hardly breathe. Hot tears filled her eyes. 'I didn't feel as if I deserved to have a child. Not after I'd done that. It was my fault, Megan. I know you're going to say that I was young, but it was totally my fault. Laying in that hospital room in Brazil, I swore that I would never ever put myself in that position again.'

Megan stared down at the wine in her glass; when she looked up again, her eyes were full of tears. 'You weren't to blame, Sophia. Lots of first pregnancies end in early miscarriages. You did nothing wrong. And I can't believe you offered to carry Millie for me. After everything you've been through. I was already grateful but now... I just can't believe you did it.'

Fragments of the guilt she'd carried for so long were

piercing Sophia's heart. If she could reach inside her chest to hold it, she would. 'I wanted to do it for you. I wanted to make it up to you. I wanted to make your life better.'

All of this was true. She'd done this for Megan. But what she hadn't known was how much it would heal her. The pregnancy, Millie's birth, the last few weeks: all of this had put her back together again, piece by piece.

A sob escaped from Megan. 'You didn't have anything to make up to me. And you didn't do anything wrong. You didn't cause your miscarriage. Unlike me.'

Sophia held out her hands to her sister. This was why she hadn't wanted to speak to her about this. 'No, Megan. You can't help your infertility.'

Megan was shaking her head. 'Four years of an eating disorder, which completely messed with my biology? How can that not have affected me? I've brought all of this on myself. On Mark. On our marriage. It really is all my fault.'

Sophia shook her head. If Megan could forgive her, why couldn't she extend the same to herself? 'You were a child, too, Megan. How did Mum not spot it before it got too bad?'

Megan's eyes were deep dark pools. 'It wasn't Mum's fault. You weren't there, Sophia. You can't understand what it was like.'

THIRTY-FIVE

MEGAN

It was so hard to listen to Sophia's history. What kind of life lottery gives a pregnancy to a scared nineteen-year-old girl and not a married woman in her thirties who wants a child more than life itself?

Sophia tried again to tell her that it wasn't her fault, but Megan held up her hand and repeated herself. 'You weren't there, Sophia. You don't know what it was like.'

Sophia sounded almost angry. 'Then tell me. I want to know, Megan.'

She wasn't sure that Sophia would want to hear all of it. But she needed her to see that their mother wasn't the villain she thought she was. 'It was really hard at home after you left. Mum and I were lonely without you.'

Sophia sipped at her wine, her voice back to almost normal. 'I would've thought it would be easier without me there "creating havoc" like Dad used to say.'

Megan shook her head. 'You were the life of that house. You always had a story, always made us laugh. With you gone, everything was so quiet. So sad. Dad was sullen and moody, but we just kept out of his way. He started disappearing for a couple of weeks, then months, at a time. And then he left for good. I was fourteen.'

Only two years after Sophia had gone. Their mother would've known where she was because of the postcards. She expected Sophia to be angry.

Instead, her voice was heavy with sadness. 'Oh, Megan. I wish I'd known. I would've come home.'

Megan needed to keep going or she wouldn't get it all out. 'Dad left us with nothing. Mum worked so hard, but we never had enough money. As well as her cleaning job, she took in ironing that she could do in the evenings. She never stopped working. But it was never enough.'

Sometimes they'd watch TV together in the evenings while her mum stood and worked. Every hour she'd give herself five minutes on the sofa with a cup of tea to rest her 'screaming' back.

For the first time, Sophia sounded as if she had some sympathy for their mum. 'That must've been hard for her.'

Hard didn't even come close. 'Mum's whole life was centred around trying to work out how she could juggle the bills to make sure that everything got paid. She'd go to four different supermarkets so that she could get the special offers from all of them.'

And how many times had Mum glued her own shoes back together so that she had the money for Megan's uniform? Not that she'd told her that. When she'd caught her at it, she'd made up some story about them being her 'favourites' and that she wanted to keep them going. Megan had done her best not to cause her mother any financial worry. Any letters about expensive school trips were screwed up and thrown away before she got home. Any parties where she knew there'd be the expectation of a gift, she'd politely declined. Eventually, friends stopped asking. It was easier that way.

Sophia held her wine glass with both hands, staring into its depths as if it was a crystal ball showing her the life Megan was describing. 'I just assumed you were okay. I thought you were happier without me.'

'No. We did our best. But we missed you so much. Our lives got smaller and smaller. One of the last winters, we couldn't afford to heat the whole flat, so we had a little electric heater in the living room and we slept in there, too.'

Something skittered through the bushes to the side of the garden. A mouse perhaps. Megan bent her legs up onto the chair and wrapped her arm around her shins. Sophia was shaking her head. 'Oh, Megan. Is that when the eating issues started?'

Even now, she wasn't really sure why it began. It hadn't been a conscious decision to stop eating, but she'd felt so uncomfortable, so overfull, when she ate more than a small plate. Food became an enemy that she was determined to overcome. Not eating made her feel calm, in control. 'It's hard to explain it. It doesn't make sense. I just know that I felt better when I didn't give in to my hunger.'

She'd been pretty ill by the time her mum had realised how bad things had got. It wasn't her fault. Her shift with the cleaning company had started at 4 p.m. – ten minutes after Megan got home from school. She'd leave food for her but wasn't there to make sure she'd eaten it. It was amazing how much a baggy sweatshirt and joggers could hide.

Sophia's voice was gentle. 'Did you have to go into a clinic?'

'No. Not as a resident. That was the threat if I didn't start to eat. They let me go as an outpatient. I didn't want to leave Mum.'

Megan could remember it like yesterday. Her mum had just kept apologising. 'I'm sorry, love. It's all my fault. Things will get better, I promise.'

And she had got well. More for her mum than for herself. There were relapses over the next couple of years. Then a new doctor had recommended she develop some interests outside the home, her mum had found the drama club, Megan had met Mark and life had got progressively better.

The darkness was getting thicker, but it looked as if Sophia was crying. Even when they were young, she'd never seen Sophia cry. In her memory, she was always laughter and enthusiasm. When their mother slipped away for the last time, Megan had left the room and she'd heard Sophia sobbing in the bedroom; she'd stood with her hand on the door, not knowing whether to go in.

When Sophia spoke again, her voice was thick. 'And what about now? Are you eating? You don't look well.'

This was why she hadn't wanted Sophia to know about the anorexia. Once people knew, they treated you differently: surreptitiously scrutinising your body, monitoring every morsel at mealtimes. 'I'm okay. But I know I need to be careful. These last few weeks, the lockdown, missing Millie's birth, it's been tough. And it's brought some of the old feelings back.'

'That's what I was worried about. It's a lot, Meg. And throwing a baby into the mix...'

She didn't need to finish. '*My* baby, Sophia. Not *a* baby.'

'I know. But I've been caring for her and it's not easy. The lack of sleep, the relentless feeds. I'm just worried that you—'

They were veering dangerously towards another argument. 'You don't need to worry, Sophia. I've got it under control. Things are different now. I have a nice home, a good job, money, Mark.'

'Mark?'

The tone of her question spoke volumes. 'Yes, Mark. He's still there. We're going to work through it all. Stay married. Stay in the same house. I know that Mark will need to... find out about that side of himself. But as far as Millie is concerned, she will have us both there.'

'Is that really what you want?'

'We can make it work.'

Sophia was shaking her head. 'No, Megan. Why do you have to make it work with Mark? You shouldn't have to compromise with someone who doesn't love you the way you deserve to be loved. Listen to yourself!'

Just when she thought they were making headway, Sophia had to act like this. 'I don't expect you to understand. We want different things, Sophia. We always have. I need this stability. I can sacrifice passion or whatever you want to call it. I want to be a mother and I want to be wife. I can do this. It's a small sacrifice. It's what mothers do.'

This seemed to make her angry. 'How is you sacrificing yourself going to help Millie? That's ridiculous. And it won't last. You won't be able to keep that up forever.'

It was too late for Sophia to come sweeping in and playing the big sister now. 'I don't want to argue with you about this, Sophia. But how would you know? Your relationships last months, not years. That's not a judgement, but I'm not made the same way. You don't need to worry about me and Mark. Millie is our baby. Let us worry about that.'

Silence wrapped around the darkness like a shroud. Sophia's voice was hard, clinical. 'You know that legally she's mine?'

She couldn't have winded Megan more if she'd punched her in the throat. Despite their recent conversations, her fear that Sophia was getting too attached, she really hadn't believed that they would come to this. 'Don't do this, Sophia. I know that you lost a baby and I'm sorry, I really am. But your loss doesn't mean that you can take my child.'

Sophia gasped. But when she replied, her voice was as strong and confident as ever. 'It's got nothing to do with that. I know that she came from your embryo, but I'm the one who carried her, who gave birth to her, who has cared for her these last weeks.'

Anxiety began to flutter in Megan's stomach. Surely she

wouldn't actually do this to her? 'That's not my fault, Sophia. I couldn't control that. It's not fair.'

'And it would be fair for you to take her from me when I've fallen in love with her?'

She was serious. The anxiety in Megan's stomach was joined by a deadly cold fear. 'It's a horrible situation, I know, but—'

'I've got to do what's best for Millie.'

Desperation clawed its way up Megan's throat and out of her mouth. 'And how are you going to explain that to her one day? When she asks where her father is? Or where she came from? Do you think she's going to want to hear what you did?'

It was too dark to see very much at all now and the cold of the evening had started to bite. Sophia scrambled to her feet and drained the wine from her glass. 'We need to stop this conversation. I need to go to bed. Millie will be awake for a feed in a few hours. Sleep well. Let's talk tomorrow.'

'No, Sophia. Please. Please don't do this.'

The door banged shut behind her. Megan was alone. She tipped the wine from her glass onto the soil and wept.

THIRTY-SIX

SOPHIA

The following morning, Megan sent Sophia a message to say that she didn't want to risk seeing Millie again until her isolation was over. It felt like a time out, an intermission, a calm before the storm. Sophia tried to treat it like every other day, not think about what was coming. It wasn't until she got in bed that night that Megan's questions returned to haunt her.

Millie, on the other hand, had slept the sleep of the innocent. For the first time ever, she'd achieved the 'dream feed' that one of Megan's stupid books had harped on about, staying asleep while Sophia had fed her, then settling immediately in her crib. How ironic, then, that Sophia had laid awake with her mind misfiring like an old engine, trying to catch onto the solution to this terrible mess.

Over and over, she'd replayed her conversation with Megan in her mind. It wasn't only what she'd said about their mother and the poverty; it wasn't even the way she'd blamed herself for the cruelty of the anorexia causing her infertility. It was what she'd said about Sophia's miscarriage.

It wasn't your fault.

As a proper adult – not the practice adult she'd been at

nineteen – Sophia knew that miscarriages happened for reasons that were not always explained. But she'd spent a long time feeling the effects of that horrendous day in Brazil. When, on that hard, cold bathroom floor, the decision about whether to keep the baby had been made for her. In her darkest days, she sometimes thought that she'd caused it to happen just by thinking about it.

Your loss doesn't mean that you can take my child.

Was that what she was doing? She hadn't wanted a baby before now. Hadn't thought she deserved one. It didn't help that the only men she ever met were temporary, drifters, nomads. How could she have known how that was going to feel? How every part of her wanted to protect and care for Millie. And it had shocked her to see how thin Megan looked. It was all very well her saying that she had her eating under control, but weren't lies and deception part of the strategy that had enabled her to keep the anorexia hidden for so long when she was young?

How are you going to explain that to her one day?

That one hit her the hardest. How would she explain it to Millie that she'd broken her promise to carry her sister's child? She could explain that her mother had been unwell. That she wanted to protect her. But, deep down, Sophia knew that this wasn't the whole truth. That the reality was more selfish. She loved her. She couldn't bear to be parted from her. Her head knew that she shouldn't keep the baby, but her heart – oh, her heart – told her to never let go.

She must've fallen asleep at some point, because she woke to a gentle knocking at her bedroom door and Alex's voice on other side. 'I've made a pot of coffee and been out for pastries. Can I come in?'

She pushed herself up in bed and rubbed the sleep away from her puffy face, surprised to find that her cheeks were wet. Was it possible to cry in your sleep? 'Yes, come in.'

She had no idea where he'd found a tray, but the flower beside the cup and plate had been plucked from the back garden. 'Your breakfast, *signorina.*'

He was a balm to her tender heart. 'Thank you. You're spoiling me.'

'You deserve to be spoiled. And I know this is a big day.'

Her stomach clenched at the thought of it. Megan's forty-eight-hour isolation would come to an end that evening. Time was running out.

Everything she did with Millie that day took on a new significance. Even the most mundane of tasks – a nappy change, clicking the poppers on her sleepsuit together, wiping milk from the corners of her mouth – were all like holy rituals. She checked the time with a religious routine as every minute ticked away closer to the moment Megan would walk through that door.

At 7.36 p.m., the knock on the door came. Alex reached out and squeezed her hand. 'I'll let her in and disappear home.'

Sophia stayed on the sofa, Millie beside her, stretched out on a crocheted blanket. Megan only had eyes for Millie as she crept forward, then crouched down beside them. When she reached out to stroke Millie's cheek, the poignancy of that gentle connection made Sophia's stomach flip over. She knew how long Megan had waited for this, longed for this, prayed for this.

'Can I pick her up?'

The was something childlike in Megan's expression and, for a moment, Sophia was back home, being asked for permission by a ten-year-old Megan who wanted nothing more than her big sister's approval. She swallowed. 'Of course.'

Every movement of Megan's was gentle and careful as she slipped her hands, one beneath Millie's back and one behind her head, slowly slowly bringing her close. As she tucked

Millie's head beneath her chin, she closed her eyes and one solitary tear escaped from under her eyelashes.

Silent and still, the atmosphere in the room was electric with emotion. Megan needed this moment, Sophia knew that. She fought to keep her hands by her sides, to stop them reaching out for her baby.

But Millie wasn't her baby. She could see that now. All the time that Megan had been at the other side of a phone screen – even in the garden last night – she could pretend to herself that Megan was not the best mother for this child. But now, watching the way that they fit together, it was impossible to see her as otherwise. An ache filled the vacuum within her, the space that Millie had left behind.

Megan broke the silence first, her voice barely above a whisper. 'I can't believe she's really here in my arms.'

Sophia didn't trust her voice, so she just nodded.

Megan opened her eyes, a thousand emotions heavy in the air between them. 'Please don't do this, Sophia. I can't lose her. I can't.'

It was a truth that Sophia had tried to avoid, but one that she knew she had to accept. But how? She couldn't bear to lose her, either. 'I know.' She took a deep breath. 'I know she's yours.'

Since she'd been born, Sophia's were the arms that'd held Millie for most of the time. Richard had occasionally held her, but the crook of Sophia's elbow had been her permanent home. Watching Megan with her made the ache inside even deeper. She was in another world right now and, already, Sophia could feel herself being excluded from it.

Megan reached out for Sophia's hand. 'I will never be able to thank you enough. Even if I say it every day for the rest of my life.'

'Well, don't, then.' It was so hard to smile, but she needed to try. If she started crying, she might never stop.

'You'll still be in her life, Sophia. You're her auntie. That's special.'

This was so painful. Whatever you wanted to call it, she'd been Millie's mother since the day she was born. Millie had come from her body. If this was going to end, she needed it to be quick. Soon. Almost as much as she needed it to be never. 'When will you take her?'

Megan looked surprised at the question. 'I don't know. Mark will sort out the details from the other end. Her passport and everything.'

'And what are you going to do about Mark? Are you really staying together?'

'He says he can do this and I don't want to parent on my own. I want her to have it all. A mum and a good dad. Something we didn't have.'

Maybe it shouldn't have been such a surprise that Megan had felt the absence of a father. 'If Mark is a good as you say he is, she'll still have a dad.' She could see from Megan's face, the small nod of her head, that she knew this was true. But it didn't seem to change anything.

'I need him, too.'

'Do you? You might want him. But need is a different matter. And will you ever really have him if he stays?'

It was like torturing her, but she had to be honest. She had to know that Megan was strong enough to deal with all of this. Strong enough to raise Millie on her own.

'I just want to have this moment, Sophia. Let me have this moment.'

She was quiet for a while longer, but it was painful to sit here with them and Megan would probably appreciate some time alone. 'I'm going to pop over to Alex's place. Give you some space.'

Megan smiled. 'Thanks. I might try and call Mark, too. See

how quickly he can get the passport sorted and book our tickets home.'

Sophia wasn't sure who was included in that 'we'. 'I won't come back with you to England. It'll be too hard.'

Megan frowned. 'But you'll have to. For the paperwork. You're registered as Millie's mother. There's no way I'll be able to get on a plane or train with a newborn baby when I'm not registered as her mother.'

Sophia felt nauseous at the thought. Wouldn't it be better to rip off the plaster in one painful movement? 'How long would you need me to be there?'

'I don't know.' Megan looked disappointed. 'I thought you might like to stay a while?'

And stand on the sidelines as 'Auntie Sophia'. No. That would be too hard. 'Well, I'll need to get back to work. Get my life going again.'

'I see. Of course. I understand. We'll try and get it all done as soon as we can, then.'

Almost immediately after she knocked, Alex opened the door to his apartment and she fell into his arms. Deep sobs soaked the top of his shoulder.

A tower of strength, he held her as she cried. 'I'm sorry, Sophia. It must be so hard for you.'

Alex had seen her with Millie. He, more than anyone, would know how this felt.

'I don't know how I'm going to live without her.'

It sounded melodramatic, even to her ears, but it was true. In a handful of weeks, Millie had burrowed into her heart and the pain of losing her was almost a bereavement. Alex stroked her back. 'I know it seems impossible now, but it will get easier. You're not losing her forever. When are they going?'

She lifted her head from his shoulder and wiped at her eyes

with the back of her hand. Despite all the tension between the two of them, this was the first time they'd had physical contact and she felt a little shy at throwing herself at him like that. 'I don't know. And I have to go back with them. Paperwork to do. Megan wants me to stay with them for a while.'

In contrast, he didn't look remotely embarrassed. 'Oh, of course. Well, maybe that's a good thing?'

He bent slightly on his knees so that he was looking in her eyes. He was so kind, so thoughtful. She didn't think she'd get through this without him. 'It'll be worse. It'll just drag it out. I want to get it over with and then just... disappear.'

She started to cry again and he pulled her in for a hug. 'Just give yourself some time. There's no need to make any big decisions. But you're welcome to come to Australia with me in a couple of weeks or join me later. It's an open invitation.'

Australia. Was that the solution? To put as much distance between her and Millie as possible. Thousands of miles away, she wouldn't have to watch Megan with Millie. And she'd have Alex. Would that help to heal her broken heart?

THIRTY-SEVEN

MEGAN

It wasn't until Sophia clicked the front door closed and left them alone in the apartment that it felt real for the first time.

She was a mother.

Though Megan had imagined this moment so many times over the years, she could never have anticipated how it felt. Even now, she half expected someone to tell her that there'd been a mistake, that she wouldn't get to keep her baby after all.

Knowing for certain that Sophia wasn't going to fight her for custody was an overwhelming relief. It had never been part of the plan for her to spend so much time with the baby. Of course she was going to bond with her; especially in the light of her own pregnancy loss.

It must've been so traumatic. Megan knew better than anyone about the grief of miscarriage and she hadn't had to deal with it alone, at nineteen, in a foreign country. Was it surprising that Sophia had turned that loss into a determination never to fall pregnant again?

She rocked Millie in her arms. 'Oh, little one. We've made such a mess of it, my sister and me. Too many secrets.'

When her mother had passed away, she'd thought that she

might never get over it. Even after she'd married, her mum had been the one she'd looked to whenever she'd needed support. How she wished she could be here right now. Through the joy she felt in Millie's birth, there was a thread of pain that her own mother couldn't be here to see her. Her mother would have helped her to know what to do. About Mark. About Sophia. About how she navigated this journey. For Sophia, too, she wished their mother was there so that she could tell her how, despite her mistakes, she had loved her very much.

But now she was the mother. She was the one who had to provide the stability for this precious little girl. To give her the strong roots she needed to grow big and strong. Was she up to the job?

Millie yawned in her sleep. Her tiny lips forming a perfect 'o'. 'Are you trying to tell me something? What do you need?'

Sophia would probably know. She would know everything that Millie needed. She'd seen the look on Sophia's face as she'd left earlier: as if had caused her physical pain to go.

But what if she didn't go? Or, rather, what if she didn't stay *here*? Was there a way that she could persuade Sophia to remain in Millie's life? To remain in *her* life? She had to try.

In the two hours Sophia was gone, Megan had plenty of time to think about what she wanted. To have her sister with her at home would be the next best thing to having their mother there. But she didn't know what Sophia wanted. When the front door opened, she was ready.

Sophia glanced at Millie before looking at Megan. 'How did the two of you get on?'

She could see from Sophia's smile how hard she was trying to be positive. Knowing what she knew now about the miscarriage, it made Megan love her even more. 'Can we talk?'

Sophia laughed as she sat on the other side of Millie on the sofa. 'I think that's all we've done these last couple of days.'

She wasn't wrong. 'I mean, can we talk about the future?'

Sophia frowned. 'What do you mean?'

'Yesterday, when you told me about Brazil, when I told you about the anorexia, it was a lot to take in. For me, it completely shifted everything I'd ever thought about you. I suppose I always thought you were invincible somehow. Like life didn't touch you. I felt sorry for myself; I thought I was the one who'd got the raw end of the deal, looking after Mum, dealing with my illness, struggling with my fertility. While you just flew off wherever you wanted, without a care in the world.'

It was a long speech, but she'd been rehearsing it in her head, not knowing how Sophia would react. But she was nodding as if she understood. 'While I thought that you were the one who had things worked out, your closeness with Mum, your caring husband, the deep roots you had to a solid, stable life.'

When she'd stayed at their house, Megan had thought Sophia regarded her life as a bore. Was that a defence mechanism, too? 'But now I see things differently. I understand things better.'

Sophia's eyes were bright when she looked at her. 'Me, too.'

This was what she really wanted to talk about. 'And I've been thinking... after we get home and sort out all the paperwork, what about if you stay longer? Come back home. Give us a chance to really get to know each other?'

She could almost see the struggle in Sophia's eyes. 'I just don't know if I can. I know that Millie is yours, Meg, but she feels like mine. Giving her back to you, I feel as if I'm giving up my own child.'

This was hard on both of them, but Megan had more to say. She just had to find the gentlest way to say it. 'I understand that. I've never given birth, but I can only imagine how that must feel. And then you've had her with you for all this time. I get it, Sophia. I really do.'

There was still guilt in Sophia's eyes when she looked at her. Guilt that had no place being there. For either of them. 'I don't know, Megan. Maybe it's too late for me to change. Alex has asked me to go with him. A new scene has always worked for me in the past.'

'Has it?' This was where she needed to tread carefully. 'Do you really want to follow another man?'

'What do you mean?'

She took a deep breath. 'It seems to be as if you've spent the last twenty years just following what someone else wants. Isn't it time to follow your dream? What is it that *you* want?'

A single tear made its way down Sophia's cheek. 'I want Millie.'

She'd known that this would be her answer, hoped it would. 'Then come with us. I'm Millie's mother but that doesn't mean you have to give her up. Come back with us. Build a home with us. Let's be family again.'

Sophia's voice was barely a whisper. 'What if it's too hard? Too painful? What if I want to go again?'

Megan had her finger encased in Millie's little hand. With her other hand, she reached out for Sophia. 'It will be hard. And it will be painful. But you can do it.'

Sophia looked at Millie and then up at Megan. 'I love you both. But I just don't think I can.'

THIRTY-EIGHT

SOPHIA

In the three weeks it had taken to fast-track Millie's passport, Sophia had tried her best to let Megan take over. It was difficult not to jump when Millie cried, to sit on her hands when Megan was struggling to wind her or when she was rocking her more quickly than she thought Millie liked. Her ways may be different to Sophia's, but Megan was her mother and she needed to find her own ways that worked.

Every morning, around ten, Megan went for a run. On the day before they were due to fly back to England, Sophia waited for her to leave before taking Millie onto her bed and laying down beside her. 'Okay, Millie, this is it. This is the last time it's going to be just you and me.'

Millie punched her little fists in the air. She wouldn't have a clue what Sophia was saying, but Sophia was the one who needed this. Time alone to say goodbye.

It should've felt silly, talking to a six-week-old baby, but she'd got so used to chatting to Millie as they went about their day, that it felt like the most natural thing in the world. 'This isn't the last time you'll see me. But, after today, we'll be back in England and you'll be in your own house with your mummy.'

Even saying that word aloud caught in her throat. One day, Millie would be able to say that word to Megan. How she wished it would be her she'd say it to.

For Sophia, there'd been so many breakups over the years. Some were a relief; some tore her apart. But there'd been nothing like this. Never in her whole life had she loved someone as much as she loved this baby. She held her toes between her fingers and wiggled them. 'I don't understand how you've done this to me. I wasn't supposed to fall in love with you, you know. That wasn't the plan. I was supposed to have you and give you to your mummy and then everybody would be happy.'

If it hadn't been for the lockdown, would she never have felt this? Would it have been possible to hand Millie over after carrying her for nine months? It was a pointless question. They *had* been isolated together, she *had* cared for her and she *had* fallen hopelessly in love.

What she'd give now for the opportunity to turn back the clock a few weeks. 'I'll never forget how it felt to have you inside me. Those times you kicked and turned around and pressed your little fists into my skin like you were ready to take on the world. Your mummy loves you very much and she is going to take such good care of you. But you grew in me, Millie, and there will always be a little space in me left empty. That's the place I'll keep for you.'

Why did this feel like a bereavement? Millie was a healthy, happy baby. Nothing was going to happen to her. Megan was going to be a wonderful mum and it sounded like Mark was going to do a stand-up job of being a dad. It was wrong that she felt so desolate, wasn't it? Tears were running down her cheeks, but she didn't wipe them away. This was the last time she was going to let herself feel like this. Tomorrow, she would be Auntie Sophia. But right now, she wanted just a few more moments of feeling like Millie was hers.

'The moment you were born, it was like... I don't know, like a switch went off in my head.' She would always have that. Millie's first moments of life were in her arms. Even now, that memory was slipping but she had to hold onto it with every part of her.

Millie gurgled at her. There was something new every day and she was changing before their eyes. She would never remember those first days and weeks when Sophia was her mother. But Sophia would never forget them. Leaning closer, she whispered into her tiny ear. 'Between you and me, I wanted to be your mummy. I didn't expect it, you know. To feel like that. I wasn't planning on ever being anyone's mummy. But you did something to me. You took my breath away and I don't ever want to let you go.'

Tears started to fall and she moved away so that they missed Millie and soaked into the bedcovers. There was so much she wanted to say, yet no words could convey the depth and breadth and height of her feelings. 'If you were really mine, I'd take you everywhere with me. We'd see the world together, you and me. All the places I've been and all the places I want to go. Just me and you and no one else.'

It was more than that, though. For Millie, she would put down roots and be the foundation, the rock, the support that she needed. 'And then I'd be that mother at the school gate who cries because her baby has to go. And I'd be the mother that taught you to ride a bike and swim and do all the things that you wanted to do. I'd wait on the sidelines at football games or ballet recitals or anywhere at any time.'

Her voice was cracking now with the pain of all those things that she would never do. These would be Megan's things. Megan's times. Millie reached out and grabbed her finger and the determination made Sophia laugh despite her tears. 'Maybe there's a little of me in you, after all.'

Wouldn't that be something? For a tiny part of Sophia to live on in Millie. A secret link that no one could take away. The cord might have been cut, but – for Sophia – she would feel the pull of that connection forever.

'I know that you don't belong to me, baby girl. But I belong to you, Millie. I'm yours forever. Whatever you want. Whatever you need. I'll be there. At 3 a.m., when a boy has broken your heart, or your friends have let you down, or you're lost. Wherever I am, I'll come.'

Still holding fast to Sophia's finger, Millie's eyelids fluttered closed and she sighed. Such a delicate precious sound. How could she give her up? It was too hard. Too painful. Too cruel. But she had to.

Tears were falling thick and fast now. She could only whisper; there was no strength left in her voice. 'Tomorrow, I'm going to be your Auntie Sophia but here—' she patted her chest '—here I will always love you as if you were my daughter.'

Millie was fast asleep now, her little chest rising and falling with her soft breaths. Sophia closed her eyes and pressed a gentle kiss on the top of her head.

Could she do this? Walk away from Millie and Megan, and carry on her life the way it'd always been? Maybe go to Australia with Alex? But then how would she keep her promise to be here always when she was almost a whole day's journey away?

No. Nothing was worth missing out on this. It would be so painful to watch Millie grow towards Megan and away from her. But the alternative – not seeing her grow up – was far worse. She had to do this. Go home. Back to the UK. Be close to her sister. Be close to Millie. However frightening that was, she would do it. She'd be there for them both.

Decision made, she waited for Megan to get back from her run to tell her the good news. The person she was not looking forward to telling was Alex.

. . .

As she'd imagined, Megan was overjoyed. 'I'm so pleased. It'll be so wonderful to have you with us.'

You. Us. It had started already. 'Well, I'll probably try and find somewhere to stay. I won't want to get under your feet.'

'We can argue about that when we get there. I'm so happy.' Megan had Millie in her arms, so her hug was one-handed, but it was firm and warm, all the same. She looked down at a wriggling Millie. 'We're so pleased that Auntie Sophia is coming, aren't we?'

Auntie Sophia. That was going to take some getting used to. But she could do it. And she would.

Alex answered the door as soon as she knocked. 'I was hoping it was you. I didn't want to interrupt family stuff but I've been desperate to speak to you.'

She hadn't realised how attached she'd got to him in these last few weeks. Being isolated together, his help with Millie, the way he made her smile when things were difficult. 'I know, it's been busy with having Megan here. All the talking.' She rolled her eyes to make him laugh. 'How's things?'

He led the way into his apartment where there were piles of clothes and books on every available surface. 'Oh, you know. Packing up. Getting all the paperwork done for medical school. I'm getting excited. How about you?'

Her stomach twisted. She hated letting him down. And would miss him so much. But this was the right thing to do. 'I'm great. Millie's passport is all sorted, and Megan and I are getting on really well.'

That much was true. It made her wish that they'd been honest with each other a long time ago. Alex's grin made his face even more handsome. 'That's really great, Soph.'

This was only making it harder. 'The thing is, Megan has invited me to stay for a while. A few months. Maybe longer. I don't know. I'm just not ready to leave Millie yet. I'm so sorry. I did want to come with you to Australia, but it's just so far.'

For a second, his face fell, but he pulled a smile back over his disappointment pretty quickly. 'I get it.'

'You do?'

'Of course. I saw you with her, Sophia. I know how much you love her. I want to go to Australia because it's a fresh start for me. But I totally understand that it's not right for you.'

His kindness and understanding almost broke her resolve. 'I like you, Alex. A lot. But I've spent my whole life following men pursuing their dreams. I need to go home. I need to work out what I want.'

She could see the sadness under his smile. 'I understand. It's just bad timing, right? In another lifetime we might have had a chance.'

She swallowed down the huge lump in her throat. 'We can stay in touch, though? I mean, this doesn't have to be the end of things?'

Even as she said it, she knew it was impossible. A long-distance relationship was one thing. But two completely different time zones would be pretty difficult to manage. She was grateful that Alex at least pretended it could happen, so she didn't have to face losing him in one hit. 'Of course. Who else will be awake for me to call when I come off a shift at 2 a.m.?'

Not following him to Australia after knowing him for a handful of weeks was undoubtedly the right thing to do, but that didn't make it easy. All through the madness of the last few weeks, he'd been a constant companion. She'd spoken more to him than anyone – even Richard. Not being able to discuss her feelings about Millie with him was going to be hard.

Megan was right. She had just followed men around rather than making decisions for herself. But what if Alex was the *right* man? What if he'd been the one who could've really made her happy?

THIRTY-NINE

MEGAN

It had been quite a moment carrying Millie over the threshold of the house on that sunny June morning. Though Megan had held her all the way home on the plane, Sophia had needed to take her through passport control as her mother. Bringing her into the house was the first moment that she'd really felt like hers.

After dropping their bags in the hall, she gave Millie a tour around the house before settling with her on the sofa. For once, she let Sophia make the tea: not wanting to let go of her daughter for a minute.

As soon as they heard Mark's key in the door, Sophia pushed herself off the couch. 'I'll give you some time on your own. I'll be upstairs if you need me.'

Was it excitement or dread that was making Megan's heart knock so hard in her chest? The thud so intense, she was surprised it didn't wake Millie in her arms.

She listened to the familiar rattle of his car keys being dropped into the ceramic tray in the hall, the pause as she knew he'd be taking off his shoes and placing them under the coat rack. Her ears strained to see which way his footsteps would go, when the door to the sitting room opened and his face appeared.

'There you are.' His voice was so soft, so intimate, that it brought tears to her eyes.

She matched his tone and smile. 'Here we are.'

Slowly and gently, he came to sit beside her and she changed the angle of her arms so that he could see the precious bundle better. 'Wow, she's really beautiful.'

Though he'd seen her on camera, Megan understood the wonder in his eyes. Seeing Millie in real life was so different. On the screen, she'd been a baby. Here, she was a work of art. The finest sculptor couldn't have crafted a more beautiful face. 'Isn't she? Would you like to hold her?'

He nodded. Sat back in the chair like a small child about to receive a coveted gift. Cradling Millie's head, she passed her carefully into his arms.

This was the moment. It was real. For the first time, it was the three of them together. The family she'd planned and wished and hoped for, for so long. She watched Mark take in every inch of her. 'Hey, beautiful girl. It's good to meet you.'

The lump in her throat was almost painful. She couldn't look at Mark. Instead, she stroked the soft down of Millie's head. 'This is your daddy, Millie.'

His intake of breath was sharp; he shook his head from side to side. 'It's so strange. I didn't expect to...'

'Love her straight away?'

He looked up at her. 'Yes. Exactly. All the times we talked about this. Even when she was born but still in Italy with Sophia. It hasn't felt real. But now... now it is. She is.'

Despite the decision she'd made in Italy, her resolve wobbled. Maybe the last few weeks had been an aberration, brought on by being locked in against the madness outside. Mark might have feelings, but it didn't mean he'd act on them, did it? And she didn't need much from him; she just needed him to be here. 'Are you happy?'

He kept his gaze fixed on their daughter. 'We can make her happy. I want her to have whatever life she wants. To do what she wants. As long as she's happy.'

He hadn't answered her question. Even so, the fierceness in his tone – the protective, primal need to protect his child – spoke volumes. He wanted for Millie what he hadn't had. The ability to choose his career, his life. Though it hurt her, there was only one thing to say. 'I want that for you, too.'

He looked up at her. 'What do you mean?'

It was crystal clear. They couldn't do this. Not in the way she'd planned. 'I want you to have the life you want, Mark. And I know that's not with me.'

With the hand that had been holding Millie's tiny fingers, he reached out for hers, gripping it tightly. 'I do love you, you know. I'll make this work.'

She didn't want him to make it work. Sophia was right. She deserved more. She deserved to be loved by someone who wanted to be with her. 'We'll both make it work. For Millie. You can be here as often as you want to, stay over whenever you like, but our marriage is over, Mark. We both know that.'

A sob escaped from his mouth. 'I never wanted to hurt you. I do love you.'

She knew that. The same as she knew that she loved him, too. But it was the love of a friend, or a sister. Though she hadn't the energy to explore it right now, she wondered if it had always been like that. 'We were good for each other.'

He nodded. 'We were. We *are*.'

She would always have a relationship with him; even aside from him being Millie's father. Because he was Mark. Her lovely Mark. The boy who'd been her friend; the man who'd looked after her all these years. This should feel like a savage wrench, but it didn't. It felt right.

For the next few minutes, they worshipped at the altar of their daughter, marvelling at the length of her fingers, the thickness of her hair. Then Mark returned to the practicalities of the situation. 'What shall we do now? If Sophia wants her room, I can sleep on the couch? Or would you rather I stayed with my parents?'

She didn't want to push him away from Millie, but there was also the need to draw a line, create some space, take a breath. 'How do you feel about that? I mean, you'd have to explain why.'

'We're due to be in Yorkshire for a couple of nights and we've an early start tomorrow. I'll just tell them that I didn't want to disturb you and the baby in the morning.'

Any other family would think that strange. Not Mark's. 'You're going to need to tell them, Mark.'

His shoulders sagged. 'They won't understand. Any of it. Telling them we're separating will be bad enough. But the reason why?' He coughed a dry laugh. 'I think my dad's head might explode.'

For her part, she was relieved that she wouldn't have to spend as much time with them. Listening to his father's opinions about the world at large and his mother's mild acquiescence to anything he said. She wanted to support him, though. 'Well, the former has to happen. They'll realise soon enough that we're not living in the same house. Whether you tell them the reason is up to you.' She reached out for him. 'But you might feel better to be honest.'

He looked at Millie. 'How do you think she'll feel about it when she grows up?'

'She won't know any different. To her, you'll just be Dad.'

His voice was thick. 'I will tell them. I don't want any more secrets. If you can deal with it, then they have to.'

She smiled at him. 'Good. And we'll be here whenever you want to come.'

He was still holding her hand and he squeezed it again. 'Same for you. If you need anything, Megan, anything at all, I'm here.'

Mark stayed for another couple of hours as they continued to marvel over every part of their daughter. She was pleased when he said he could see her mother in Millie's face; she'd thought it herself, but wondered if that was just her being sentimental. When he stood to go, it was hard – this really was the end. At the door, with Millie in her arms, he reached out and circled both of them. 'I love you so much, Meg.'

It was impossible not to cry. 'I love you, too.'

Sophia must have been listening out for him to leave because she came downstairs within moments of the front door closing. 'Everything okay?'

Megan wiped away the tears from her face. 'Yes. It will be.'

Sophia knew not to press her, she just nodded. 'Cup of tea?'

'Yes, please. I'll follow you out to the kitchen.'

Once the kettle was on, Sophia leaned back against the counter. 'What have you decided to do? Is Mark coming back later?'

She shook her head. 'He's gone to his parents' house. We need to find a way through it all, but I think it's going to be okay. You were right. I can't pretend to live a life that's based on a lie.'

Sophia nodded. 'It's hard. But you'll be okay.'

She would. She really would. 'What about you? Alex? Do you think there's any future there?'

Back in Italy, it was clear how heartbroken he'd been when he'd dropped them to the airport. The attraction between the two of them was there for anyone to see. But Sophia shook her head. 'I don't think so. I like him. I really like him. But Australia is too far away.'

'I'm glad you're here with us. I was thinking about our conversation in Italy. Have you considered going back to university?'

Her eyes widened. 'University?'

'You have your A levels and if they're not good enough, you can do an access course. You could do your art degree. Or something else. Whatever you want.'

For a few moments, Sophia didn't answer. Had she pushed too far? The last thing she wanted was an argument. But when she spoke, it was quiet and thoughtful. 'I would actually love to do that.'

Thank goodness. 'Well, I can help you to look into it. There's loans and things and you can obviously live here if you go to a local university.'

Sophia tilted her head. 'It this just a ploy to make me stay?'

Maybe there was a little bit of truth in that. 'Not in the way you think it is. I just want you to know that you have a home here.'

'And I want you to know that you don't need me here, or Mark, or anyone. You can do this on your own, Meg.'

If she heard it enough times, she might start to believe it. But that didn't change the fact that she wasn't ready to lose Sophia again. 'I know. But I want you in my life. In Millie's life.'

Sophia's eyes misted over as she leaned in to stroke Millie's cheek. 'And I want to be here. I want to be close enough to see her grow up.'

Sophia looked more vulnerable than she'd ever seen her. Strangely, that made Megan more confident, more sure. 'Then stay. Let's be a family.'

A long pause meant she wasn't sure that she hadn't scared Sophia off again, but she needed no other confirmation than the smile that spread like sunshine across her sister's face. 'I'd like that. I'd like that very much.'

FORTY

SOPHIA

The next day, Sophia slept in late. She'd been up until the early hours of the morning, looking up all the information about art colleges – and funding for mature students – that she could find. Even the prospect of setting down roots in one place for at least three years wasn't filling her with fear: that baby had a lot to answer for.

She woke when she heard Mark arrive. Rather than go downstairs and interrupt their time together, she had a look on a local job site, looking for something to tide her over until she could apply to college. That's when she saw the advertisement for a temporary art technician in a local secondary school. The pay wasn't great, but how wonderful would it be to be spend her days around paints and pastels? Once she heard Mark leave, she emailed herself the link to the job application and swung her legs off the bed.

Downstairs, Megan was talking to Millie who lay in a bouncy chair, kicking her legs. Megan looked up when Sophia walked in. 'Morning, sleepyhead.'

'Oh my word. You sound like Mum already.'

Megan laughed. It was good to hear. 'Mark brought pastries. And cakes. They're in the tin over there if you'd like one.'

She resisted the urge to ask Megan if she'd eaten already. 'Do you remember what Mum would do if we were cutting a cake to share?'

Megan mimicked their mother's voice: 'One of you can cut, the other can choose.'

How bittersweet was memory? How much pain in the pleasure of nostalgia? 'And whoever would cut the cake would be more precise than a ruler because they knew that if one was bigger the other one would choose it.'

Sophia smiled. 'Good memories.'

There *were* good memories from their childhood. With their mother gone, she needed to focus on those. Trying not to stare, she was pleased to see Megan polish off the last of a croissant. Hopefully, she'd worried needlessly about her slipping back into a bad relationship with food. If she said she had it under control, she'd have to trust her.

Millie started to fuss in her chair and Megan glanced at her watch. 'It's not time for her feed yet; maybe her nappy needs changing.'

As she bent down to pick her up, the doorbell rang, so Sophia held out her arms. 'Do you want me to change her?'

She understood the reluctance on Megan's face; she wanted to do everything for her baby. 'Actually, can you get the door? It's likely to be Mark having forgotten something.'

But it wasn't Mark at the door.

For a moment, she froze. Out of context, she almost didn't know him. The navy t-shirt made his eyes bluer than she'd remembered. On a step below the door, he was almost exactly the same height as her and her heart reached out before her mind caught up. 'What are you doing here?'

Alex grinned at her. 'Lovely to see you, too.'

'Sorry, I was just...' She threw her arms around him. Pulled him close. Breathed him in. And then he kissed her cheeks and found her mouth and his hands were in her hair and she never wanted it to end. Every part of her wanted to touch a part of him. *He was here. Alex was here.*

When she let him go again, those blue eyes of his made her stomach flip. His smile was even wider than before. 'I've wanted to do that for a very long time.'

It was so good to see him. She'd only given him Megan's address so that he could forward any mail that came to the apartment. She hadn't thought for a second that he would turn up here. She pulled him into the hall and reached for him again. 'Me, too.'

As she led the way through to the kitchen, she could barely keep herself from touching him, almost breathless with the pleasure of having him here. 'Do you want coffee?'

He pulled off his scarf and draped it over the kitchen chair, his eyes never leaving her. 'Yes. Thanks. I had something nasty in a paper cup on the plane here.'

She wagged a finger at him. 'Never have coffee on the plane. It's always dire. There's pastries and cakes if you'd like one.'

Why did she feel so nervous? This was Alex. He'd seen more of her than men she'd dated for months. A few days apart and she felt like a kid on a first date.

'This is some house.' He looked around him at the cavernous kitchen. 'I can see the attraction in staying here.'

It was a lovely house. 'But that's not why I'm here.'

He rolled his eyes. 'I know that. How's our little girl?'

She knew it was just a turn of phrase, but it brought tears to her eyes. For a while it'd felt exactly as if Millie was their baby. 'She's great. Megan's taken her up to the nursery to change her nappy. If you think the kitchen is impressive, you should see Millie's room. She's got a proper changing table up there with a hundred little drawers for all the toiletries and nappies.'

He raised an eyebrow. 'You mean she doesn't just chuck a towel on the sofa and do it there?'

That made her smile. 'No, Megan likes to do everything properly. She's getting Millie into a routine.'

They were so different. Where she'd liked to go with whatever Millie seemed to need in the moment, Megan had a place and time for everything. Neither was right or wrong. It was just a different way of doing it. Judging by Alex's laugh, however, her face might not be expressing her acceptance of that. 'You'd better be careful. She'll be getting you into a routine next.'

'Never.' She crossed her arms and frowned dramatically. 'Disorganised 'til I die.'

She'd missed this so much. The teasing, the easy chat. Was he here to persuade her to go with him to Australia? Did she have the strength to say no? She saw Millie in her mind's eye: she had to.

He took a small cinnamon swirl but didn't eat it. Instead, he stared at it as he spoke. 'Are you settled here, then? In England? Are you definitely staying?'

He *was* here to persuade her. Every atom of her wanted to follow him, to have another adventure. Except one. The space in her heart where Millie lived. 'I think I have to. I can't leave her, Alex. Even when I move out of here, which I will, I don't want to be so far away that I never see her.'

He nodded but continued to stare at the pastry. 'Good.'

That was surprising. 'Good?'

He lifted his eyes, but they were unreadable. 'Yes. Good. Because I've spoken to a friend who's a consultant in a London teaching hospital. They're desperate for junior staff. When I offered, he bit my hand off.'

She didn't dare to hope. 'Offered what?'

'To come and work there. There's some stuff to sort out, paperwork and so on, but he thinks it'll be a cinch to get me back on the programme. Finish my final year. Live in London.'

He looked at her intently, as if asking her a question. She almost didn't trust her voice. 'You're going to live over here?'

'I thought a lot about what you said in Italy. About not wanting to spend any more of your life following a man around. But when you left, I found that I couldn't quite live without you. So I decided that I'd follow you instead. If that's okay with you?'

Now the tears wouldn't stop. 'Okay with me? This is so wonderful, Alex. I can't believe you'd change your plans from Australia to London just to follow me here.'

He opened his arms to pull her towards him. 'Well, you can start believing it. It was an easy decision to make. You're worth following, Sophia.'

And then he kissed her again.

FORTY-ONE

MEGAN

After meeting Alex, Megan decided to take Millie out in the pram so that they could have some time together.

It had been lovely to meet him properly and thank him for all he'd done during the birth. He'd been really sweet with Millie, too. There was something about a man with a baby which was so tender. She hoped that, in time, Mark would be as comfortable with her as Alex clearly was.

Sophia looked so happy to have him here. When he talked about getting an apartment, Megan had felt a little less happy. Selfish though it might be, she wanted Sophia to stay with her. At least for the next few months. She was doing her best to learn how to be a good mother, but Sophia seemed to have a natural confidence with the whole thing. It was like having a safety net.

There was a slight breeze in the air, but it wasn't unpleasant, and the June sun was doing its best to find a way through the light clouds. Realising that she was marching like a woman on a mission, she made herself slow down.

Though she'd walked – and run – these streets hundreds of times before, she saw everything so differently walking at this pace. The vibrancy of the flowers in the hanging baskets outside the pub, the intricate metalwork at the top of the gates to the park, the neat borders around the gardens of some of the houses. Everything was alive to her in a way it had never been before.

As she reached the shops on the High Street, she caught sight of herself in a shop window. Just an ordinary mother and her pram. Nothing unusual. Nothing to take notice of. But, oh, she saw a beauty in the reflection that she'd never known before. This – pushing her baby in a pram – was a moment in time that she would cherish forever. She slowed her steps even more, relishing every moment, until she reached the baby clothes shop four doors down.

Disappointed that the shop had still not reopened, she paused to look in the window. Last year, she would hurry past this display, not wanting the striped sleepsuits and soft leather boots to mock her empty arms. Now, she drank in the riches of the window, then smiled down at Millie. 'We're going to have so much fun in here, little girl.'

She'd turned back to look in the window when she heard the reedy voice of an older lady next to her. 'What a beautiful baby you have.'

She was keeping a respectful distance, and was wearing a mask, but Megan could see she was smiling from the kindly crinkle in her eyes. 'Thank you. This is her first trip out in the pram.'

'How lovely. I remember doing that when mine were small. You enjoy it, my dear. Nothing better than when it's just you and your baby.'

The eyes crinkled again and she was gone. Megan stayed where she was, letting the pleasure of that moment really settle on her. For the first time she really felt it: she was Millie's mother. The first few weeks of her life had been unorthodox, strange, even lonely. But now she was here, they were together and she was her mother.

As she pushed the pram away from the shop, the sun peeped from behind the cloud and the warmth on her face matched that in her heart. Even though her mouth was hidden, she smiled at every person she passed, trying to beam that smile from her eyes. *I'm happy. I'm a mother.*

Maybe Sophia had it right all along. Maybe you didn't need to tie yourself to rules and responsibility. All this time she'd been scared of being lonely and alone. But it wasn't frightening any longer.

The whole country was coming out of lockdown, but Megan felt as if her own personal lockdown had lifted. She could be whoever she wanted to be and so could Mark and so could Millie.

The future was uncertain. Mark might meet someone. He might not be around as much as he'd promised. Sophia might decide to move in with Alex. Or follow him abroad. But it didn't matter. She had Millie. She had everything. And it was wonderful.

FORTY-TWO

SOPHIA

A shaft of light cast a yellow glow across the pale carpet.

'You really have made a good job of this room. It's beautiful.'

Megan rocked gently from side to side, Millie asleep in her arms. 'I'm sure you would've done it better. You've always been more creative than me.'

Sophia wasn't sure that was true. 'She's a very lucky little girl. When will you move her from your room into here?'

Megan frowned. 'The book says six months, but I'm not sure I'll be ready by then.'

Sophia laughed. 'You don't have to do everything by the book, you know.'

Megan arched an eyebrow. 'Have you actually met me before?'

Had she imagined it, or was Megan different these days? She seemed... looser somehow.

On one wall, a white bookshelf was full of the gifts she'd been sent. Stuffed animals and board books and a silver hairbrush which Megan had rolled her eyes at when Mark's parents had brought it yesterday. They'd worn masks and kept their distance but had managed to drop several hints about Megan and Mark 'patching things up'.

From behind her back, Sophia pulled out the yellow scrapbook, which she'd finally finished yesterday. 'I have something for you.'

Megan's arms were full, so she opened the book for her and slowly turned the pages, watching her sister's eyes scan the pictures and fill with tears. 'Oh, Sophia. That's beautiful. Thank you so much.'

Sophia laid the book on the top shelf and ran a finger down its spine. 'Will you tell her the story of her birth? About me carrying her?'

'No.' Megan's voice was firm. But when she looked up, she continued. 'We both will.' She smiled. 'It's a special story. She'll know that she was a special baby who was wanted so much that even her auntie was willing to carry her.'

Sophia's throat tightened. 'I do love her.'

'I know. And I'm sorry if this is difficult for you. I really am.'

She brushed a tear away; this was no time for sadness. 'I think it's shifting. My feelings for her. When I look at her, I'm beginning to feel more like her aunt than her mother.'

Megan stopped rocking and looked at her, searching her eyes to test whether she meant her words. 'Really? Is that true?'

The mess of feelings in her chest were too complex to explain. 'I don't know if I'm totally there yet. But I want it to be. I want to be able to enjoy her as her auntie without feeling the loss. I want her to feel like yours and not mine.'

If it was difficult to say those words, it must be difficult for Megan to hear. But they'd promised to be honest with one another from this point on. 'Because you want to leave again?'

She hadn't realised that Megan would jump to that conclusion. 'No. I don't want to leave. I want to stay here, with you. I want to look after you both. I want to be your big sister. I want to look out for you and help you.'

Megan's smile was tentative. 'What about your life? What about Alex?'

Alex had been playing the situation just right, sending her flirty little texts and keeping her updated on his progress with somewhere to stay, but understanding her need to be with her sister right now. This was a new thing for her: a considerate boyfriend. She liked it. 'I think he'll be sticking around. But it goes Millie—' she moved her hand down an imaginary list '—then Megan, then Alex.'

Megan reached out and squeezed her hand. 'I'm glad. And it's okay if you still feel like she's yours. You can tell me if there's things that I need to do differently. You know her better than I do.'

It felt as if she knew Millie better than she knew herself. 'I carried her in my body. She'll always feel like part of me. But she's made from you.'

Megan nodded. 'She belongs to both of us.'

That wasn't quite what she meant. 'She belongs to herself. But maybe we both get to borrow her for a while.'

They stood quietly, watching Millie sleep. Who knew that watching a baby could be so captivating? 'What about Mark? Is he going to stay at his parents? Will he not be coming back?'

'He's a good man and I know he'll be a good dad. But it's over between the two of us and we both think it's best if we live separately. We'll always be friends.'

She really seemed okay with that. 'Really? Do you think you can manage that?'

'To be honest, I think that's what we always were. Good friends. I loved him. I'll always love him. Just not in the way I thought I loved him.'

It really did seem that she was okay. Not panicking. Not crumbling. Not even crying. 'It's a big change.'

'Yes. It is. But, for now, being a mum is enough. And being a sister.'

She felt the same. Yes, she had Alex, but it wasn't like any other relationship she'd had. She wasn't going to lose herself in him. This time she had a strong anchor. Two of them. 'Do you remember Mum saying something like that? When I told her that she should get out more? *You two girls are enough for me.* I never believed her.'

Megan smiled and nodded. 'To be honest, neither did I. When Dad left, I used to worry about her. She seemed so lonely. But you can be in a relationship and be lonely.'

The truth of that hit home. 'I know exactly what you mean.'

Megan looked down at the sleeping bundle of perfection in her arms. 'But you'll never be lonely, little one, because you'll always have us.'

Sophia leaned in and pressed her lips to Millie's forehead. 'Both of us.'

A LETTER FROM EMMA

Dear reader,

I want to say a huge thank you for choosing to read *She Has My Child*. If you did enjoy it and want to keep up to date with all my latest releases, just sign up at the following link. Your email address will never be shared and you can unsubscribe at any time.

www.bookouture.com/emma-robinson

For a long time, I've wanted to write a story about two sisters. As Elsie's sister says, the relationship with a sibling is likely to be the longest relationship in your life, but it is often the most complex. Though raised in the same family, siblings can be very different from one another, and it was this that interested me most in writing this story. In addition, both Sophia and Megan are forced to reconsider – and reevaluate – events from their past through each other's eyes; a fascinating challenge for any character, real or imagined!

The idea to have the sisters separated by Covid restrictions came from my very clever editor, Susannah Hamilton. Revisiting that period was a strange experience and I tried to keep a very 'light touch' approach to the details. Knowing that it was a very difficult time for so many people, I hope I have been sensitive to this while keeping as close to the facts and timelines as possible.

KEEP IN TOUCH WITH EMMA

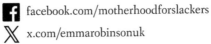 facebook.com/motherhoodforslackers
x.com/emmarobinsonuk

ACKNOWLEDGMENTS

First thanks go to my fabulous editor Susannah Hamilton for pushing me to go deeper and further with the story and for such insightful input to every element of the plot and character. Thank you to Sarah Hardy for PR and to everyone else at Bookouture. You are all so lovely to work with and I really appreciate how hard you work for our books.

For helping me to polish the prose and minimise mistakes, thank you to Donna Hillyer, Deborah Blake and Carrie Harvey for your attention to detail. Thank you to Alice Moore, for this eye-catching cover which will look lovely on the wall of my writing room!

The book is dedicated to my wonderful pals Anita Hole, Ashlie Hughes, Felicity Squire, Hayley Lill, Kerry Enever, Louise Hoskins, Theresa Allen and Tracy Harper. Anyone who has followed me on social media from the beginning will have seen the fabulous book-themed gifts they've showered on me but, more importantly, they have supported and believed in me from the very beginning. I love you all very much.

Lastly, as always, to my family. Your lack of drama gives me no material, for which I'm very thankful.

PUBLISHING TEAM

Turning a manuscript into a book requires the efforts of many people. The publishing team at Bookouture would like to acknowledge everyone who contributed to this publication.

Audio
Alba Proko
Sinead O'Connor
Melissa Tran

Commercial
Lauren Morrissette
Jil Thielen
Imogen Allport

Data and analysis
Mark Alder
Mohamed Bussuri

Cover design
Alice Moore

Editorial
Susannah Hamilton
Nadia Michael

Milton Keynes UK
Ingram Content Group UK Ltd.
UKHW040618200324
439767UK00005B/152

9 781837 908776